From the Library of Joanna French

BY SUSANNA MOORE

MY OLD SWEETHEART
THE WHITENESS OF BONES

THE

WHITENESS

OF BONES

THE

WHITENESS

OF BONES

SUSANNA · MOORE

DOUBLEDAY

NEW YORK · LONDON · TORONTO · SYDNEY · AUCKLAND

Published by Doubleday,
a division of Bantam Doubleday Dell Publishing Group, Inc.
666 Fifth Avenue, New York, New York 10103

DOUBLEDAY and the portrayal of an anchor with a dolphin are trademarks of Doubleday, a division of Bantam Doubleday Dell Publishing Group, Inc.

Lyrics from "Honolulu Hula Hula Heigh," "Nani Kaua'i," "He'eia" and "Hula" from *Na Leo Hawai'i Kahiko,* reprinted by permission of Bishop Museum Press, Honolulu, Hawai'i.

Lyrics from "Every Night at Seven" by Burton Lane and Alan Jay Lerner © 1951 Chappell & Co., & SBK Entertainment (Renewed). All Rights Reserved. Used by Permission.

Lyrics from "This Is Always" by Harry Warren and Mack Gordon © 1946 WB Music Corp. (Renewed). All Rights Reserved. Used by Permission.

Lyrics from "The Girl from Ipanema" (Garota De Ipanema), Music by Antonio Carlos Jobim, English Words by Norman Gimbel, Original Words by Vinicius De Moraes © Copyright 1963 by Antonio Carlos Jobim and Vinicius De Moraes, Brazil. Rights administered by DUCHESS MUSIC CORPORATION, New York, N.Y. 10019 for all English Speaking Countries. All Rights Reserved. Used by Permission.

Robert Van Gulik, excerpt from *Poets and Murder* Copyright © 1968 Robert van Gulik. Reprinted with permission of Charles Scribner's Sons, an imprint of Macmillan Publishing Company.

Library of Congress Cataloging-in-Publication Data

Moore, Susanna.
    The whiteness of bones / Susanna Moore.— 1st ed.
        p.   cm.

    I. Title.
PS3563.0667W4   1989
813'.54—dc19

T H E

WHITENESS

OF BONES

ONE

It is still said, in those small towns on the island of Kaua'i that have remained unchanged for years, that if the legendary *menehune* do not finish a task in one night's work, they abandon it forever at dawn. Anthropologists tell us that this is because the *menehune*, the tiny men and women who lay hidden in the wet forests through the long, hot days, were afraid to return to the same good *taro* field or water ditch, night after night, lest they be caught and bound into servitude by the lazier, bigger, more ferocious Tahitians.

The *menehune*, who were the eleventh-century forebears of the more arrogant and more recent invaders from Tahiti, died out hundreds of years ago. They do not believe this in Waimea town. There are several sightings each year of *menehune* and many of the old people leave food out for them, papayas and *'opihi*, and the yams that the *menehune* love so much. There are royal fish ponds and ancient roads and black lava-rock temple sites hidden all over the island and to the initiated, the children who are born there and live there, these locations are revered and kept secret from outsiders.

The irrigation ditches cut into the sides of the mountain

by the industrious *menehune* were eventually built over by the industrious white men who came long after them to plant the lovely sugar cane, to sell it and to ship it far away. In place of the *menehune* ditches, diligently made by hand of cut-and-dressed stone, there now were aqueducts, wooden half-barrels laid on their sides and elevated on rusty trestles, to rush the icy spring water down the mountainside to the fields.

This system of irrigation through flumes was simple, but effective. There were miles of flumes and, although they were difficult to reach and often hidden from view in thick stands of *'ohe 'ohe* and *pili* grass, the children of the island used the flumes as water slides.

The location of certain especially fast and dangerous flumes was kept secret in families for generations and passed on in unquestioned solemnity. It was against the law to use the flumes as water slides, but since the land and the water were owned by fathers or mothers or cousins, punishment, if one were so careless as to be caught, was seldom very severe.

The children had been fluming all day in Makaweli. Mamie Clarke, twelve years old, sat on the front bumper of an old army jeep as Lily Shields, in the driver's seat, let the heavy jeep coast recklessly back down the winding mountain road. Tōsi, Lily's adopted brother, who was Japanese, held his muddy feet on top of the strawberry guavas careening back and forth on the floorboard to keep them from rolling under the clutch pedal. Mamie jumped off at the bottom of the mountain, where the dirt track met the highway. She was covered with dust and the *pakalana* lei she was wearing when she started out had only a few crushed green flowers left on its string.

"Meeting tomorrow afternoon," Lily yelled back into the

wind. Mamie held up her hand to show that she had heard. They belonged to a club.

Mamie walked home through the sugar cane. The fields had been planted by her father's grandfather. Sugar grew tall and pale green up the soft slopes of the mountains behind her. It swayed and bent over her as she splashed through the water in the bottom of a shallow ditch. The red, silted water was cool. The old, crooning sound of the cane came to Mamie. The cane knew different songs. That day, Mamie recognized "Tell Me Why" by Neil Young.

It had not rained in three weeks and some of the cane, the growth farthest from water, had begun to turn brown at the roots. The dust made the inside of her nose dry and tight. She could see the Filipinos in their straw hats coming back to the cane fields from lunch in the workers' camp.

The camp glinted suddenly as the sun struck a rippled tin roof. There was a flash of bright red, too, from the leggy poinsettias that poked along the peeling wood porches of the old camp houses. Giant ferns and allamanda pressed densely around the little ramshackle houses that were like the forts a child might build with odd pieces of wood and the corroded sheet metal of abandoned cars.

She took the dirt road that ran through the camp. Piles of rotting mangoes, black with drunken fruit flies, lay under the big trees. The branches drooped low, heavy with fruit. The spoiled mangoes smelled like sweet jam.

Mamie's hair was cut very short. Despite her boyish head, her arms and back and neck had a tender, lithe refinement. She moved with the easy grace of a child who has been brought up under the sky. In the bright sunlight, her eyes seemed as if they were yellow, but inside her father's palm grove, in the shade, her eyes were brown. Her skin was the color of home-made taffy.

It was much cooler in the grove. Another song was serenaded there, "Waimanalo Blues," as the rushing, rustling branches creaked and groaned above her. She picked up two coconuts, two cents, and carried one under each arm.

The palm grove had been planted by the Chiefess Deborah whose land it once was, before she removed herself and her large retinue to the more convivial, more temperate, climate on the banks of the Wailua River. Long-horned cattle brought in sailing ships by Captain Vancouver once grazed in the palm grove. There were more than five hundred trees, and generations of workers had eaten the milky meat, plaited rope from the hemp, carved bowls from the shells, and woven prized floor mats from the green, sharp-edged fronds. Now McCully Clarke paid his children a penny a coconut to collect them. The Chiefess, when she abandoned the Waimea plantation, had tired of the heat and the muddy water. She weighed two hundred and forty pounds and ten young men were needed to carry her litter to the little dock. She took the long-horned cattle with her.

Through the palm trees, Mamie could see her mother, Mary, bending in the flowers at the side of the plantation house. She was transplanting the delicate Tahitian gardenias she had brought from Hanalei the day before and watering them from a big, square tin that once held soy sauce.

The house, long and low, sat on a wide expanse of lawn between the Pacific Ocean and the palm grove. With its damp, brown sand, glittering with mica, the beach hemmed the land like a bejeweled lace ruffle on an old green gown. The rich iron silt from the Waimea River one mile to the east and the irrigation runoff from the cane fields made the ocean the opaque color of coffee with milk. It was not a beautiful beach, with its slow, small breakers, and the children rode their bikes through the bending cane to swim instead in the dangerous white surf at Polihale. Several people drowned at Polihale each year, usually young servicemen in tight nylon bathing suits. Cheap hotels, the children called the suits. No ballroom.

The house had a peaked, corrugated-tin roof and long verandas running the length of both sides, so that a fresh trade wind blew through the cool, open rooms day and night. On the veranda facing the ocean were rocking chairs and big *hikie'es* where guests would sleep at night. Leaning against the inside wall of the ocean veranda were canoe paddles made of *koa* wood, some of them one hundred years old. They were used whenever McCully and the boys took the outriggers to the reef, and during the months spent training for the canoe races. Some of the paddles had been won in races, and the dates of the victories were carved on their long, smooth handles: 1903, 1928, 1931, 1952, 1969, 1971, 1972.

The flowers that surrounded the house were white flowers. Mary had planted white ginger five and six plants deep under the bedroom windows so that you fell asleep and awoke to the heavy, narcotic smell of ginger. She had not planted them outside the dining room, as she knew that the odor would be too strong, so white oleander and spider lilies, only mildly scented, were allowed to grow there. The children could eat without getting flower-headaches. The faint smell of the deadly oleander always reminded Mamie of the afternoon that Hiroshi, the gardener, found a man, woman and two children lying dead in the sea grape. They were holding in their hands sticks of leaf-stripped oleander. Perfectly grilled hot dogs swayed on the tips of the sticks. There were several bites in each of the hot dogs, or so Gertrude, the maid, had whispered to Mamie. Gertrude's boyfriend was a part-time policeman. That the dead people were tourists was evident immediately. Not much sympathy was felt for the visitors from Denver, so stupid as to roast hot dogs on poisonous sticks. In Waimea town, the strange deaths only strengthened the islanders' instinctive disapproval of outsiders.

Mary planted the white, trumpet-shaped datura that grew to fourteen feet along the grove veranda. It was another deadly plant, but the gardenia with its sturdy, shiny leaves did not seem to mind, for it grew happily alongside. Only the edge of the lawn, near the eucalyptus, was left unplanted, as Mary, after years of Hiroshi's warnings, had finally admitted that only the sea grape and the creeping purple morning glory, clinging to the sand, were able to withstand the spray from the ocean.

Mary worked in her garden all day long. She was from Oklahoma. Mamie wondered if there were any flowers or trees in Oklahoma. Mary worked in the moonlight, too, especially when the thorny, night-blooming cereus, on its three-winged stem, was opening on the lava-rock walls. She corresponded with the Horticulture Department of the University of Hawaii and botanists from the mainland came to visit her. Mamie did not fully understand, or appreciate, perhaps, just what her mother did, as it seemed to Mamie that the difficult task was to keep things from growing. If you happened to spit guava seeds on the path, it was not uncommon to see a guava shoot sprouting there a few days later. Perhaps if Mary had shown as much interest in her daughter as she showed in her plants, Mamie would have been less confused.

As Mamie stepped onto the thick lawn, she saw Hiroshi sitting in one of the folds of the banyan tree, eating his lunch from an aluminum *bento* box. Ever since her father told her that in India entire families, entire villages, lived in enormous banyans like the one in their garden, she had been particularly interested in the tree. She did not like the smell of the banyan, a smell of rotten fruit and sap-stained leaves, but she liked imagining Indians tucked into clefts in the branches, taking sodas from an icebox wedged into a bend of the trunk, tying their turbans to air roots when it was time to sleep. She dropped the coconuts outside the laundry door and went to sit with Hiroshi.

He had been with her mother and father since before Mamie was born. After World War I, he had come from Japan when his father, working as an indentured laborer in the cane fields, had finally saved enough money to send for his family. McCully's father had recognized Hiroshi's gift for growing things and had given him to McCully and Mary as a wedding present.

She sat next to Hiroshi in the shade. He was eating cold cone sushi, *agé,* and he handed Mamie the damp, wrinkled end of it, the part that resembled an old woman's elbow. She ate it as he neatly repacked his box, folding the used waxed paper precisely into fourths, shaking out the last drops of *gen mai cha* from the bamboo thermos, burying in the hard dirt the big, hairy seed from the mango. The skin on his fingers was so calloused that it was cracked and split. He had a wispy white chinbeard that Mamie liked to comb. The tufts of hair were like thin ribbons of smoke. His face was very wrinkled from years of squinting in the bright sunlight.

Mamie watched him in adoration. He patted his lap. She slid over and sat on his legs. She noticed that someone, probably Orval Nalag from the camp, had scratched "I Fock Tiny" on the trunk of the banyan.

"We're going to Koke'e tomorrow. You coming?" Hiroshi

tucked Mamie's thick brown hair behind her ears. His old fingers trembled.

"For plants?"

"She like move down more ginger."

"No," Mamie said. She felt very comfortable leaning back against Hiroshi. He, too, had an odd smell, like camphor wood and *kim chi*.

He rested his hands on the elastic waist of her faded red *palaka* shorts. The water in the bottom of the irrigation ditch had rinsed the red dirt from her feet, but a henna anklet of dried mud prettily encircled her brown calves.

"You got *chawan* hair," he said, fondly stroking the back of her head.

"I don't like *chawan* hair," she said. She shook her head to push his hand away. *Chawan* hair was hair that had been cut under an inverted rice bowl. She could hear him chuckling behind her. She laughed, too.

He slid one of his old hands inside her faded shorts and moved it down inside her warm, white cotton underpants until it was resting softly on her labia.

She turned to look at him. She was not frightened of him. She was confused. There were tears in the wrinkles of his face. She took his big, hardened hand by the wrist and pulled it away from her. There was a little snap of the elastic waistband as both their hands came awkwardly out of the shorts. She placed his hand palm-down in the dirt.

She could see her mother, Mary, binding the straggling, willful shoots of a cape jasmine to a post of the veranda. Her younger sister, Claire, was standing on the veranda steps with her mongoose, Jimmy. She could hear Gertrude loudly singing a maudlin Filipino love song in the laundry room.

She lifted herself from Hiroshi's bow legs. She walked slowly across the lawn. She felt as though her body, by some mistake or accident, had passed out of her keeping. I did not have it very long, she thought.

She padded noiselessly through the cool forest of Norfolk pine, the dry brown needles cushioning the earth beneath the bare feet that used to belong to her, and went through the banana plantation, the banana leaves tattered and flapping, and the heavy, purple, inflorescent banana blossom hanging from its notched rope. The cone was like a part of the human body not meant to be exposed, a heart swinging on a spiny string of vertebrae or the pink tip of a dog's penis emerging harmlessly from its sheath.

She followed the dirt road into the workers' camp. The wooden houses were silent in the middle of the afternoon. There were big fishing nets thrown to dry on porch railings. A smell of brine and salt fish came from the nets. Rows of pale blue Japanese glass balls lined the rickety steps of the houses. A spindly papaya tree grew in each small, pretty yard. Mangy, happy dogs with protruding hip bones rushed out, yelping, to sniff her hands. She could smell fried Portuguese sausage. The bare legs and feet of Orval Nalag stuck out from under a two-tone, turquoise-and-white 1959 Chevrolet. The soles of his feet were blotted with motor oil. Coffee cans planted with pink bougainvillaea closely marked the neat boundary between Daldo Fortunato's house and the house of his first cousin, Ray. These plantings in old oil drums and tin cans, the plants outgrowing the containers quickly, made her mother furious.

"Why can't they plant them in the *ground?*" she would ask.

"Perhaps because it is not their ground," McCully would answer quietly.

Mamie was looking for McCully.

She found him in his office at the sugar mill.

```
‾‾‾
˙ ˙ ˙
```

They walked slowly back through the camp. McCully had to stop only once to admire the sweet-smelling wooden weather vane of two men fighting with machetes that Daldo Fortunato, one of the mill foremen, had just finished carving. McCully patiently helped Daldo attach it with chicken wire to the top of Daldo's aluminum mailbox. Then they all made small bows to Mrs. Nagata, standing on her tiny green lawn, more like a baby's quilt than a lawn, watering her vanda orchids.

Mamie took McCully's hand as they came nearer to the house. She was relieved to see that Mary was no longer on the veranda. McCully stopped at the edge of the garden. They both saw Hiroshi at the same time, still sitting in the fold of the banyan, smoking his stained ivory pipe, his torn straw hat in his lap. He looked as if he were waiting for them.

She watched from the screened window of her bedroom as McCully and Hiroshi stood under the banyan tree. McCully was much taller than Hiroshi, and from a distance it looked as if McCully were talking to a child. Hiroshi held his hat respectfully in both hands. They were not there long, McCully with his hand on Hiroshi's rounded shoulder for a moment, nodding his head as he listened to the old man. Then McCully put his hands in the pockets of his baggy khaki pants and turned to stare at the calm brown sea and Hiroshi looked back at the house once. Looking for me, Mamie thought. "Looking for me, my sweet Hiroshi," she said aloud, weeping. Her face burned with shame.

She knew that she would never see him again.

When Claire banged her way into the room, flinging open the screen door, and saw Mamie standing at the window, she said loudly, "Oh, no, don't tell me you've been reading *The Constant Nymph* again!"

Mamie wiped her face quickly, the face that used to be her own, said yes, and vomited.

TWO

Mamie and Claire were accustomed to walking each late afternoon into Waimea to the Dairy Queen, where they would buy two enormous root beer floats and one cheese dog and carefully carry them back along the quiet two-lane high-way to the palm grove. They would then untie the pacing Jimmy from an old gate and sit in the grove while the sun went down behind them. Some of the palms, planted to commemorate great events, long forgotten now, had been trained to grow crookedly and Claire liked to sit on an old tree that grew horizontally, its long fronds shading her like a parasol.

Mamie would read aloud. She tended to choose mysteries or suspense stories that would best lend themselves to serial reading. It was understood that the book was only to be read together in the grove, and even though Mamie was often tempted to read ahead on her own, she never cheated. She read from a Judge Dee mystery: " 'She was clad only in a transparent underrobe; her white, muscular legs hung down on to the floor. Her thin bare arms were flung out, her broken

eyes stared up at the ceiling. The left side of her throat was
a mass of blood that was slowly spreading on the reed-matting
of the bench. Fingermarks in blood stood out on her bony
shoulders. Her heavily made-up, mask-like face, with its long
nose and distorted mouth that showed a row of small sharp
teeth, reminded the judge of the snout of a fox.' "

Mamie paused dramatically and they slowly sipped their
cool drinks, eating the vanilla ice cream with long plastic
spoons. Jimmy had already eaten his cheese dog in two snapping bites.

While Mamie completed the day's episode, the hundreds of
curving palm trees were silhouetted blackly against the streaked
rose sky. Mamie stopped when there was no longer enough
light to read. The girls and the mongoose looked as if they
had been set on fire.

"Orval likes you," Claire said.

"No, he doesn't."

Jimmy whined and nervously wound himself around them.
He was still hungry. McCully said that Claire had unbalanced
the poor animal by forcing him to change his nocturnal habits.
Claire didn't care. She was not troubled by things like the
sleeping habits of small animals.

"He has *cho-cho* lips, anyway," Claire said.

"Who?"

"Orval. What is wrong with you? You've been weird all
week."

Claire seemed to be made more delicately than Mamie.
It was a deception. Her hair, cut short like Mamie's, was
a lighter brown and her small, quick eyes were green. She
was not as brown-skinned as Mamie. She stayed out of the
sun because it gave her freckles. She had small, plump hands
and feet.

"I saw you walking through the camp this afternoon. You know what Mother said last time," Claire said.

"She doesn't understand. It's because she's not an island girl. Father doesn't mind."

"He grew up in the camp practically."

"Well, that's what I mean," Mamie said irritably. "He knows it's safe there."

"Not with Orval around." Claire stroked Jimmy with growing passion. "Oh, Mamie, Mamie, Mamie . . ." she moaned. Jimmy watched her fearfully as she twisted and massaged his little peaked ears.

Mamie stood in the now gloomy, dark grove. "You don't know anything," she said.

Claire writhed provocatively against a palm trunk as a terrified Jimmy twisted to get away. He scratched her.

"No mice for a week!" Mamie heard her sister say furiously to the confused, frightened animal.

Mamie found her way home through the maze of black trees.

In the living room, open to the verandas, Gertrude was turning on the lamps. There were no shutters or curtains, as the deep veranda eaves provided all of the shade needed during the hot day, and at night, the house was isolated between the dark ocean and the dark grove. Mamie could see Gertrude moving indolently from room to room. Gertrude's coarse black hair, hanging to her waist, swayed back and forth as she moved.

In the kitchen, Mitsuya, the cook, was grating coconut for the icing of a warm yellow cake, and her helper, Sharlagne, whose father worked at the mill store in town, was washing rice. Mary had told Mitsuya many times that rice no longer

needed to be washed, but Mitsuya, who was seventy-eight
years old, liked to do things the old way. Sharlagne counted
aloud as she swished the rice in the cold, cloudy water. It
made a pretty sound, like the tumbling rush of small rocks
and shells left behind by a wave.

"That's eight washings," Sharlagne said, wiping her hands
on her *muumuu*. "I like go now." Sharlagne's brother had
returned the day before from Vietnam and there was a party
that night at the Fire Station.

Mitsuya smiled. She had no teeth. "No need," she said.
"You *pau* now. See you bumbye."

Everyone on the plantation spoke Pidgin English. Mamie
and Claire could speak Pidgin, and McCully, of course, spoke
Pidgin most of the time. Mary did not, out of principle,
and she wondered aloud what the girls would do when
they were in the "real world" and had to speak in complete
sentences. "As if this is not real enough," Mamie said to
Claire in astonishment. "As if I am ever going to leave
Waimea!"

Claire seemed to take her mother as she found her, with
ironic calm, but Mamie was baffled by her. The puzzling
thing to Mamie, as well as to McCully, was that Mary
was not affected by the island itself in that passionate way
that so moved them. Mary admired her island flowers, but
Mamie could imagine her mother loving flowers in Eugene,
Oregon, or Cuernavaca, Mexico. McCully's pious great-great-
grandfather had made the long, dangerous journey of one
hundred and sixty-four days around the Horn in order to
convert the natives in Hilo. He had stayed on, less pious,
but far happier, to buy up all of the land and to plant coffee
and sugar, and to bring more heathens from Japan and China
to work in his fields and to pray in his churches. McCully
was as much a part of the island as the trees in the grove

or the coconut on Mitsuya's cake. But Mary never came under the spell.

Perhaps she was a bit frightened of it, the spell, and could not have succumbed to it even had she wanted to. Perhaps it had to do with the air, the unusual feel of the air, so thick with fragrance and moisture that it was almost tangible. It was the same temperature as the body, so there seemed to be no difference, no separation, between body and atmosphere. You were the air. That is what Mamie and McCully felt, and Orval and Sharlagne and Hiroshi and Claire. But Mary wore gloves when she gardened and, strangest of all, shoes. In fact, she wore shoes all of the time. Mary clearly did not feel that she and the air were one.

Mamie knew that something had happened to her mother many years before, and she was willing to take into consideration the unhappy circumstances of her mother's early life, but, try as she might, what information she did possess was not ever enough to justify her mother's apartness, or as she would have put it, that Mary was not that finest thing, "an island girl."

She knew that as a child in Oklahoma, Mary and her younger sister, Alice, had been left orphans when their mother died of pneumonia and their father ran off to Alaska to work on a fishing boat. They were adopted by a Miss Henrietta, a kindly, elderly spinster and Christian Scientist, who lived in the biggest house in town. She had raised the two girls, sent them to school, and accompanied them on holidays to Santa Fe and Pasadena. When she died unexpectedly, leaving her estate to the Christian Science church, Mary was stranded once again, this time at Stanford University. Alice, who was still in high school, took the first train east to New York City and a job as a hat model.

It was at Stanford that Mary met McCully. He was studying agriculture in preparation for the time when he would manage the plantation at Waimea as his father had done before him. To the surprise of his family, who did not ever imagine that he would return with a dry, quiet mainland girl to an island where there were as many beautiful, riotous girls as beautiful, riotous flowers, he brought Mary home as his bride. As far as Mamie could discover, she went right to work in the garden.

Mamie did not blame Mary for her resistance to the tropics, but she was depressed by it. It seemed so much against her mother's best interests. She talked these things over with her friend, Lily Shields, who lived at Koloa in the Big House. Like Mamie, Lily was under the spell. As she was also extremely interested in her own mother, the two girls had formed The Mothers Club. They held secret meetings at the Big House. These meetings would have seemed dangerously morbid to the casual observer, especially as Lily's mother had died mysteriously a few years before. The girls locked themselves in the dead woman's perfumed, humid rooms for days and talked to each other in a big seventeenth-century gilt mirror propped against a lacquer screen looted from the Forbidden City. They innocently adorned themselves in the most priceless Chinese bridal robes, once belonging to the Dowager Empress, Tsu Hsi; wrapped Fortuny silks and brocades around their thin necks and waists; flung strands of Burmese cabochon rubies over their soft shoulders; and pretended to smoke the black, oily pellets of opium they found in the toe of one of Lily's mother's handmade satin shoes.

They held these meetings regularly, and all in all, it was probably a very good thing for both girls. Once, Lily's father, Dr. Shields, had come into the room looking for a Japanese sword and found the girls side by side on the bed in crepe negligées and big black pearls. He politely apologized for disturbing them and excused himself. He, too, was under the spell.

Mamie went into the kitchen through the back screen door. Mitsuya was icing the cake and looked up when Mamie idly opened the door of the refrigerator. Mamie seemed sad, and Mitsuya looked at her again, squinting.

"You going to da pahty bumbye? For Lyle?"

Mamie nodded. She could hear McCully and Mary arguing on the ocean veranda. McCully's voice was calm and low, but her mother sounded very angry. Mamie could only remember their having argued once before. It was the summer when Mary's sister, Alice, arrived from New York City with a house party of eight people in the hope of spending the month of July with them. McCully, who was not a rich man by their city standards, had offered them employment cutting cane after the second week, and the glamorous Alice had furiously called him a feudal dictator, mixing it all up historically. Hadn't there been a Constitution for just this thing? She'd thought the camp cunning and sweet at first, but now, she was very sorry to say, she saw the advantages of Communism, a statement that thrilled her with its boldness. To McCully's astonishment, she even stamped her foot. They left on a yacht that very afternoon to visit Dick Stratton at the Parker Ranch. Mary had been embarrassed. Mamie had been fascinated. One of Alice's guests, an interior decorator from London, left Mamie two books, *South Wind* and *My Dog Tulip*. They were certainly not to be found at the Waimea Library and she had been very flattered to be given them. She read both books the night they sailed.

Mary was shouting at McCully, "Are you sure? Are you sure of this?"

Before Mamie had time to close the refrigerator door, Mary ran into the kitchen and shouted angrily, "Do you know what you are talking about?"—mindless of Mitsuya, gaping, with the cake balanced precariously on the palm of one trembling hand; mindless of Claire who had wandered into the kitchen with Jimmy slung around her neck; mindless of Mamie's terror.

Mamie's face flushed bright red. She could not open her mouth. Of course, she thought, it is not my mouth to open.

Mary forced herself to speak more calmly. "Do you understand the consequences of your accusation? He is gone, you know. Why would he want to come back now?"

McCully came into the kitchen. He stood behind his wife. Mary reached around Mamie and it seemed as if she were going to strike her, but she only closed the refrigerator door with great force. Claire's eyes dilated with fascination. Mamie was unable to look at her mother, which made her seem guilty and ashamed.

"Why would you want him back now?" McCully asked quietly.

"Why? Why?" Mary turned to him.

Mamie burst into tears. She covered her face with her hands.

"I don't think you quite understand what has happened. You can't have, Mary," said McCully.

"What did happen?" asked Claire. Jimmy was hypnotized by the coconut cake, still held in Mitsuya's weakening, outstretched hand.

"Did you ever—" Mary began to say.

Luckily for all of them, something in McCully's face warned Mary that it would be dangerous for her to continue, that she could not win this contest. "Oh!" she said and left the kitchen.

McCully awkwardly put his arm around Mamie. She was sobbing. Mitsuya, gums bobbing, edged the cake shakily onto the counter. His prey lost from view, Jimmy's eyes flickered sleepily with the kitchen heat. He yawned with a high, sliding whine.

"So what happened?" Claire asked plaintively, but no one could tell her.

The grief that overcame Mamie that night smothered her and soaked into her. She never spoke of it to anyone, and she bore the loss of her friend, Hiroshi, and, it might be said, the loss of her mother, without complaint. It was her nature to be fair. But she suffered greatly nonetheless, perhaps even because of her fair-mindedness, and it was days before she could speak to her mother without shaking, so strong was her sense of the injustice done her, and it was years before she ever even approached the banyan tree. The pain held a certain interest for her because it was, to her surprise, an actual physical pain in her heart. She had read about such things, maidens who felt sharp pangs in their hearts, but she had not, until then, understood that hearts really could break.

Mamie did not blame her mother for not believing her. Mamie did not even blame Hiroshi. She had not been frightened by his putting his hand once on her vagina. She had known that she had to tell her father because she had known that what Hiroshi had done to her was wrong and dangerous. What she had not known was that the almost unbearable weight of grief and regret brought on by her assumption of responsibility would nearly crush her.

Surprisingly, Claire was kind to her, and that first night and for many nights after, Claire and Jimmy slept in Mamie's bed with her. They would lie back together on the small pillow and gaze out the big screened window into the palm grove to watch the stars drift through the dipping branches. Offshore, the small, dry island of Ni'ihau floated like an abandoned war junk. One yellow moonlit night, Claire enticed Mamie into the grove, and they read Archie and Veronica comic books by the light of the moon while Jimmy ecstatically killed toads. He did not eat them, perhaps knowing that they were poisonous, and the girls let him wander off in his sinuous, stealthy way. Now and then they would hear the pop of an exploding toad as he tossed it up like a ball and caught it in his little dry teeth. They were not squeamish or sentimental girls.

Toward the end of the summer, when Mamie was sleeping calmly enough for Claire to remain in her own bed, there suddenly arrived at the plantation the two stepchildren of their Aunt Alice. They were Courtney, who was twelve, and Brooke, who was eight, and they had been sent straight from camp in New England to the middle of the Pacific Ocean. It is possible that they did not even stop one night at home in New York, so eager was their stepmother to have nothing to do with them.

They were, understandably, in a daze. McCully was in the fields all day, and Mary, as she pointed out, had more than enough to do now that she was without a head gardener, so the stepcousins were left to Mamie and Claire. They were sweet-tempered and malleable. Claire and Mamie were amazed at the girls' timidity and their fear of adventure, such as stealing and eating the grave-offerings from the Chinese cemetery. Claire and Mamie realized that the girls had been ordered and shunted about all of their lives. They were astonished when they made this discovery, and felt sorry for them and did not take advantage of them.

They were picked up one hot afternoon at the edge of the palm grove by Lily Shields and Tōsi. Tōsi was driving the jeep, and Lily sat in the back on top of a pile of towels, a large tin can held between her legs.

The children were dressed in blue Kauaʻi work shirts, buttoned tightly at the wrist, and jeans. Tōsi headed straight up into the mountains behind the plantation. He did not stop until they reached the first gate. Courtney and Brooke looked on curiously as Lily and Mamie jumped out and expertly jimmied the lock and opened the gate.

"We're not supposed to do this," Claire said nonchalantly to the two girls.

"Do what?" Courtney asked. "Open the gate like that?"

"All of it," Claire said. She yawned, having been up very late the night before with Gertrude.

They passed through several more gates in the same way, and Courtney and Brooke were just beginning to enjoy the windy lawlessness when Tōsi stopped the jeep with a lurch. Their heads jerked forward into the back of the seat.

They were in a thick stand of mountain apple. The crimson-feathered *'apapane* in the high native forest above them were feeding on the nectar of the *'ohi'a lehua* blossoms. At the edge of the trees, by an underground spring, a ditch fed fresh water into a flume. A long line of half-barrels, elevated on trestles, ran for miles down the side of the mountain. Narrow slats of wood were nailed at intervals across the top of the open flume.

To the cousins' amazement, Tōsi and Lily and Claire slid down into the cold water. Lily Shields held the tin can in one hand as, shoulders hunched from the chill, she waded across the ditch to where the water poured into the barreled flume. She took a big breath and lowered herself deeper into the water. With her head just above the surface, she allowed her legs to float before her into the flume. She grabbed onto the first wood slat with her free hand to stop herself from being sucked down the flume by the fast fall of the water.

"Last one down is a rotten egg," she said and she let go of the slat and disappeared in a wake of water. By the time Courtney stepped tentatively to the edge of the ditch, Lily was halfway down Green Valley. Tōsi and Claire waited in turn to shoot down the flume.

Tōsi said, "Mamie, you go last, behind them, just in case."

"Yes," Mamie said to the girls, "it is very important that you get out in time. You'll be going downhill very fast so when you see Claire pulling herself up through the slats, you must be ready to get out."

"Get out?" Brooke asked in dumb wonder.

"You stick your arm up," Tōsi said. "Through the slats. And hold on."

Courtney started back through the grove of mountain apple trees. Mamie could see her disappearing through the tufted myrtle.

"Did you tell her about Lorraine Mitsuda?" Claire asked Mamie angrily. Lorraine Mitsuda had not stopped herself in time and had been swept into the reservoir. She was mangled to death in the big pump. Benjie Furtado was there when they pulled out her legs, or so Gertrude said.

"No, of course I didn't."

"Who's Louise Mitsuda?" Brooke asked.

"I'm going," Tōsi said impatiently. As he hung from the

slat with both hands, his pants filled with air and streamed out before him. Then, with a shout of happiness, he, too, disappeared.

Claire, screaming with excitement, went down after him.

Mamie looked at Brooke and then she took her hand and they walked back to the jeep together. Courtney was sitting in the jeep. They played Twenty Questions and ate tiny mountain apples until they saw Tōsi, Lily and Claire hiking back up the steep dirt road.

Their clothes were wet. Tōsi carried the tin can. There was a tiny, watery trickle of blood on Tōsi's neck, behind his ear. Lily held her right wrist tenderly in front of her. Claire held long spears of yellow ginger and Mamie could smell the flowers long before they reached the jeep. Tōsi put the can in the back and Brooke and Courtney helped wrap Claire and Lily in the towels. Brooke looked curiously into the tin can. She screamed with such terror and disgust that Lily forgot for a moment the intense pain in her wrist.

In her rush to escape the horror of the can, Brooke overturned it and the black leeches inside flopped out onto the back seat.

"They can't stick to tin," Claire said sympathetically. She gently plucked the leeches off the seat. "They're for Jimmy."

"But where did you get them?" Courtney asked. She noticed a red welt on the top of Claire's bare foot.

"Where do you think?"

"In the flume?"

"This is why we wear clothes," Claire said, her patience nearing its end.

Courtney covered her mouth with her hand.

"You barf and you're walking home," Claire said, dangling the last leech over Courtney's head.

The island children were without fear. They grew up in the mountains and in the water, without benefit of organized games or even toys—in the Clarke household there were only a couple of packs of greasy old playing cards and some clumsy but fast home-made skateboards—and they drew their inspiration and pleasure from the ocean and valleys around them.

Lily Shields broke her wrist fluming that day. That is how she came to be able to write with her right foot, an accomplishment she later mysteriously claimed saved her from many awkward situations.

Mamie had proved herself a kind friend, never regretting that she had remained behind with her stepcousins. She would go down the fast flumes many times in the years to come, and the sisters from the mainland, who had never before eaten the wild apples that tasted like roses, or seen black leeches, went back down the mountain with a gratifying sense of their own awakening courage.

Claire and Mamie had been taken early to the dentist in Lihue, and the two tender girls, left on their own, decided to have a morning swim in the muddy waves in front of the house. Perhaps they wanted to test their daring and prove themselves to their new heroines. It was not necessary, for Claire and Mamie loved them, but it is possible that they did not know that.

As they walked through the kitchen with their beach mats and nose plugs and plastic eye protectors for sunbathing, just some of the extensive equipment that fascinated Mamie and Claire, who would never have taken even a towel to the beach, a sleepy Gertrude said casually, "Watch out for da shock."

"Oh, we're used to it," said Courtney politely. "We go to camp in Maine."

Gertrude watched dreamily from the big kitchen window as the girls gingerly edged their way through the eucalyptus trees and wandered off, on tiptoe, down the beach.

They were brought back to the house three hours later by two embarrassed Japanese fishermen who had been surfcasting off the Point and had had some trouble at first making out what the two babbling children were trying to tell them. The men had kindly carried them to the plantation house, reasoning soundly that there were not too many places in the area that would claim two convulsive white children.

McCully was called from the mill office, the fishermen given lemonade in the kitchen, and Courtney and Brooke were put to bed and coaxed back to life with little sips of warm *saké*. McCully was able to learn, finally, after Dr. Shields came down in a rush from the Big House, that they had been attacked, although it is really too strong a word, by a school of baby hammerhead sharks. They had been nuzzled and butted in the muddy water by the nearly blind but curious sharks, and although the sharks would not have caused them grave injury, and would certainly never have eaten them, Sheridan Shields said that they had nearly died of fright.

When Mamie and Claire ambled into the house, pleasantly absorbed with the thawing of their jaws, they were startled to find the two girls in bed, covered with blankets, Gertrude stroking the pale pink hands laid limply on top of the blankets like rabbit paws, and Mitsuya feeding the girls from bowls of *miso* soup.

In the kitchen, McCully, who was rarely angry, asked a frightened and bewildered Gertrude why she had let the girls go into the water.

"I told da kine, watch out for da shock. Watch out for da shock," she said, "an da kine went anyway."

"They thought you meant the shock of the water, that it would be cold. They don't speak English the way you do, Gertrude."

"But, that's what I say, da *shock!*" Gertrude did not understand why he was angry, and McCully knew that it was unfair to blame her. She was accustomed to the usually harmless independence of Mamie and Claire, and she had warned the two little girls in her fashion.

Despite Claire and Mamie's begging them to stay, and Mary's promise of a trip to the caves at Ha'ena, Courtney and Brooke left two days later, as soon as they regained the full use of their arms and legs. They would be several weeks early at their boarding school in Switzerland, but special arrangements had been made by Aunt Alice, and the school, though staffed only by building maintenance, would be delighted to see them again. After all, as their stepmother had explained to the headmistress, they had been "mauled by wild sharks."

Mamie and Claire were very sorry to see them leave. Mamie had been reading *The Wilder Shores of Love* aloud to them and Claire had even taught them how to catch crayfish in the flume reservoir (white bread balled up and wadded onto the end of a palm-frond spine). They felt for years after that they could have turned their stepcousins into barefoot Kaua'i girls if they had only been given the chance.

"Children recover quickly," Mary said dryly to her daughters. She was trying to make them feel better. She allowed them to kiss her on the cheek. "I know," she said.

But she was hardly a good example and even Mamie knew better than that.

‾ ‾ ‾

It was not long after the incident with the sharks that Mary reminded McCully that it was time for Mamie to go to school in Honolulu. There probably was no connection between the "attack" on the two mainland girls and her reminder that Mamie be sent away, as it was a tradition in those families who lived on outer islands for the children to attend the Punahou School in Honolulu as soon as they were old enough, but Mary's sudden interest in household matters did not go unmarked by McCully or Mamie.

McCully felt sorry for the girl, not because she was going to Punahou, that had been done in his family for generations and he knew that she would be well-educated there, but because he saw that she was always misunderstood by her mother. The child had bad luck. It was not that she tried to please her mother, or even to anticipate her approval. Just getting Mary's attention would have been more than enough to thrill Mamie. It would not have mattered much, however, what Mamie did, for Mary was unable to be very interested in either of her daughters. She had tried when they were babies, but the intimacy had terrified her and she had lost heart. They exasperated her.

McCully and Mary went to Honolulu for ten days, McCully to make the arrangements for Mamie to go to school, and Mary to search for older and stranger varieties of plants. She was still trying to find a gardener to replace Hiroshi.

Mamie and Claire were left in the house with Gertrude. Mitsuya came each morning to cook and the days were lazy and peaceful. Mamie wandered home from school the long way, through the town, hoping, as she still did, to catch sight of Hiroshi or to hear some news of him. He had disappeared. She stopped in at the feed store with its dry, pleasant smell of manure and bird seed, but no one had seen him. She stopped at Yumi's Menehune Inn to buy some *li hing mui* and a Spam sandwich. No one had seen him.

The evenings were spent watching reruns of "Gilligan's Island." Each of them picked the part she wanted to be that night. Claire kept trying to change her part, but Gertrude and Mamie were adamant once the roles had been chosen. Claire would watch in petulant dissatisfaction, stroking Jimmy. "I don't see why I can't be Ginger Grant if I want."

"You have to pick at the beginning of the show," Mamie said. "You can't say, 'I have dibs on Ginger' halfway through when Gertrude is already Ginger. It's not fair."

"Why do you make the rules?"

Mamie thought for a moment. "I don't," she said. "That's just how it is. It's just right, that's all."

Claire could think of no further argument, and besides, once the program began, they were so happily immersed in the plot, it was difficult for Claire to remember that she was angry.

A few days went by before Mamie noticed that Benjie Furtado, Gertrude's boyfriend, was keeping them company at unaccustomed times of the day and night. Benjie was very handsome. He was small and slight in that girlish, delicate way of young Filipino men, with black hair greased back into a d.a., and a thin black moustache. He wore tight tank tops with PRIMO BEER and MAUI NO KA OE printed on them and slippers with thick black rubber soles. Gertrude, who was plump and soft, adored Benjie, and Gertrude, with her good nature and easy ways, knew that Benjie was her destiny. Mamie was surprised to see him at the house so often, but Gertrude explained that he was on sick vacation.

Soon Benjie was watching "Gilligan's Island" with them. He sat in McCully's leather chair and drank San Miguel beer from the brown bottle. Then Gertrude began to want to sit in the chair with him. This was impossible, so they moved to the big *hikie‘e*. They necked while Mamie and Claire sat in front of them on the floor, painting their short nails, eating sweet and sour preserved apricots with just the tips of their fingers, so as not to smear the polish. Despite the occasional moan or burp from the lovers, the girls were very content. They were not in the least disturbed by the voluptuary sweetness that slowly overtook the house. Jimmy was slightly frenzied, perhaps because of the erotic, sweaty scent that padded the air around Gertrude and Benjie whenever they stirred. They did not stir much. From the *hikie‘e* in the library to the refrigerator to, eventually, the big bed in McCully and Mary's cool bedroom. Gertrude very kindly gave a grumbling Mitsuya the week off.

Benjie's cousin, Cecil, began to drop by after work. He had been in Vietnam and, according to Gertrude, he had come back a "hang-loose keed." Mamie asked him about the war while they played slap dominoes and he said, "The big things in my life, good things and bad things, happened there. What I dream about is the smell. There was a smell there. I smelled it as soon as I got off the plane. It was like what the food smells like in the back of a Chink restaurant after it's been there a week."

He came back the next evening for a rematch and before Mamie could even say hello or double-or-nothing, he said angrily, "Don't ask me no more about Nam. You started me thinking about it," and she said, "Sure, Cecil," and calmly set up the tiles.

Four days after Mr. and Mrs. Clarke boarded the plane for Honolulu, the girls stopped going to school. Mamie no longer read. Benjie and Gertrude spent most of the day in McCully and Mary's bed. At two in the morning, a tousled, sated Benjie, clearly nude under McCully's roomy bathrobe, barbecued *char siu* pork for them and fried bananas, and Gertrude taught the girls how to crack gum. Gertrude could crack gum louder and faster than anyone in Waimea. This was a feat proved at the last Captain Cook Festival when she'd won first prize in a gum-cracking contest. The local newspaper begged her to reveal her special formula, two Juicyfruits? One Hubba Bubba? But she refused to tell. Gertrude no longer bothered to dress when she staggered out of the bedroom every evening. She waddled happily to the kitchen in her big black brassiere and big black panties, and rustled up a few bags of Fritos and bottles of Coke for the girls.

Mamie and Claire were virginal odalisques, if such a thing is possible. They, too, moved in a dream of languorous stupefaction. It is to their credit that they never, even later, saw the slightest immorality in the situation. Perhaps they were simply fulfilling their true natures, and the competent, but sterile, years of their parents' rule had left them porous and expectant for just this sort of innocent sensuality.

The house was a mess. Dishes coated with plum sauce and dried *lau-lau* leaves were on every tabletop, and every chair held empty white cardboard take-out containers and jars of hair cream and saucers overflowing with cigarette butts. Jimmy gained five pounds just from licking the dirty plates. Since they had unconsciously restricted themselves to only a few rooms of the house, it could not be said that they had spent the time in filth. It was untidy, but not sordid.

The night before the Clarkes were to return, they seemed to realize that their idyll had come to an end. They felt no dread at the return of McCully and Mary because they felt no guilt. They did feel, all four of them, a luxurious and intimate regret. Mamie hoped that they would be together like this for the rest of their lives, as soon as the girls could get away from their parents.

Gertrude washed the badly stained sheets until four o'clock in the morning.

It was Cecil and Benjie's job to collect and burn the trash—the beer cases, boxes of See's candy, Dairy Queen cups and rib bones of various unidentifiable animals. The enormous bonfire on the beach burned exuberantly through the night.

Mamie and Claire cleaned the kitchen. Every glass, every plate, pot, utensil and cup had been used and left, encrusted and glazed, in the sink and on the counters for the whole, happy ten days.

There were a few things that they had left until it was too late, such as the cigar burn in McCully's bathrobe, and the empty bottles of California wine that McCully was saving for a special occasion, but there was nothing to be done about it.

They went about their chores happily. Claire said she felt like the elves in *The Shoemaker and the Elves,* and Benjie asked, "What's an elve?"

While Claire gaily told him the story, Mamie scraped the last of the cold *malasadas* into Jimmy's greasy, smiling mouth.

THREE

Several weeks after McCully and Mary returned from Honolulu, Mary asked Mamie if she would like to help her in the garden. Mamie was very pleased to be asked and worked quietly at the small chores that Mary gave her—weeding under the milky *plumeria* trees and watering delicately by hand the trembling young *liliko'i* shoots.

Mary may have suspected by then that Hiroshi had done exactly what Mamie told McCully he did, for how else could his disappearance be explained? Mary was also not so removed from her daughter that she did not know that Mamie was an intelligent and honest child. She had behaved rashly when Hiroshi was dismissed, Mary told herself, and she considered that she may not have been kind to Mamie. That she had profoundly altered Mamie's view of the world and herself in it did not occur to her. She was less honest and less intelligent than Mamie. She did feel sorry that the whole thing had ever happened. She should have told Mamie.

Mamie watched Mary expertly divide the root stock of a *ti* bush. Mamie admired her mother's ruthless pruning. Mamie was always a little afraid that she was hurting a plant, but Mary hacked and snipped with a clear conscience.

"That is why you're a good gardener," Mamie said aloud.

"What?" Mary was entangled in a vine.

"You're not worried about hurting the plants."

Mary looked at her as if she had lost her senses. "Of course I'm not. What a funny idea." As if to prove it, she ripped the vine from an old wood fence. Mamie was sure she could hear the tiny suckers on the vine whimpering in pain as they popped off the wood rails.

"I think you'll like your roommate next year," Mary said, panting a little with the effort of yanking the stubborn vine from the fence. "She's from the Big Island. McCully went to school with her uncles." She passed one end of the vine along to Mamie. "And Lily Shields is there, too, a few years ahead of you. Such a strange girl. I saw her the other day in Lihue dressed all in black and wearing white rice powder all over her face. I'm surprised her father lets her go out looking like a ghost."

"That's what she is."

Mary looked up from her work. "What?"

"She is a ghost."

"What *are* you talking about?" Mary was irritated. Mamie should have been more cautious. It was well-known that Mary loathed anything fanciful.

"In the school play," Mamie said. It was a lie, but she would rather protect her best friend than ever explain The Mothers Club to Mary.

"Her mother was strange, too."

Mamie turned back to the weeds. There seemed to her to be many things that she could never explain to Mary. She had loved Lily's mother.

"Did you see Auntie Emma in Honolulu?" she asked to protect Lily and her dead mother.

"Twice. We went to dinner at George Brown's and she made him play the ukulele and she danced all the old hulas."

"Father must have been happy."

"I'm afraid he danced, too." Mary gave a last, mighty tug on the vine, and she almost fell over backward as it finally gave up and came fast off the fence. The word "too" came out of her like a shout.

"I love when Daddy does the hula."

Mary roughly coiled the vine in an unruly, leafy circle.

Mamie saw that she had lost her attention. "Can't you see how terrible that is for the vine?" she asked quietly. "Can't you hear what is going on around you, what Mr. Griep, my science teacher, calls the 'music of the spheres'?"

"What, Mamie?"

Of course, the question that Mamie most passionately yearned to ask, and the question that was implicit in all of the others, was, Why do you not love me? But she merely said again, "the music of the spheres, the music of the—"

"There!" Mary said with satisfaction.

She had subdued the heavy vine, like a snake charmer. Heedless of the child who sat motionless in the grass, watching her solemnly, she went off to spray the fruit trees.

Exhausted by the effort of trying to keep her mother's interest and failing, Mamie walked listlessly back to the house.

McCully was sitting in the library in his leather chair, Benjie Furtado's leather chair, and he looked up when he heard Mamie on the veranda. He came outside. Mamie could hear Sousa marches on the record player.

They sat down in chairs facing the ocean. Behind them was an old bookcase with glass doors. It was filled with the dark, gleaming *koa* calabashes given to Mamie's ancestors by the Kings and Queens of Hawai'i. Heavy stone poi-pounders sat in rows on the bottom shelf, next to thin sheets of brown-and-white *kapa* cloth. McCully had been asked several times to donate these artifacts to the Bishop Museum, but he withheld his decision. He liked the idea of giving them to Mamie some day. He always said that she would know what to do with them.

When Mamie was younger, McCully would hold her in his lap in an old *koa* rocker and she would watch the changeable sea, the birthplace of the moon, as he told her the heroic tales of Kaua'i, the oldest, most verdant, and most sacred of the islands. He told her the legend of the young woman, Pele, who begged permission of her mother and father to leave home. She took with her an egg in which her sister was hatching. Pele carried the egg carefully under her warm arm until the egg broke open and her sister was freed. Although Pele was blessed with the gift of magic, she did not foresee the sorrow her sister would someday bring her. Pele was too distracted. She was looking for fire, island to island.

"Daldo Fortunato tells me he's making you a new surfboard," McCully said.

"In exchange for taking over his son's paper route."

"The one who just joined the marines?"

"He wants to go to Vietnam."

"Now I remember. He's the one who was kicked out of Castle High."

"They're sending him instead to California and so he tried to resign from the marines, but they said no. You can't just resign, they said."

"Why did he want to go to Vietnam?"

"Orval said it's because of the grass. He has a plan to develop a new kind of marijuana seed."

McCully looked at her. She was not trying to be funny, although she knew that what she was saying was funny. Besides, she was telling the truth.

"You've always talked about the importance of our agricultural economy," she said, trying not to smile.

"Didn't anyone else want the paper route?"

She shook her head.

"But it's worth a surfboard?"

"Daldo makes the best sticks on Kaua'i." She pronounced it in Pidgin, "steeks," and he finally laughed.

They could hear Mitsuya chopping vegetables in the kitchen. The chopping was surprisingly in time with the Sousa march.

"Something quite mysterious has happened," McCully said. He had temporarily restored her frail sense of well-being, so she was not prepared when he went on to ask, "Were there people here in the house when your mother and I were away?"

"I think so," she said, very low and still.

"Was there a party or something?"

She was silent.

"Some things are missing, there are burns in my clothes. It doesn't make sense." He was not trying to entrap her, but in his guileless way, he was mystified. "I found a pair of woman's undergarments in the pocket of my bathrobe, and I don't believe they belong to Mother."

Mamie felt herself begin to perspire. She looked at him, forcing herself to stare into his sunburned face. She was afraid. She had awakened every morning since Hiroshi disappeared with the anxiety that something just like this would happen. She would lose Gertrude now, and whatever was left of her mother's affection, and, worse, even McCully would be disgusted by her. She had instinctively come to realize that although she and Claire had been deliriously happy on their honeymoon with Gertrude and Benjie, McCully, and especially Mary, would be shocked by it.

"Someone was here, but it was all right. Not a party."

"Someone?" He was so intent on the curiousness of it that he still did not notice that she was very upset.

"I cannot tell you," she finally said.

"You can't tell me?"

"It was Gertrude and Benjie," she said, hanging her head.

"Benjie Furtado, the cop?"

Her father's slowness to understand made it worse for Mamie. She wanted to leap to her feet to shout angrily that it had been blissful while they were away, shouting as if it were his fault that she had been so happy.

McCully shook his head in amazement.

"Gertrude is going to marry him," she said, wringing her hands.

McCully finally saw how much she suffered. "Well, good," he said cautiously, trying to understand her distress. He took her hand.

"I couldn't stand it, Father," she whispered, "if anything happened to them because of me."

"Nothing will happen, dear," he said, stroking her arm.

She let him calm her, and she believed him when he said that he would take care of everything. He made her promise that she would not worry. She saw that he was still mildly troubled by what he could only guess had happened, but she knew that she could trust him.

They walked across the lawn to the beach. He had his arm around her shoulder. It was windy and some Hawaiian children waiting for the boat to Ni'ihau were throwing sand. They ran away when they saw McCully, as if they were not allowed to play on his beach.

McCully and Mamie walked down to the wooden dock and were back in time for dinner.

Mamie and Claire were both good readers and because their parents were not, their reading went largely unremarked. Very little that was stimulating was offered to them at school, so their eager imaginations depended on the books that Mamie brought home daily from the small public library. Claire was partial to books from the adult section. Mamie told the dubious librarian that Claire's selections, *Forever Amber* and *Valley of the Dolls,* were for her mother. Mamie was a serious, mature reader, and although she had read most of Dickens and all of Dumas, she had a special fondness for books about desert isles. She read *Robinson Crusoe, The Swiss Family Robinson, Lord of the Flies,* and even *Peter Pan* with deep pleasure.

It had something to do with what she later called the "white bone-fantasy." It was an image of herself washed up on a beach, as smooth and as white as a bone. It was a notion she had first had from Lily Shields' mother, Anna, who had often taken the girls to distant, isolated beaches—they had to struggle down steep cliffsides, hanging dangerously from the horizontal roots of the *'alula*—where she would encourage them to remove their bathing suits and pretend they had been shipwrecked. Given Anna Shields' notorious charm, it is not hard to see that this game would have been very alluring to Mamie. The girls would hunt in the *naupaka* for dried husks and pieces of torn net to use as loincloths and tools.

This fascination with desert isles was perhaps a reaction to the assault Mamie's body was suddenly undergoing, as black hair began to grow under her arms, and on her rounded pubis, and swellings like little green peas began to ache under her nipples. This would be the conventional interpretation. Mamie yearned for and sought a kind of purity. In another family and another time, Mamie would have eventually entered the convent, taking the name of one of the more intellectual, masculine saints like Jerome.

It was a matter of temperament. Claire thrived on turmoil and intrigue with a heartless exuberance, but Mamie had begun by innocently trusting outward things to play their part. Lately she had come to realize that there was no promise that things would, or even could, play their part and her body was proving to be the most unreliable thing of all.

Perhaps it was this feeling of tentativeness and isolation that led her one hot afternoon into town and into the dusty photography studio of Mr. Yasunobu Tsugiyama. Mr. Tsugiyama's modest business was to take photographs of Japanese wedding parties and small family groups, photographs to be ceremoniously sent back to Japan to provincial parents and grandparents. The solemn faces in the portraits could be framed, at the sitters' choice, in hand tinted pink cherry blossoms or red temple gates. The photographs were used, too, as burial cards. Mamie had looked at them closely whenever she was in the Buddhist cemetery, pasted onto the gravemarkers, and prettily decorated with silk flowers and paper inscriptions when the grave was fresh.

Perhaps that is where she first had the idea of being photographed. Mr. Tsugiyama was certainly very surprised to see the *haole* girl come into his little store that humid day. He did not speak English very well, only a few words, but she spoke to him in English as if he could understand her, and she did not raise her voice or speak very slowly in a way that would have patronized him.

He ushered her through the faded calico curtain with elaborate politeness and sat her in a wooden folding chair and gave her a pink plastic mirror and comb.

She smoothed down her hair, and ruffled up her eyebrows with saliva the way Gertrude had taught her to do. She was wearing a lei of *pikake*. He moved her head, tilted her chin this way and that, and straightened her collar. She allowed him to pose her as he liked and then she froze obediently, holding the pose, while he studied her. The poses were not very sophisticated—an index finger held to the chin, cocked head resting on a fist—but Mamie did not know any better. She was concerned that his deep frown meant disapproval, but when he finished fussing and backed away from her, smiling, pleased with his work, she saw that it was only concentration that made him look so serious.

He disappeared under his black cloth. He took far more photographs of her than he would customarily have taken of the shy Japanese bride in her heavy wig and wedding kimono who was his usual subject. This odd, solemn child was altogether something out of his experience, and if he spent more time with her than was usual, it was because she interested him.

When they finished, they shook hands and bowed low several times. He watched her with curiosity as she went out into the harsh light. When she reached the corner, she looked back and bowed again.

In the middle of the afternoon, when Gertrude had an hour off, Mamie and Claire often went to Gertrude's room at the back of the house, next to the garage, to lie on her small bed and entice her into telling them secrets. Whatever they knew of seduction, conception, abortion, betrayal, murder and seemingly, but not necessarily, less serious things such as how to keep a man or how to pierce ears with an ice cube and a lei needle, they learned in those happy afternoons with Gertrude. Sometimes it rained and the noise of the heavy, plump drops falling on the roof of the greenhouse made Mamie feel reassured and happy. Gertrude's radio was always on and they listened to Golden Oldies and the surfing report: "Mahalepu has heavy swells, no crests; breaking to the left at three to five feet." There was the sickening sweet smell of Lilac Vegetol hair cream on Gertrude's pillow. It gave Mamie a headache. It was a man's hairdressing, Mamie knew, very greasy and very popular with the straight-haired, black-haired boys from the camp. The camp boys called *"bilat-bilat"* to Mamie when she self-consciously pumped past them on her bike. When she'd asked Gertrude what *bilat-bilat* meant, Gertrude matter-of-factly said "cunt."

Mary forbade Mamie to shave her legs, even though the dark-haired Mamie was always in shorts or a bathing suit, and embarrassed by the hair on her legs. Gertrude secretly took Mamie aside to show her how to remove the black hair with a sharp stone brought up from the beach. Gertrude had learned the primitive technique from her mother on her home island of Ilocos Norte. The hair removal was painful, the stone acting as a pumice. It removed the skin from Mamie's legs as well as the hair. Mary had not noticed, even though Mamie's legs were bright red for several days. Claire, of course, had the nerve to wonder, after the terrible suffering Mamie endured while Gertrude vigorously planed her raw calves, why Mamie did not buy a razor with her allowance.

"This is how her mother taught her," Mamie said, trying to be patient. "It is authentic, and even romantic. Like being a castaway on a lonely isle."

"Romantic? Your legs are bleeding, Mamie."

"You are more modern than I am, Claire. I like to pretend I live in a distant past."

"You act like you're someone in a story." Claire would have soaped and shaved her legs in front of her mother if she'd felt like it. She was not cautious, as was Mamie, but her assumption that she was entitled to have her way did rob her of a certain tenderness.

Gertrude was full of other kinds of lore as well, requiring less physical pain, perhaps, but just as thrilling to Mamie. She told them, for example, that Orval Nalag's older brother, Clinton, who played first string football at Castle High, had made Ann Portago, the fifteen-year-old daughter of the state senator, pregnant. Or, as Gertrude put it, "knock-up." Ann Portago had disappeared from the face of the earth two weeks earlier and the girls had been told that she had mononucleosis and had been sent to Santa Barbara, California, so the girls knew that Gertrude was telling the truth.

Gertrude had been born a twin. The other baby, a girl, had died at birth. Gertrude's mother came every year from the Philippines to visit her, bringing a suitcase full of the same hand-embroidered placemats as presents. Gertrude's mother took on new importance to them when Gertrude nonchalantly said that when her mother had felt the birth contractions begin, she had ignored their warning, as she was having her nails done at the time (What color? Claire asked) and they were not yet dry. That was Gertrude's mother's explanation for the death of Gertrude's own other self and Gertrude accepted it with a passive and uncritical literalness. That this explanation of the unnecessary death made sense to Gertrude, that it had a kind of sympathetic logic, that it was, most importantly, without blame or sorrowing guilt, was an amazement to Mamie. Gertrude knew that grief and bereavement took up an unreasonable amount of invisible energy. Both sisters admired her deeply

—Claire, because she recognized another realist (wet nails are, in the end, as good an explanation as any for blind tragedy) and Mamie because she recognized her opposite, her happy opposite.

Mamie was trying not to let the smell of the hair cream make her sick as she watched Claire sing along with James Brown, "(Get Up, I Feel Like Being a) Sex Machine." Claire used Jimmy as a microphone, switching his tail back and forth with her free hand as if it were a microphone cord. She made Mamie laugh. Gertrude passed her Vicks nose inhaler to Mamie for a good, head-clearing pull on it.

Gertrude said that Sharlagne had told her that morning that Dicky Herbert, whose father had bought him a surplus army tank, had taken a pipe of hashish and two green bananas and a girl from the Koloa Camp named Imelda, in honor of the wife of the Philippine president, into the tank and driven to the waterfall at the end of Knudsen Gap, destroying the Knudsens' famous plantation of rare croton bushes.

"He refuse to let da girl, Imelda, out da tank," she said, her eyes wide.

There was a quiet knock on Gertrude's door. All three of them jumped. Claire put Jimmy on her shoulder. The door opened and McCully stuck his head into the room.

"May I see you a minute, Mamie?" he asked. He did not come into the room, having a democratic idea that it was Gertrude's room, even if it were his house.

Mamie followed him through the house to the little room he used as an estate office. Rain had brought hundreds of small toads onto the lawn. Mamie was always interested in this phenomenon because she could not imagine where the toads kept themselves when it was dry. She watched the toads assembling in the rain. It had something to do with insects, she knew. When the rain stopped, the toads would disappear as if summoned away by a sorcerer.

McCully did not speak and because Mamie was diverted by the toads on the grass, she did not at first notice his silence or the stiff way that he stood behind his desk.

It was a *koa* wood desk made for McCully the year he had given a workshop to the high school. He had wanted those boys who did not do well in the academic classes, and this would have included most of them, to have the pleasure, tactile as well as emotional, that came from making something good with their hands, something that was not a furrow for sugar cane or a ditch for irrigation. The cabinetmakers he found to teach the boys were local Japanese artisans whose beautiful work, in a more sophisticated and acquisitive market, would have been sold in galleries rather than roadside garages. The boys must have recognized what it was that McCully had done, for by the end of that first year, they had made the desk for him.

If it is possible, the desk grew more beautiful in those years it spent in McCully's room. Perhaps it was the damp salt air, that air that turned new bicycles to rust two days after Christmas, that breathed mercifully on the lovely desk. It had grown more beautiful each year.

The boys who had made it were grown men now and one of the carpenters who had taught them, Mr. Yomashiro, was an old, old man, and because no one ever left the town, McCully would have seen these men all the time in the fields or in the town. None of them had become craftsmen or artists, and they were not unhappy doing the work their fathers had done before them, planting furrows and digging ditches.

McCully bent down, out of sight on the other side of the desk. "Did you do this?" Mamie heard him say.

She walked around the desk. He was squatting before a drawer, rubbing his fingers against the wood, not looking at her. She did not understand. She bent down next to him. He turned to look at her, close to him, as he reluctantly pulled his fingers away from the wood. There, in deep, precise letters were the words MARY WILDING CLARKE. It was her name.

Someone had gouged the letters with a strong knife or a chisel. It would have taken time to do it so clearly and deeply. There would have been shavings and sawdust and the sound of the tool scraping and digging. There would have been sufficient time to reconsider; to stop and run away after the first *M*. All of this became more and more clear to Mamie, as it had become clear to McCully.

It also went through her mind that she was named Wilding after the spinster lady who had adopted her mother. The desk was made the year Mamie was born, McCully had told her many times.

She turned to McCully. "I didn't do it, Father."

He nodded slowly. She did not know what he was thinking, or if he believed her.

Mamie touched the words of her name. "Do you believe me?" she asked quietly. Her eyes filled with tears.

He stood up. Mamie heard his right knee crack. He shook the creases out of his trousers. There were bits of red Kaua'i dirt stuck in the crenulations of the rubber soles of his work shoes.

"Yes," he said.

It never occurred to either of them to try to discover who had defaced McCully's beautiful desk, a gift from the Waimea High School Shop, Class of '61. Years later when Mamie did learn who had laboriously carved MARY WILDING CLARKE in the desk, she was only a little surprised at the revelation. She had already convinced herself that she, Mamie, had done it.

She used to wake in the hot nights after McCully showed her the defacement and whisper to herself, Maybe I did do it, yes, perhaps I did. I must have. I did.

It might have seemed to an outsider, or someone who lived in a city, that Mamie and Claire's days were long and lonely. That their most intimate companion was a lackadaisical, superstitious Filipino housemaid, or that Claire spent a large part of her time talking to a mongoose, might have been significant in a different setting. But there, on the westernmost boundary of the United States, on the very edge, it did not seem strange at all.

Mamie did have her best friend, Lily, the co-founder of The Mothers Club, but Lily lived an hour's drive away in Koloa. That Lily also seemed to live contentedly in a kingdom of her own making, several light-years away, only enhanced her in Mamie's eyes. They wrote letters to each other, part rebus, part rhyme, and left the letters in hollow tree trunks, to be picked up and delivered by one of the many unusually devoted servants of the eccentric Shields family. Lily even tried sending messages by her brother's carrier pigeons, but it was not a successful experiment.

Mary did not approve of the friendship. Even when there was the possibility of Mamie's hitching a ride with one of the ranch hands into Koloa, Mary would find a way to prevent Mamie's going. Lily Shields, even though she was just a girl, made Mary very uncomfortable. It is possible that Mary was a little jealous of the child.

Mamie had another friend, Sherry Alden, who was the daughter of the English teacher at the high school. Sherry played the 'cello and knew about such things as withdrawing troops from Vietnam (yes) and B. F. Skinner (no). She was Mamie's first leftist friend. She was two years older than Mamie, which gave her mystery and prestige, and it was Sherry who gave Mamie her first hint that there was a big, alluring world awaiting them. They would lie on the cool floor of Sherry's untidy room and listen to a bossa nova record that Sherry had sent away for, Stan Getz and João Gilberto, and it was during these delightful sessions that Mamie took Sherry's hint about the world. Listening to the sweet Brazilian music with intense pleasure and identification, Mamie began to see that she might find a place in that lovely universe beyond her cane fields.

The more she listened to the music, the greater was her longing, and she imagined herself in the poignant, erotic world of jazz sambas and men who loved you so crazily they wrote songs about you: "Tall and tan and young and lovely, the girl from Ipanema goes walking, and when she passes, he smiles but she doesn't see . . ." Sherry introduced her to other music, too. She liked to listen to the St. Matthew Passion at full volume and she insisted on playing Edith Piaf while they read Raymond Radiguet with a French dictionary, but it was the seductive Brazilian music that entered Mamie's soul and stayed there.

Mamie was very impressed by what seemed to her to be the very bohemian and intellectual pursuits of the entire Alden family. Mr. Alden was writing a novel on the weekends, and the mother, who made her own candles, taught a sculpture class at the university extension in Lihue. Mamie was fascinated by them. Unlike her own family, they did things together. Sherry's mother kept a shell-encrusted casket, that she had made herself, in the center of the cluttered dining room table into which they all dropped their loose change and the odd dollar bill in the hope that they would put enough away to enable them to emigrate to Bali.

Despite the charm of the family itself, Mamie always felt a

little uneasy when she was alone with Sherry. Sherry wanted to massage her back or arm wrestle or brush her hair and Mamie felt guilty that Sherry caused her to feel so uncomfortable. There was a time in the fall, when school resumed, when Sherry would telephone Mamie every evening. Mary was pleased because she hoped that Sherry would replace Lily Shields as Mamie's friend.

Then, suddenly, Mamie refused to even come to the telephone when Sherry called, and she would no longer go to Sherry's house after school. Mamie would have nothing to do with the Aldens.

Mary, who was constantly levying petty punishments on Mamie for walking through the workers' camp—she was convinced that Mamie would be assaulted by one of the local boys—and who would never understand that the workers' camp was the safest place that Mamie could be, was angry that Mamie would not be Sherry's friend. She was further upset when Mamie refused to explain her sudden loss of interest in the Aldens.

It would have been impossible for Mamie to explain to her mother just what had happened. Mamie knew that Mary would not believe her. Mamie herself had some difficulty believing what had happened, even though she went over it many times in her mind.

She had been invited to spend the night at Sherry's house. Sherry's parents had gone to a Kundalini yoga class after dinner and Sherry and Mamie had played cards, crazy eights, and made a marble cake in ice-cube trays. They picked *pakalana* flowers in the dark garden and Mamie pinned them in her hair. Sherry began to act a little silly right before bedtime and Mamie had insisted on undressing and taking a shower alone.

In the bedroom, Sherry had waited nervously for Mamie before getting into bed. She had even waited for Mamie to turn down the cotton blanket. When Mamie, her dismay growing like a flowering tree inside of her, did turn down the blanket, she uncovered a sheet that was marked with a huge brown stain.

She stood next to the bed, the hem of the blanket held high in her hand, staring at the stain for a long time. For the briefest moment, Mamie thought she must be mistaken, but when Sherry began to giggle spasmodically, Mamie forced herself to admit that the stain was dried blood. Sherry had begun to menstruate and she had saved the proof of it for Mamie.

She was giving it as an offering to Mamie.

Mamie did not want it.

Her only thought had been how to get away. She wanted to sleep in her own clean bed. She could already see herself running down the black highway in her nightdress. She could see herself scratching at the back door for Gertrude to let her inside (she would have to sleep in Gertrude's room so that her mother would not ask any questions). She could see herself writing to Lily Shields in the morning, not to tell her what had happened, but to reassure herself and to fortify the only friendship she would ever, ever have—she was thinking all of this, still holding the blanket, when Sherry's parents came cheerfully into the room.

Mamie had slept on the floor, or that is pretended to sleep, while Sherry wept loudly. Mamie had listened, horrified and ashamed, until Sherry had fallen asleep. In the morning, Mamie sneaked away before anyone else was awake.

Mary never could reconcile herself to what she saw as Mamie's willful refusal to be friends with the right kind of girl. Because Mamie never would explain why she no longer wanted to see Sherry, Mary decided that Mamie was a secretive child. Mamie knew that her mother thought less of her because of this, but it would have been impossible for Mamie to save herself simply by telling the easy truth.

She went back several times to Mr. Tsugiyama's photography studio to look at the proofs and select the poses she liked best. Mr. Tsugiyama had his own particular favorites and they spent quite a bit of time over their final choice. At one point, Mr. Tsugiyama went into the back and made green tea for them. In the end, although she preferred a rather perky shot that was not at all like her, at least in spirit, she succumbed and agreed with Mr. Tsugiyama that the serious one of the girl (it was hard for her to think that the photographs were of herself) with the hopeful gaze was the best one. He was very pleased that she agreed with him. She ordered five prints.

She returned only once more, to pick up the finished portraits. She had never once considered where she would find the money to pay for them. When she told Mary that she needed forty dollars cash money (an expression she had learned from the workers), Mary, perhaps because of her constant state of benign distraction, gave it to her without question.

Mamie never told anyone about her sitting with Mr. Tsugiyama. She kept the photographs under her clothes in a drawer in her bedroom. She took them out when she was alone and lay on her bed and stared at them. She was not vain. She was not interested in the length of her lashes or the sweet curve of her lower lip. Mamie was trying to understand just who she was, and how she came to be that way.

F O U R

One quiet afternoon, three police cars from Waimea Township turned into the fields. The cars bounced slowly up and down the dirt lanes of the camp. The officers' voices were calm over the loudspeakers as they advised the startled residents to evacuate immediately to higher ground. A tsunami, originating in the cold waters of the Sea of Japan, was rapidly approaching the island. The tidal wave was expected to strike the south shore in less than two hours.

Stores and houses were closed and boards hastily hammered over glass windows. Livestock was brought in from the low grazing lands and, roped in single file, led reluctantly up the winding road of Waimea Canyon. There was no time to lure them into horse trailers and cattle vans, so the cavalcade looked more like placid animals being led to the Ark than animals in flight. School buses drove slowly through the town, doors open, and people jumped onto the moving buses, pulling children and dogs and cats behind them.

There was no panic. The only indication that some unusual manifestation of nature was about to alter the world was the gradual but steady change in the wind and sky. The dance of the trees grew more violent as the trees made deeper and more ecstatic bows. The sky darkened as a watery black ink stain seeped slowly north from the horizon. The animals, too, began to tremble and howl, heads cocked toward the ocean, listening to some silent, terrible warning.

Benjie Furtado was on the end of the dock, helping the returning fishermen to fasten their rocking boats. There was not enough time to take the boats out to sea. The water grew more muddy and turbulent. It was as if the shallow ocean bottom were being stirred violently. The siren from the Fire Station keened out over the bay.

McCully was at the mill. He came back to the plantation with Officer Higa, who dropped him at the grove. There were only two good roads into the mountains, and there was a danger that the townspeople would be caught and drowned in their cars. McCully had arranged for Daldo Fortunato to meet him at the plantation house with his truck.

When McCully reached the house, a little more worried now that it had taken him so long to get there in Officer Higa's slow-moving patrol car, he found Mary and Claire throwing seedlings and plants onto sheets of burlap. Gertrude, a little hysterical, was walking in circles. Mitsuya was tying up the corners of the burlap. Claire had Jimmy on the end of a long clothesline, and the mongoose accompanied Gertrude in her pacing. The siren made it difficult to hear.

Daldo pulled up in the truck and helped the women heave the burlap sacks into the open back.

"Where is Mamie?" McCully asked.

Mary looked up, worried, as she realized that Mamie was not with them.

Claire pulled Jimmy, hand over hand, into her arms. Jimmy was chattering and biting the air. Daldo lifted Claire into the back of the truck.

"Where is she?" Mary asked Claire.

"I thought she was with Gertrude."

Gertrude began to whimper. McCully grabbed her by the shoulders.

"Where is she?" He shook her.

She shuddered and said, "Orval came during lunch and told her he seen Hiroshi at da reeva." She started to moan again.

"And?" McCully spoke low. He pressed her shoulders as he held her firmly before him.

"She went to da bridge to try find Hiroshi."

She fell forward into McCully's arms and he helped her climb into the back of the truck with Claire, while Daldo took Mitsuya and Mary into the front with him. McCully slammed the heavy door, and the truck creaked and bounced through the grove and onto the highway that was already blocked with cars and school buses. Through the swaying and creaking trees, McCully could see a winding line of cars and animals and people climbing the soft slope of the mountain. It looked like a pilgrimage.

He rode Claire's small rusty bike through the camp. The bridge was on the other side of Waimea, near the old Russian fort. The Waimea River, wide and deep at its mouth, was the natural harbor where Captain Cook had dropped anchor and stepped ashore for the first time to greet the curious, unsuspecting Hawaiians.

In the camp, dirt was swirling in circles, and loose pieces of tin and palm branches flew in the air. Through the siren sound, there was the groaning and snapping sound of trees splitting and roofs and fences ripping away. A fishing net was blown across his path, and damp laundry fell heavily on the flattened hibiscus bushes and broke the blossoms from their stems. The animals left behind, chickens and goats and cats and dogs, herded together in terror and raced in a pack through the abandoned camp.

Then McCully heard another sound through the siren and the baying trees and the baying animals. It was the water, in its first surge backward to the edge of the planet, leaving in its perverse wake thousands of flapping, startled fish; banks of red coral suddenly burdened with wiggling, gasping eels; old outriggers encrusted with barnacles like Sherry's mother's shell casket; and one white enamel washing machine.

McCully stopped the bike by the seawall. He could see the cement bridge. He could see, for the first time, the deep clay bottom of the river. He turned away from the land, to the roaring horizon. He could see his destruction.

Although the garden was badly uprooted, the house and the banyan tree stood firm. The ocean veranda was washed out to sea. The inside of the house was damaged, but there was nothing that could not be repaired or replaced. Mary set to work at once, and McCully's relatives were impressed by her strength. What had once seemed to some of them as cold detachment now stood her in good stead, and some even understood that it had stood her in good stead all of her life.

Mamie, who insisted on remaining with Daldo and Benjie for the three days and nights that the search parties looked for survivors, was with them when they found Hiroshi's body. It was entangled in a net of seaweed and driftwood trapped under the bridge. McCully's body was never found.

With the one ancient calabash that had somehow escaped the deadly pull of the ocean, and with Claire, whom Mamie convinced Mary to let go one year early, Mamie left Waimea for school in Honolulu. Both girls were very happy there.

FIVE

Aunt Alice, or Alysse (accent on the second syllable) as she now preferred to be called, decided to give a small dinner party the night of Mamie's arrival in New York. She always did things on the spur of the moment. It was one of her own favorite character traits. She thought it made her seem headstrong and that this made her seem young.

It didn't occur to her that Mamie might be tired after her trip from Los Angeles. The truth was, Alysse was regretting just a tiny bit her invitation to her niece. After all, she had not seen her in nine years, since McCully's funeral. Because of her mild regret, she could think of no reason to delay Mamie's debut. The dinner was, in fact, a little test.

She had the idea from her second husband, who had once said, "I don't know if I should, but I judge people by their picnics." It was a trial that worked well for Alysse. You might have ordered the saturation bombing of small, neutral countries or made your fortune selling missiles to an African government or, on a less dramatic level, you might enjoy having sexual intercourse with persons no longer living, but if you could hold your own at one of Alysse's dinners, and by that is not meant anything so elementary as knowing which fork to use, you became a dear friend.

Mamie, a little pale, was shown into the red library. Alysse was on the telephone. At first glance, she seemed like an alert, blond bunny. She was wearing a pink angora sweatsuit. A big pink ribbon held back her pale curls. She had not as much hair as she might have liked to have, and the loops of the ribbons stood up on her head like rabbit ears. She gestured excitedly to Mamie and pantomimed her boredom and impatience with the speaker, but she did not end her conversation. There was a strong smell of orange peel and clove in the lacquered room.

The maid, Lydia, stood impatiently in the doorway, holding Mamie's bag. Alysse, pointing and waving exaggeratedly, finally made them understand that Lydia was to take Mamie to the guest room.

She said, with a sudden shriek, "He's the most eligible married man in New York," and Mamie turned back because she thought that Alysse was speaking to her, but Alysse was standing at the window with the telephone, looking down at Park Avenue, laughing.

Mamie followed Lydia. Her room was at the end of a narrow, winding hall. The curtains were drawn even though the sky was still blue and full of light. Mamie sat on one of the beds. Lydia began to unpack her bag. The curtains and chair material and bed coverings were a blue hydrangea-printed chintz. There were horticultural watercolors on the chintz-papered walls, each gilt frame hanging from a moiré ribbon attached to the ceiling molding with a big bow. There were Chinese pots of pale blue hyacinths in the empty fireplace and their thin smell, too sweet, hurt Mamie's head.

"I'll do that," she said to Lydia. Lydia looked at her in satisfaction, as if Mamie had committed her first mistake. "I prefer to," Mamie said, smiling with embarrassment, and Lydia shrugged.

There was a bottle of mineral water, for aware French women, it said on the label, on a silver tray on a table. There were little hard pillows in the shape of cats and pug dogs in the corners of the chintz-covered chairs. There was a blue-and-white plaid mohair blanket on the arm of a chair.

"Do you need anything, miss?" Lydia asked.

"No. No, thank you."

Lydia refolded the mohair blanket and turned around one of the cat pillows. Mamie wondered nervously whether she was supposed to tip her, but before she could reach for her handbag, Lydia was gone.

She looked more closely at the watercolors. They were very beautiful—grapes and yellow pears, signed Withers. Mamie was bending close to the watercolors, studying them, when Alysse rushed into the room and took Mamie forcefully into her arms.

"I am *so* glad to see you at last. So happy. So pleased." She was not so tall as Mamie so their sudden hug was awkward.

Mamie was aware that she was being studied very carefully, quite in the same way she had been examining Mrs. Withers's *Duchesse d'Angoulême* pear. I'm not as good as the pear, she thought.

"You're seated next to Mr. Zimmerman tonight," Alysse said. She beamed. *"Lucky* Mr. Zimmerman." She thinks me good enough, at least, for Mr. Zimmerman, Mamie thought.

Alysse whirled around and around, looking for something. She stopped when she saw Mamie's suitcase.

"I have all the clothes in the world, all of them, although I'm not quite so tall as you, even without those shoes," Alysse said. She was looking at Mamie's feet.

Mamie looked down at her zebra-skin high heels. Her mind

seemed not to be working with any speed. It had not really been working in its accustomed way for the past few months. Her aunt was moving too fast for her. Even the maid had been moving too fast. "My shoes?"

"You can, and must, borrow anything of mine you need. Coming straight from college, you must have nothing but kilts and cashmeres." Alysse was pulling clothes out of Mamie's open suitcase.

"They wear jeans now."

"Of course they do." Alysse said. "I wear jeans."

She threw Mamie's clothes across the bed.

"There are two other bags downstairs. The doorman said he'd send them up. I'd feel much better if you went through those, too."

Alysse turned slowly to take another look at her niece. Mamie was smiling. Her face, which had looked tired when she arrived, was a little flushed and her eyes were clearer.

"Well," Alysse said, shutting the suitcase. "I can see you'll do just fine." She came closer to Mamie and she, too, smiled. She had a big, beautiful smile. "You're not at all like Mary, are you?"

"Mother is smaller than I am."

"Yes," said Alysse, looking at her through shrewd blue eyes. She snapped on a pink-shaded lamp on a little table. "My guests arrive at eight-thirty and we dine at nine-thirty. The way they do in Europe."

"I like the pears so much and the grapes," Mamie said quickly.

"The pears?" Alysse looked around.

"The watercolors. On the wall. They are very beautiful."

"Are they? Willy Russell-Davis gave me those years ago."

"Uncle Bill?"

"You can't remember him."

"He was with you on that big boat when you came to Waimea. None of us had ever seen a yacht before. Claire still tells the story of Uncle Bill and the moray eel."

"He wasn't your uncle. Your mother made that up." Alysse, clearly not interested in any tall tales about old lovers and eels, went to the wall to look closely at the lovely watercolors, possibly for the first time. "He always did have wonderful taste. His awful wife gave everything to the Museum when he died. Just to spite me, I'm sure. These *are* good, aren't they?"

She took one of the paintings from its moiré ribbon and tilted it to catch the light. Distracted by this find in her very own guest room, she wandered out, leaving Mamie standing there. She took the watercolors with her.

Mamie had to fight up to the last minute to wear her own dress, a pale lime green voile of Hungarian embroidery, rather than the dress that Alysse wanted her to wear, a fire engine red taffeta with big black pom-poms that made Mamie look like a rather intimidated Carmen. Of Mamie's own dress, Alysse said dismissively, "at least it's *eau de Nil.*"

During dinner, Mamie won a wide smile from her aunt when she made Mr. Zimmerman, an investment banker, laugh out loud during the first course, a *Roulade au Fromage*. Mr. Zimmerman was very interested in what he called the "real Hawai'i," his experience being limited to the Kahala Hilton and the nightly Korean call girl. He had an idea that anyone whose family had lived there for generations was rich and aristocratic, and Mamie, who had never thought her family to be either, amused him with a description of going to see her Aunt Emma.

As a McDougal on her mother's side, Aunt Emma was the

possessor of as revered a local name as it was possible to inherit. Aunt Emma lived in an enormous, wood Victorian house in such disrepair that it was considered dangerous to walk on the second-story floorboards in 1920. She refused to leave the house and downtown Honolulu had been built around her six filthy, entangled acres. She told Mamie and Claire that when she died the land would belong to them. Mamie and Claire were not fond of visiting Aunt Emma.

"She is very boring and she smells bad," Mamie said to Mr. Zimmerman. "We're given weak tea and stale Ritz crackers."

Aunt Emma confined herself to one crowded room, and it was not unusual to see a large black wharf rat (the docks were at the end of Ward Avenue) trot boldly past on tiptoe, hugging the moldings more out of custom than fear.

"Aunt Emma always watches the rat calmly and says, 'Those rats first landed here with the ancient Tahitians who sailed due north in their huge double-outrigger canoes, as big as longhouses, searching for new islands . . .' Once she begins one of her lessons in Hawaiiana, it is awfully hard to stop her. Claire once said that the rats in Aunt Emma's room must have been very, very old."

After dinner, Mamie was left on the sofa with a beautiful red-haired woman. Alysse whispered to Mamie that the woman, Dodo Hennessey de Santiago, had been the most famous model of her day and Mamie was surprised to learn that "of her day" meant only a year earlier. She had not realized that Dodo was six months pregnant until Dodo said, "I've never had tits before and it's the only thing that makes this bearable." Even though she was wearing a tightly cut dress, Mamie could barely make out a swelling stomach through the Lycra sheath.

Mamie asked Dodo all of the polite questions as she passed her a demitasse and cream and English rock sugar.

"Is this your first child?"

"And last."

"Are you hoping for a boy or a girl?"

"It doesn't matter, I just want a healthy baby."

Despite Dodo's optimistic remark about her new breasts, Mamie was not really prepared when Dodo casually said, "I'm having a Caesarean delivery so as not to stretch my vagina."

"How sensible," Mamie said, sipping her coffee.

"*I* thought so," said Dodo, and asked the butler for a tequila.

In her aunt's mirrored bathroom, mirrored toilet and walls and floor and ceiling, Alysse asked Mamie about her dinner partner, perhaps in the hope of catching Sid Zimmerman in an indiscretion, and Mamie was able to say, with a clear conscience, that it had been very interesting.

"You say that a lot," Alysse called out from on top of the mirrored bidet.

"Well, it *is* interesting," Mamie said. "It's not like having Sunday dinner with the headmaster."

"What?"

"That used to be my standard of worldliness. Sunday with Dr. Fox."

"Dodo finally got smart," Alysse said, drying herself in the mirror. "If she didn't have this kid, all the dough would go to the younger brother. She's so smart she's even naming it after the grandfather. Walter. Such a bad name. And for a child, too."

"But she doesn't know if it's a boy, does she?" asked Mamie in surprise.

"She's known it was a boy for months. She had that test. Dodo did not get where she is just on her looks, you know."

Mamie wanted to ask Alysse just where it was that Dodo had got to, but she stopped herself when she realized that

Alysse might think she was being sarcastic. She was right to stop herself. Mamie, an apt student, was beginning her course of New York lessons, and while it cannot be said that Alysse was the teacher one might have wished for her, she was the only one available. At her best, Alysse, in her impatient and practical way, might have been a tonic for Mamie. Alysse could keep Mamie afloat, as long as she held Alysse's interest, and she could make Mamie, at least in her terms, a success.

Mr. Zimmerman found Mamie perfectly charming, or so he told Alysse, with whom he was sleeping later that night. Alysse was relieved. Mamie had passed her first test.

When Mamie told Alysse that she wanted to stay in New York and that she was going to look for a job, Alysse was, in her own words, *"très, très* delighté."

"And find an apartment," Mamie said. "I can't live with you forever."

"At least until you're organized," Alysse said, reassuring her. She opened a bottle of champagne to celebrate Mamie's decision to stay and the two of them settled girlishly into the green velvet sofa in the library to discuss Mamie's prospects. Her prospects were limited, for despite the genuine charm of her dinner conversation and her intelligence, she had no particular accomplishments.

"You have to graduate from Harvard to get a job sharpening pencils at one of the magazines," Alysse said. She regretted now that she could not telephone Carter Schmidt, who owned one of the networks, but she had, she admitted, accused him of giving her a local infection and he probably would not take her call.

Mamie was unaccustomed to the sweet, cold champagne. She liked the taste of it very much. "I can handle a machete," she said. "I can roll a cigarette." She laughed. "I can graft an orchid. I can do a back dive. I can talk a little bit about books. But that's it. Not much to go on." In the course of reciting her talents, she had managed to discourage herself.

"You don't understand, Mamie," Alysse said, pushing the loose brown hair back behind Mamie's flushed ears. "What good would typing do you? You'd only have to type. What we want to do is make a list of everyone we know, and who owes favors, and who will be willing to help and who won't. You leave it to me."

Mamie leaned back against a needlepoint pillow and drank her champagne. Perhaps this is what I need, she thought happily. It had been a long time since she had taken for granted, as do most children, that everything would be all right, that there were grown-ups out there acting busily in her interest. Alysse's seductive confidence was misleading to Mamie. She did not know that conviction, on its own, did not necessarily mean wisdom.

"You just leave it to me," Alysse said again, terribly excited at having the young woman in her care.

Alysse did not bother to tell Mamie that as one of Deardorf's best customers she felt it only right that the most expensive women's store in New York take on her niece as an assistant lingerie buyer. Nor did she tell her that she had given Mr. Deardorf a very thorough, as thorough as Alysse could be, account of Mamie's family connections in the islands. These social attributes of Mamie's were not seen as handicaps to selecting satin bedroom slippers and terry-cloth bathrobes. Generations of barely educated, well-born young women had skipped across Deardorf's elegant floors for that awkward two- or three-year period between college and first marriage, and their sponsors—wealthy grandmothers, fathers' mistresses, trust fund executors—had been relieved and lucky to place them there.

Mamie believed that she was fortunate to have been given the job. She resignedly gave up any individuality and passively placed herself in the plump red hands of the head saleslady, Miss Magda. She never complained or imagined that there was anything else she would be able to do. She understood that there were things she *could* do, such as work at a publishing house as a reader, but she had no idea how to even find a job like that. She walked during her lunch hour, unable to afford lunch in a restaurant and too self-conscious to eat alone in the noisy store cafeteria with the other solitary women. She willingly fetched vanilla yoghurt from the corner delicatessen for the middle-aged, middle-European salesladies who ordered her about; tirelessly replaced on satin-padded hangers the silk crepe nightgowns dropped carelessly to the floor of the dressing rooms (she was not yet trusted with the keys on the pink grosgrain ribbon used to lock the customers into the dressing rooms); and conscientiously sorted out, at the end of the long day, the size-five panties from the size-six panties and returned them to their "proper drawers," as Miss Magda called them, seemingly unaware of the bad joke she had made. Mamie decided that it must be Miss Magda's unfamiliarity with the idiom, even though Miss Magda had lived right on West Fifty-seventh Street for the last thirty years, a fact she pointed out to Mamie nearly every day.

She made friends with a very pretty blond girl named Selena. Selena's mother, a baroness, had moved to Calcutta to work with an order of silent nuns for the poor and dying. Selena had none of her saintliness, if, in fact, it was sanctity that had led the baroness to impulsively leave everything behind in Munich.

"She hasn't given it up forever, you know," Selena said irritably whenever Mamie asked about Calcutta and the nuns. "It's just what she's doing now. She used to live with a cargo cult in New Guinea."

Selena wanted to marry. She lived with her rich grandmother in a big apartment on Fifth Avenue. Her father, an extremely handsome businessman who was divorced from her mother, often came to New York and took Selena to lunch. For those occasions, as well as for her many dates, Selena stole her clothes from Deardorf's. Selena told Mamie that it was not really stealing, because she sometimes returned the clothes the next day, although Mamie once refused to take back a red satin corset that Selena sneaked back badly stained and slashed. Mamie would never have reported Selena, but she did not want to steal clothes from Deardorf's. Selena was irritated by this, especially as she disapproved of the way that Mamie dressed. Mamie, by choice as well as by economy, found her clothes in second-hand stores. She wore one of the printed *muumuus* from her collection of silk aloha shirts and sundresses, cinched around the waist with an alligator belt. If it were a chilly evening, she added one of her elaborately beaded cashmere sweaters from the 1950s, her favorite being an ivory-colored cardigan embroidered with pastel insects. Selena could not understand why Mamie refused to take advantage of the extraordinary opportunity offered by Deardorf's open racks. When Mamie tried to explain that she liked the way she looked, Selena accused her of being "deeply out of it."

"You're in New York now," she said. "Not some hokey little farm town."

Mamie was not happy at work. She was not unhappy, either. She recognized that it was something she must do in order to earn money, so that she could take care of herself. She received a small allowance of two hundred dollars a month from her mother and she knew that she could not stay at Alysse's too much longer, but she was worried when she read the advertisements for rental apartments in the newspaper. She did not know how she would make her way.

Although her mother had never written much to Mamie when she was away at boarding school and college, she now began to write to her every week.

Dear Mamie,

I was naturally quite surprised by your decision to settle in New York City. You probably don't remember but when you were a child, you said that you were going to be famous and Claire said she was going to be a nun. We never knew where she got that, although McCully said it was probably Gertrude, because she was so religious.

I was in Koke'e yesterday, cleaning out the wild hydrangea, and I was tempted by the possibility of finding some *maile* on the path near the Wiliwili Camp, so I lay down my tools and let myself be drawn deeper into the canyon. There was a faint humming sound, like a swarm of mosquitoes, but I could not see them. I spotted, at a height, a tendril of *maile*, and I pressed against the *lehua* to which it had attached itself, and I saw that the trunk was covered with hundreds of *kahuli*, those little red-striped shells which attach themselves to trees and begin to sing, scritch, scritch. It was the humming sound I had heard. I forgot all about the *maile* in my pleasure of listening.

Charlie King died yesterday and I must drive to Ha'ena Wednesday when they scatter his ashes on the reef. I never know quite what to wear for those occasions, as you do get wet in the canoe. A raincoat would look disrespectful, I think.

I have had an offer from a Japanese hotel company to buy some of the beachfront here to build a hotel. They would have to dredge the beach, but we would retain a beach right-of-way. They wanted to build a swimming park where the palm grove stands, with water slides and lagoons. The minute I heard that, I said no. I don't think he meant to tell me. He was Japan Japanese.

Give my aloha to Alice.

Love,
Mother

Mamie was reminded again of her mother's curious literalness—settling in New York City, Gertrude religious. It made her smile.

Alysse wondered indignantly how her sister could have turned down the Japanese offer to buy the palm grove.

"How she can live on that lonely island, I'll never know. Their idea of a good time is weird Mexican-sounding music and dinner at five o'clock. I remember going down the road with your parents to someone's house for dinner and they actually served coffee with the main course, the only course, as it turned out. Can you imagine? Always a bad sign, coffee with pork chops. Besides," she went on, "you'd be rich."

"Rich?"

"Loaded."

Mamie did not mind the idea of being loaded, as Alysse put it, but like Mary, she did not like the thought of Chiefess Deborah's grove being bulldozed for a swimming park. She wrote back to her mother that she thought she had made the right decision in declining to sell the land.

She wondered where it was that Alysse had been so disturbingly served coffee with pork chops, but she didn't think she should ask. She refrained from asking Alysse many things and let her talk on in her irresponsible, absolutely certain way. It was not that Mamie accepted everything that she heard (she was still amazed at the inaccuracy of the belief that childbirth left your vagina a vast marshland), but she kept quiet and listened. Part of it was what she considered the polite behavior of someone who was a guest, but part of it was also an astonished interest in her aunt. Although Mamie did not yet understand that Alysse's seeming sophistication was really a kind of crude expediency, she did see that Alysse was a woman who would get her way.

Perhaps she believed that she might take on some of Alysse's audacity during those cozy winter nights when Alysse was not engaged and she invited Mamie into the library and opened bottle after bottle of champagne and instructed Mamie in the fundamentals: "never, ever let your maid work for a friend and do not be overly familiar with the help, for example, you should not have introduced yourself the other night to Mrs. de Coppet's chauffeur; never sit on *any* toilet seat, *anyone's,* I don't care whose, besides, it's great for the thighs to pee three inches above the seat; try to use the old form of a word, looking-glass, for example, or frock; do not ever get caught changing the place cards at someone else's dinner; *do* underdress, it makes the other women look older and vulgar; *do, do* flirt, with everyone, children, husbands, wives, especially wives as they're the ones who invite you back; try to remember that having a child is nothing better than giving birth to a living insurance policy, you never can tell, it might come in *très, très* handy; never, never underestimate anyone—you can never be sure just who they are. You paid not the slightest attention to Louise Hathaway at lunch, but you must remember it was

Louise who was singlehandedly responsible for bringing the sport of water-skiing to France."

She was really the first mature woman ever to pay any attention to Mamie. Her own mother had never really had a conversation with her. How could she help but sit mesmerized at Alysse's knee, drinking the champagne, taking it all in? After the drudgery of her day at Deardorf's, Alysse was funny and titillating. Mamie was flattered by Alysse's interest in her. She didn't realize, of course, especially when Alysse began every conversation with the warning, "Don't dare tell anyone this," that Alysse had just had the same conversation with her masseuse or one of her best girl friends, and one might say, looking back, that it was unfortunate that Mamie was so naïve as to think that Alysse really favored her, but how could she have thought otherwise?

Although Alysse was not very curious about Mamie's life, correctly assuming that there was little there to interest her, she did not hesitate to tell Mamie about her own. She had married a Mr. Buddy Klost, an industrialist from Detroit, with whom she lived in New York and Islamorada, Florida. Mr. Klost, an ardent sportfisherman, set the world record for black marlin, caught in the waters off Peru. He worked hard and played hard and fucked hard; a real man, in Alysse's words.

"We were married in an old church in Birmingham, Michigan. It was a very famous church with catapulted ceilings, and I wanted awfully to impress his grandmother, who really ran the show and controlled everything, so I rented the bridesmaids. That's when I first met Dodo. She was seventeen and I said she was my younger sister."

"You rented her?" Mamie laughed.

"It *was* funny. But it worked. I just called a modeling agency in Chicago and I picked the girls, and the dresses were made to order, divine white organdy from Dior, with little vine baskets of lily of the valley and white French roses and old Mrs. Klost, who wasn't too happy about Buddy's choice, me, took off her famous pink pearls during the reception, you haven't seen them yet, they're in the safe, and put them around my exquisite white neck and everyone applauded."

On other nights when there was too much champagne, Alysse would succumb to a little sentimentality and sniffle into her handkerchief, careful not to smear her mascara, genuinely moved by the beauty and drama of her own life. Buddy had been beheaded in a head-on car crash in Georgia.

"All they gave me when I flew down to identify the body was a gold sailfish he used to wear on a chain around his neck. I gave it to him for Father's Day."

"Was he Courtney and Brooke's father?"

"Oh, no," Alysse said. "That was my second husband, Harry Shannon, the handsomest Irishman you ever saw. They were the children from his second marriage. Not mine. Oh, you would have adored Harry Shannon."

"I liked his daughters. I hoped to see them——"

"I met him in the South of France at a party. His wife was having an affair with Betsy Tyndal, the Marchioness of Drummle, and he shoved his foot between my legs at dinner. I slipped my hand down and somehow managed to remove his shoe. I put it in my sewing bag, we all carried big tapestry bags then because it was a fad to do needlework after dinner, you know, like Queen Victoria or someone, and I wouldn't give the shoe back to him. When we got up from the table, he, wearing one patent leather shoe like in that nursery rhyme, followed me from room to room, hopping. It was very funny, because he was considered quite a dandy. You've heard of him, I'm sure. He was the one who first wore his wristwatch right on his shirtsleeve cuff, so fabulous, and all the young men at the party thought Harry was setting a new fashion by wearing only one shoe. Several of them turned up at dinner the very next night wearing one black evening shoe. He followed me back to the Eden Roc and stayed three weeks."

Because most of her stories were about sex, Mamie thought at first that Alysse liked men very much, but as time went by, she began to suspect that Alysse wasn't really interested in men, and that she was not interested in sex at all. She had no understanding of pleasure, certainly not anything so un-selfish as shared pleasure, and even had she been interested, she would have seen her own pleasure as something that might, to her disadvantage, get in her way. This practical view of romance was a new and not altogether likable one to Mamie. She often felt uncomfortable when Alysse laughed about her husbands or boyfriends, as if she, Mamie, should be defending them, and it wasn't until years later that Mamie discovered by accident that Alysse had left out entirely a certain Mr. Vic "Big Cat" Cattani, her first husband, who drowned mysteri-ously off Staten Island.

"Of course, after Jack Fitzjames had that umbrella duel at the Opera with the man sitting in front of us, I couldn't possibly see him again," Alysse said in her slight, careless way. She said about another admirer, "He fought in that war in Spain in the thirties, I forget what it was about, and ever after he insisted on wearing this ludicrous Basque beret. I did every-thing to get him to change, took him to Lock in London, everything, but he was unnaturally attached to that goddamn hat."

"Perhaps someone gave it to him," Mamie said, sympathetic to the man in the beret. She would have liked to have given it to him.

"I doubt it." Alysse said, snorting. "His wee-wee was the size of a thimble. I found *that* out."

Mamie went one night in a snowstorm to have drinks with Alysse's second-best-friend, Bones Washburn. Whether Mrs. Washburn's nickname came from her celebrated figure or her ability to stop, with a single shot, a charging rhinoceros at a hundred feet, Alysse did not know. She had never thought about it, she told Mamie on their way up to the hotel suite that Bones had kept for twenty years. Bones was what used to be called a dame, and she was smart enough to be proud of it. She was one of those tolerant women with a raucous laugh and heavy gold charm bracelets who could hunt and ski and fish and drink all night with her man. She was a good sport. As Alysse put it to Mamie, "She could 'fuck, fight or hold the light.' " It was not an expression familiar to Mamie.

Bones had met Alysse and Buddy Klost in the bar of the Norfolk Hotel in Nairobi. She took Alysse in hand after that first drunken night in Africa, and showed her how to dress and how to order food and hire servants, and Alysse always credited Bones with enabling her to hold on to the restless Buddy. Alysse, fresh from an illegal divorce in Juarez, thought she could never do better than beef Stroganoff and gladiolas. Her idea of shopping was an afternoon at Gump's. Bones changed all of that, and if Alysse never acquired Bones's natural talents, she knew better, after Bones, than to wear white python cowboy boots or to pass Vienna sausages as hors d'oeuvres.

Bones liked Mamie so much that she grabbed her by the hand, right in the middle of cocktails, and pulled her into a closet and filled her arms with a big pile of clothes that she insisted Mamie take home with her—Bones's driver, Mohammed, an Arab boy she had adopted, would take the clothes for her. Without wanting to appear rude by looking through the clothes, Mamie did manage to spot a leopard-skin cape and a pair of green suede *lederhosen*. Mamie also noticed a small needlepoint sign hanging from Bones's bedroom doorknob that read PAS CE SOIR CHERI.

"Mamie asked me on the way up how you got your name," Alysse said to Bones. She was drinking vodka and cranberry juice. "It's very good for your female parts," she had said confidentially to Mamie.

Bones was biting chocolates from a box sent to her weekly from Zurich. She did not offer any to Mamie or Alysse. She licked her fingers, then wiped them on her gabardine trousers. Her face was dry and wizened from too much sun and too much drink.

"It's short for boners." She searched for a caramel, poking in the lace-lined box with a big, handsome finger. "I was good at boners," she said, turning over a piece of chocolate to look at the bottom.

"You sound like my friend Gertrude," Mamie said, laughing.

"You know," Bones said, "rich men are really shits about money. Turds. They have to be, I suppose, or women would never stay with them. Olympia Lecci had to pawn her watch every time she needed an airplane ticket to visit Senator Guslander, you'd have thought he'd have sent her the goddamn ticket himself, and Princess Francini had to borrow money from Fifi Lewis just to get home, the last time she had a fight with the Prince. Of course, he's always despised her. He's in love with his sister. Me, I always believed in cash *and* boners. It works every time." She tossed the box of chocolates onto a sofa. "Did you ever have a walk-out with Guslander?" she asked Alysse.

A newcomer to the world of the rich might be forgiven for thinking that Bones Washburn led a life of irresponsibility and pleasure. Bones had complied uncomplainingly with the selfish whims of every lover and husband. She had paid with every stupefying dinner party; every aggrieved and vicious stepchild; every arduous performance of fellatio (tens of thousands of them); every holiday spent killing scared, hot, plains animals; every perjury; every bad beating.

She did not complain because she understood that those were the terms of her arrangement. The women who were jealous of her, and said viperish things about her, did not have any idea of the discipline required by Bones's line of work. They would have changed places with her greedily. It is hard to know if Bones would have changed places with them. She did marry five times, each husband richer and meaner than the last, as she made her way through the hard world. It would be interesting to know, in the end, if she thought that it was worth it. Bones had heart, unlike Alysse, so it is possible that she might have thought that it was not.

Mamie tried to make her aunt talk about Mary and Mc-Cully. Alysse was not particularly interested in anything that did not concern herself. Naturally, this rather personal historical view excluded her sister. She never spoke of her and few of her friends even knew that she had a sister.

Mamie had noticed about Alysse and her women friends that they did not really seem to have come from anywhere. Nothing from the past adhered to them. There were no regional accents or phrases, no references to bayou or mesa. There were no stories told about family or even childhood. Mamie longed for some clue from them, some slip of the tongue that would allow her to identify and place them; some memory, accidentally released, that would give them individuality. It was not that Alysse did not have an early life, it was that it didn't matter. Alysse might be from Maine or New Mexico; it was impossible to know.

Alysse had been fond of McCully, although she described him as "the dull farmer." When Mamie said to her, without taking offense, that McCully had been neither, Alysse said, "Dear child, he listened to bagpipe music. He wore funny shoes. And his idea of a good time was to hike up that stream or river, whatever it was, in those mountains. I thought I was going to die, really die."

"You insisted on filling the thermoses with champagne and one of them exploded."

"McCully was quite cross."

"No, he wasn't," Mamie said.

"I suppose you could say that I never look back. Is that so terrible? When that sexual hysteric Miss Henrietta adopted Mary and me, I was as comfortable in that big, gloomy mansion as if I'd been born there. And when she died suddenly and all the money went to those loathsome Christian Scientists, I was here, right here in New York City, in four days. I can't imagine living any other way. Your mother was the opposite. I don't think she looked either forward or back—she lived in some incredibly boring present. She never made plans. She had *no* ambition. *Rien*." Alysse shook her head in disgust. It was the worst thing she could say about anyone.

"I realized the other day that I have never seen her naked," Mamie said.

"No, you wouldn't have, not with the scars."

"Scars?"

"Didn't you know?" Alysse asked dramatically. She wiggled

into a more comfortable position on the sofa and poured champagne into their already full glasses. She was excited by the discovery that Mamie did not know about the scars. "Didn't you wonder why she never went swimming?"

"All the time."

"When we were little, before we were sent to Henrietta, your mother dressed up one Halloween as a bride. She wore a white tablecloth as a veil and she caught on fire."

"Caught on fire?"

"She had a jack-o'-lantern with a candle inside of it. They didn't have those wonderful plastic ones in those days. And her costume, the bridal veil, caught on fire. She had terrible, terrible burns all down her back and because we were poor and there weren't any particularly brilliant plastic surgeons in Boxcar, Oklahoma, she had bad, bad scars. She was the girl at the Senior Prom in high neck and long sleeves. Pale green. Not her best color."

"What *was* her best color?"

Alysse looked up from the *House and Garden* she had restlessly opened while she told Mamie about the time her sister went up in flames. Alysse could never be quite sure about Mamie, and because Mamie was quicker than her aunt, she was often able to disguise her true feelings from Alysse. Alysse, with that characteristic belittling of hers that reduced everybody and everything to the same low level, said many things during those few months Mamie lived with her that she would never otherwise have admitted had she known how much the girl would remember.

"Did I ever tell you about the time Bones dropped a diamond earring out the window? She had to have it copied in twenty-four hours or Giancarlo would have killed her. He had already broken her arm for letting the tub overflow at the Beverly Hills Hotel and flood the entire third floor. Poor Bones."

"Poor Bones," said Mamie sympathetically.

During the day, Mamie used her lunch hour to explore the city. She would walk purposefully down one street and back along the next in order to look at the architecture. It was the end of winter, and on weekends, when she had more time, she would walk all the way to the river, sometimes east and sometimes west. She regretted that the city did not have more of its life on its rivers. It was not like other big cities where the river was a lively, lovely symbol of the city itself. New York, moored in its fast rivers, was little interested in them and, perhaps because of this, the rivers at first seemed ugly to Mamie. She had been comforted to read in her guidebook that the Hudson River flowed from Lake Tear of the Clouds, high in the northern mountains. She often stood at the iron railing at the embankment at Gracie Square and wondered if she would see a corpse float by, or the bloated body of a dog.

It was while standing on an abandoned pier and looking across the flat, chilly Hudson that she had realized the importance of a view. In her first month in New York, before she discovered the rivers, she had been inexplicably melancholy. She realized that it was the absence of any perspective that was making her feel uneasy. She needed perspective. She needed a foreground, middle ground and background. It was not simply a matter of temperament. As someone who had spent the first eighteen years of her life in the open, she needed sudden storm clouds and the running currents of neap tides.

She found it at the rivers. And one night at a cocktail party standing before a glass wall in a new, transparent building.

And she found it looking out through a snowstorm at the lighted city from Bones's tower suite. Wherever she discovered it, it always made her feel calmer, a little less squared off and boxed in and, oddly enough, it made her feel very nostalgic for that possibility of glamour and sweet romance that the very name Manhattan had always held for her.

She bought a guide to literary sites and roamed through Mrs. Wharton's Chelsea, and Gramercy Park. She stood outside Marianne Moore's house in the Village and she remembered that at this time of year, the end of March, she once would have been imagining, as she walked to classes in Westwood, the lonely new shoots of *Sanicula sandwicensis,* the rare perennial in the parsley family, sending up its little yellow flowers in the high, cool mountains of east Maui. Once, the sound of California jays had reminded her of the *pueo,* the high-flying Hawaiian owl that made a sound like a woman lost in the forest. But she now found herself able to identify the more prosaic smells of this new city—urine, diesel fuel, warm pizza, dry-cleaning fluid and even the occasional blossoming pear tree on a side street—without immediately sinking into a daydream of the past. Things seemed to be just what they were and this was very soothing to Mamie. She learned some things about herself, as well as New York, on her long walks.

Heading north on Madison Avenue, she saw in the window of a flower shop a bouquet of wildflowers and grasses—goatsbeard and meadow rue and jack-in-the-pulpit—tied with a length of twine. It is just the thing to keep me company tonight, she thought. At first, she saw the modest bouquet on the too small marquetry table by her bed, then she thought perhaps it would be rude to buy flowers for herself, even if they were the kind of roadside weeds one might absentmindedly collect on a walk after Saturday lunch. Although they were not exactly Alysse's style—she liked Georgian silver wine buckets jammed with *damascena* roses (Flowers must look as if you've just had them sent in from your garden in the country, she told Mamie)—Mamie thought that she would buy them as a present for her aunt.

The man in the shop told her that the flowers would be six hundred dollars.

"They're native wildflowers," he said when she looked at him in amazement.

All she could think of was her mother. Mary would have been furious. "They're very eighteenth-century," she said to the man.

"I know," he said without interest.

On her return one evening, she found a special delivery letter waiting for her on the hall table. It was from Claire. It was short and quite to the point. She had left the University of Hawaii. She had not had her period for four months. Orval Nalag refused to give her money for an abortion and she was understandably unable to go to her mother. She needed Mamie to send her seven hundred and fifty dollars as soon as possible. She knew she could count on Mamie. "Help, help, help!"

Mamie immediately sent the money she had put aside to rent an apartment. She did not tell Alysse. She thought how strange it was that Orval, the boy Mary feared would attack them walking through the camp, was the father of Claire's child. She wondered if they had made love many times. She convinced herself that it must have happened only once. It was hard to imagine them dating, given Mary's prejudices.

Mamie did not hear again from Claire, and although she knew better than anyone Claire's ability to take care of herself, she did think of her often. She imagined Claire sitting in the huge waiting room at the mill clinic with the skinny, restless children of the laid-off sugar workers. She imagined the beautiful, fat Hawaiian women who waited gaily with all of their sisters and all of their cousins and all of their girlfriends. She even imagined what a child made by Claire and Orval Nalag would look like, brown and sturdy with black hair slicked back with Lilac Vegetol.

What she did not imagine, and could not have imagined, was that, a few weeks later, Lydia would grumpily call her from her room one night when Alysse was at the Kabuki to ask her if she knew anyone by the name of Claire. The doorman was on the intercom. There was someone in the lobby named Claire who wanted to come upstairs.

SIX

She stood in the paneled entrance hall, in baggy khakis and a pale pink sweater. She wore new white Keds. She had obviously said something funny, or fresh, to the porter, Mr. Rodriguez, because he was still laughing and shaking his head as he put down the good leather suitcase that had once been McCully's and went back downstairs in the elevator.

Mamie was very happy to see her. Lydia stood peevishly to the side, fists clenched in her apron pockets. She watched the two girls suspiciously. Claire handed Mamie a shopping bag.

"Sweet and sour apricots. *Manapua*. A guava chiffon cake from Aloha Bakery. Two new Gabby tapes and your mail. I already read your letters."

Mamie took the bag and kissed Claire on the cheek. "They do it on both cheeks here," she said smiling, suddenly self-conscious.

"Where's the bathroom?" Claire asked, pushing past her. "There's blood running down my leg and fuck knows what else. *Who* else, actually."

While Mamie helped her sponge the blood from her thighs, Claire told her that Gertrude had induced a miscarriage by feeding her tea made from the bark of the mountain apple. They peeled it off the trees in the very grove where Mamie once waited with the sisters who would not go down the flumes. She used Mamie's rent money to buy her ticket and some new clothes in Honolulu.

"You mean the tea really works?" Mamie asked in astonishment.

"Well," Claire said, "the tea and several long workouts on the trampoline at McCully Clarke School."

Mamie thought about Gertrude. She was not like a mother to them. She was a shaman.

"Aunt Emma sends you her love. She gave me an incredibly long message for you about how the *kolea* plover is a metaphor in old Hawaiian stories for independence and mystery. She said you'd understand. She also insisted that I put *ti* leaves in my suitcase for a safe journey." Claire had taken off her soiled pants and thrown her bloody underpants onto the bathroom floor and was sitting half-dressed on the edge of one of the beds in Mamie's room.

Mamie was relieved that Alysse was not at home. She worried that Claire would bleed on Alysse's chintz bedspread. She brought a towel from the bathroom for Claire to sit on, but Claire pushed it aside.

"And Gertrude made me pack some of those placemats her mother brings her. I thought I could give them to Aunt Alice."

"I don't think so," Mamie said quickly. She tried once again to tuck the white towel under Claire's legs. "And it's A-lysse now. She has only very beautiful things. She and her friends spend quite a bit of time tracking down the best little places to buy things. The best place for gloves in Milan or a little shop in Paris for stationery. I don't think she'd like coconut-husk placemats from the PX at Clark Air Force Base. She—"

Mamie stopped when she noticed the surprised expression on Claire's face. She shook her head and smiled in embarrassment.

"This is what happens when you have no one to talk to. Except Miss Magda at work, of course."

"You've got me now," Claire said. She jumped up and opened the closet. Mamie anxiously looked to see if there was blood on the bed or on the back of Claire's legs. She could see the tan line made high on Claire's hip by her bathing suit. Claire bent over to open a drawer in the bureau. There was no blood.

"Everything is scented!" Claire said. She stuck her head in the drawer to have a good smell. "The hangers, the drawer paper, the toilet paper. It smells terrible."

Mamie nodded. "I've had a headache for three months. Like Mrs. Nagata's silkworms." Mrs. Nagata's silkworms, while indifferent to climate, were not particularly fond of noise and Mrs. Nagata had always hushed the children irritably whenever their play brought them too near her house. She needn't have troubled, as it was odor that most offended them and she had lost all of them one humid afternoon to the smell of fried fish.

"Alysse has been very generous," Mamie said. She sighed. "She sees me as an untapped resource—she's not sure there's anything there, but she's willing to give me a chance."

"You *are* an untapped resource. I've always said so." Claire was going through the drawers in the bathroom. "Even the cotton balls are scented."

"How is Mother?"

"Oh," Claire said from the bathroom. She was sitting on the toilet.

"I'm glad she didn't sell the land," Mamie said.

"It was such a preposterous idea. How long has it been since you've been home? Eight months? Were you there when she brought down a cabin from Koke'e? On coconut logs. And there is a new bamboo grove, three acres with a hundred strains of rare bamboo and a little wooden 'thunder house' in the center where you sit in a storm to listen to the bamboo and the thunder. How could she possibly sell it? What would she do?"

"Alysse says we'd be rich."

"I always thought we *were* rich. People always acted like we were rich."

Mamie laughed. Claire came back into the bedroom. She had stuffed some of Alysse's good linen hand towels into her clean underpants.

"You know, Mother is one of those people who justify themselves by saying that they're just as hard on themselves as they are on others. Well, fuck that," Claire said.

"Did she know about Orval?"

"No. Wait 'til you read your letters. Lily is in Italy with Tōsi and she swears they're never coming back. She says none of us are really Americans anyway. And Sherry Alden has left Berkeley and run off with a dancer from the San Francisco Ballet."

"She has?" Mamie was surprised.

"A *ballerina.*"

It was only recently that Mamie had thought again about Sherry. The massages and arm wrestling of years ago had slowly begun to make sense, the truth working its way up through her memory.

Claire looked at her. "Didn't you know?"

"I must have," Mamie said, laughing at herself.

"The muff-diver who taught tennis in Koloa went down on her every afternoon last summer behind Court II."

"How do you know?"

"Mamie. Please. You're so dumb."

"I mean about the details. How do you know it was Court II?" Mamie didn't like that Claire made her feel stupid.

Claire just laughed. "Does Aunt Alice have a record player?" She was restless.

"I'm not sure we should use it when she isn't here. Besides, you wouldn't like her music. You know, Diana Ross and Lionel Richie." She was trying to discourage her.

"You forget you're talking to the first president of the James Brown 'Funky President (People It's Bad)' Kaua'i Fan Klub. Mamie, *I've* got the music."

Claire had been there an hour and she was already commandeering the music system. She was wandering through the apartment in transparent underpants, Porthault hand towels wadded between her legs, handling carelessly the carnelian elephants and jade monkeys from Olga Tritt, sloppily pouring herself a big drink from the Russian gilt decanter on the silver tray in the library, reading the engraved invitations on heavy white paper that lay on Alysse's chinoiserie desk.

Mamie sensed that Claire's presence—an unpredictable, volatile, attractive presence—would change everything. Mamie recognized in Claire a Darwinian adaptation. She was a girl-helot in Claire's service. She admired her and wished she could be like her, but she was afraid.

"When do you go back to school?"

"Never," Claire said distractedly. She was reading a letter she had picked up from Alysse's desk. She reminded Mamie of someone. Claire dropped the letter, bored. There were pictures of Alysse in silver frames on the red lacquered desk. "Is this Alice?" she asked and Mamie realized that Claire resembled Alysse—she was like her aunt.

"She's good-looking," Claire said.

"I wanted to ask you about Orval," Mamie said.

Claire was behaving as if they had lived together uneventfully in the scented apartment for years. Mamie wanted to talk about what had happened, but Claire was far ahead of her, settling easily into the future. Orval and the camp, and even the palm grove, were seeping away, held only in Mamie's tireless imagination.

"Oh, I forgot to tell you! You'll love this, Mamie. You remember Benjie's cousin, Cecil, the one who was in Vietnam and used to play dominoes with you? You used to ask him about Vietnam. Well, there were reports of lost pigs and Mrs. Takaki's *hibachi* was stolen, and the old people in town said it was the *menehune* or the displaced spirits from the lot where they built the new post office, but it was Cecil! He was living in the mountains in full camouflage with an automatic rifle. When they brought him down, Benjie and Clinton and Mike Fayé, he thought it was 1969 and he was in some place called An Khe. He thought Benjie was the Vietcong."

"Will he be all right?"

"Mamie. Please."

It was not inconceivable to Mamie that Cecil would be all right, especially in a small village like Waimea. It was one of the things that she liked about Waimea. Perhaps it came from the big nineteenth-century novels she read in which certain plot points tended to hang on the actions of feeble-minded but harmless boys. There had always been people wandering about the town suffering from mental illness and congenital birth defects and alcoholic delirium, so it was possible that Cecil Furtado, still wearing his fatigues, might turn up working in the gas station. It might very well be Cecil, without his AK-47, who pumped your tires. She was about to say this to Claire, when she noticed that Claire was moving with great charm and vivacity to greet her surprised, amused aunt.

"Oh!" Alysse said. "You've lost your pants!"

Mamie went nervously to put the jade tortoise back in its row.

As Alysse had been caught by surprise by Claire's visit, she had not had time, even with her legendary impetuosity, to plan a dinner party. She did not waste any time, however, and the day after Claire's arrival, she arranged a lunch with the two sisters and her third-best-friend, Apollonia, a charming and ignorant Brazilian. Alysse had told them, as if to ensure their admiration, that Apollonia was the heiress to all of the high heels in Brazil.

Mamie, who had to join them at the restaurant from the lingerie department, liked the idea of being a shoe heiress. Despite her first anxiety, she was happy and relieved that Alysse had liked Claire. Claire was very clever with Alysse, falling instantly into a girlish colloquy of squeals and squeezes and secret-telling. Mamie had not known how good Claire could be at that kind of intimacy.

They were already seated when Mamie arrived and as she sat down and began to apologize for keeping them waiting, Alysse interrupted her.

"Apollonia was just telling us about her rape."

Mamie looked at Claire, but Claire was staring at Apollonia with sparkling, interested eyes.

Apollonia had been traveling near Taroudant in southern Morocco, hoping to see some of those Blue Men, when she was assaulted by her two young guides. "One of them, Aziz, was very good-looking," she said. "I was taking a bathe, eh? And they were watching me. Can you imagine this shock?" Mamie thought Apollonia was going to spit in disgust.

Mamie looked around the crowded restaurant. It was full of

middle-aged men and women, all a little pink in the face with good health and satisfaction, not unkind or unintelligent faces, but unworried and complacent. They all seemed happy to be there, and at the same time, clearly took their presence in the peach-colored, pretty room as their due. As Apollonia talked on about her rape with great simultaneous explosions of hilarity and outrage, Mamie began to think of the two Arab guides who had, in Apollonia's words, "ravage" her in the back of a jeep. No camels, Mamie thought. Too bad.

"I wasn't able to screw for weeks after," Apollonia said with a pout.

"Because you were so sore?" Claire asked innocently. Mamie kicked her under the table.

"My dear, it had nothing to do with that. The dirty pigs had upset my mind, eh?"

Mamie, who worried about the seeming inability of men and women to really like each other, felt an unexpected relief that men and women did not, after all, understand each other better. It is the only way the world can work, she thought. If they really knew, really understood, the fear and contempt, all of the women in this restaurant would be obliged to leap to their feet to cut off the penises of their lunch partners with the grape scissors, just as the men would be forgiven for lunging across the tables in a final attempt to settle their fingers tightly around the inflamed throats of the women. I got off easy, Mamie thought. An old, calloused hand in a pair of *palaka* shorts.

The women were talking about houses. Apollonia had taken a wing in an *hôtel particulier* in the Marais and she invited them all to come to stay.

"I suffered greatly in the childhood from big houses," Apollonia said.

"Poor thing," said Alysse. She gestured to the waiter to pour more champagne.

"I was thinking about this the other day," Mamie said. "I've never believed that suffering makes you a finer person, have you?"

They looked at her. She had abruptly altered the tone of the lunch. She saw that Claire was watching her with an amused, challenging smile.

"This whole notion," she went on quickly, "that suffering gives strength of character. Isn't it just the opposite—that strength of character is what enables you to undergo suffering?"

"I know where you're coming from," said Claire, just to make Mamie crazy.

"Where *am* I coming from? Iowa? Switzerland? I wish *I* knew," Mamie said, blushing.

"I'll be in Gstaad in January," said Apollonia. "You must come to stay with me, eh?"

These people are always inviting you somewhere, Mamie thought.

"Lady Studd is here," Alysse said in a low voice to Apollonia. "Two tables down. With that Iranian."

"You mean Persian, no? *Nada mais* Iranian."

"Is she the skinny woman in black?" Claire asked. "I've been watching her eat. She ate everything on her plate, then everything on his plate, all the bread and butter, then three desserts. She should weigh three hundred pounds."

"Oh, she'll be home in an hour vomiting," Alysse said dismissively. "She taught me how to do it years ago: you drink two glasses of milk or eat some ice cream to coat your stomach—"

"*Exactement!*" said Apollonia with approval.

"And then you put your fingers down your throat. Of

course, it eventually ruins your digestive system and leaves you unable to control some parts of your body. Poor Georgiana. There have been complaints about stains on tapestry chairs."

Although Mamie was fairly hypnotized by this information, as well as by the matter-of-fact tone of her aunt, and while even Claire was set back a bit, the two older women, pleased with the world, gazed contentedly around the room. They did everything but lick their paws and velvet muzzles. People were finishing lunch and standing to say good-bye, and there were blown kisses and pantomimed promises to telephone and to soon meet. The women held their eyes open very, very wide, which gave them a startled, slightly insane expression, as if they were feigning extreme interest in something that bored them very much, and the men had a benign, sated look, as they took out their cigars for a quiet smoke on the drive back downtown, more than delighted to leave all of the fuss and exaggeration and exclamation to the animated women. The men were there as angels, as theatrical investors; the show that day simply being "lunch."

Alysse and Apollonia carefully took it all in while they sipped their double espressos. Apollonia reapplied her fuchsia lipstick by looking into a knife blade held horizontally before her beautiful, placid face.

Lady Studd stopped at their table on her way out of the restaurant. She was very thin. "How *are* you?" she asked Apollonia in the barely disguised, avid tone of someone longing to hear bad news. "I know how *you* are!" she said gaily to Alysse.

Alysse laughed loudly and asked for the check.

Later, lying on their beds, Mamie forced Claire to admit that, like herself, she had had to use all of her self-control not to stare at the back of Lady Studd's dress.

"It looked all right to me," Mamie said, somewhat disappointed.

"You never can tell with black," said Claire.

SEVEN

Mamie and Claire spent quite a bit of time lying on their beds. Alysse was invited out almost every night and the girls did not expect, or want, a begrudging Lydia to prepare dinner for them. With the last of Mamie's saved rent money, they bought a cheap cassette player and Mamie carried home food they could eat out of a bag. She also bought long stalks of tuberose to put on the little table between the beds. The room smelled like the tuberose and french fries.

They stretched out on top of the covers and ate their greasy, delicious dinners and listened to the tapes Claire had brought from home—Coleman Hawkins, Mamie's Brazilian sambas, James Brown, and the Hawaiian slack-key guitarist, Gabby Pahinui. Mamie worried only briefly about their nutrition. They were careful to throw out the grease-stained bags and paper wrappings when they were finished so as not to offend Alysse, and they sometimes had to light scented candles when the smell of the food (pepperoni pizza, sauerkraut) overcame the smell of the tuberose. Claire, who was looking for employment, read the want ads aloud while Mamie took off her shoes and stockings and washed her hands.

There were letters from Mary, separate letters, for Mamie and
Claire. Claire started to read her letter, but did not make it
through to the end. Mamie read her letter dutifully.

Dear Mamie,

I certainly think it is nice that Claire is visiting you
during her school break. She deserves a vacation. She was
studying so hard. Every time I would telephone, her
roommate said she was in the library. How nice that it
is open all night.

Boar hunters sighted in Na Pali a nest of the rare Laysan
albatross. They are sending a team from the museum to try
to track them and some of the old people here think it's a
bad idea. No bracelets on holy birds, Mrs. Kaona told me.

The 'akala raspberry is coming into fruit at Koke'e and
even though I love its early bitter taste, it is a dangerous,
invasive plant. After the tidal wave, I used to prize the
specimens labeled "invasive" in my horticulture books—
they would do the work for me and overnight. I don't
think you will remember how bare the garden was, on
the Kekaha side. Beautiful in its way, but not as beautiful
as now with the bamboo that never stops moving and
whispering.

I am going to Wainiha, to the cottage where old Malia
Kaanehe spent her girlhood summers. She says it is so
changed now, but, of course, I don't see it, and I'm rather
glad I don't. I do think lovely Hanalei must have been
the Garden of Eden.

Love,
Mother

Mamie asked Claire if she could read her letter, dropped to
the floor, but it was already lost in the daily scree of crumpled

wrappers, tear-out magazine subscription cards, underwear and Dos Equis beer bottles.

The letters made Mamie depressed because they reminded her of all the things she was trying so hard to keep tamped deep in her memory. Mamie remembered that Mrs. Kaona had named her after the albatross, *Ka'upu,* the bird that observes the ocean, because Mamie was so watchful. She remembered that *'akala* was prescribed by the herbalists to obtain forgiveness.

While Claire ate Cheez Doodles and watched "Three's Company" on the little television in the armoire, Mamie tried to understand just what it was in her mother's letters that filled her with such grief. The very words "Wainiha" and "girlhood summers" were enough to fill her eyes with tears. I must be homesick, she thought. It is only that, nothing more. She had already noticed that a recording of Louis Armstrong singing "Do You Know What It Means to Miss New Orleans?" caused her heart to feel as if it were being crushed between her ribs. Even though it is the kind of sentimentality I most dislike, it is only homesickness, she said to herself. I will get over it.

Mamie had all the courage of her naïveté. It was lucky that she did, for it was neither homesickness nor sentiment that were slowly breaking her heart. It was something that had begun, years earlier, under the gummy, dusty boughs of a banyan tree.

Mamie had so far managed to learn little from Claire of the extraordinary circumstances that had brought her sister so happily and unexpectedly to Sixty-fifth Street and Park Avenue. Claire was not very forthcoming. It was more a matter of temperament than a need to conceal or a desire for privacy.

She tended not to reconsider. She did not sift through the past for clues. Mamie had learned long ago that Claire saw things in a way altogether different from her own view, so Mamie was always very interested to hear Claire's version of things. She questioned Claire ceaselessly about the past, not because she required pure information, nor to reinforce her own cool, fastidious memory, but because the variations in the story thrilled her.

"You must have sneaked out to see Orval that time you said you were going to paddling practice."

"I never made the crew and Orval was with his grandmother at McBryde Plantation."

"I thought his grandmother drowned in that accident."

"No."

The constant surprise of this freshly created past confirmed Mamie's suspicion of her own individuality, and the individuality of others. It gave her, too, the beginning of an idea: memory, happily, was not the same thing as truth.

"Well, how did it happen then?"

"What?"

"With Orval. How did you get pregnant? It's awfully hard to get pregnant these days, isn't it?"

Mamie's own sexual life was limited. That is to say, the act of sexual intercourse had so far played only a small part in Mamie's life, while her sensuality was unexplored and unlimited. The best part, it seemed to her, had been the kissing. The hours and hours, all through the night, that she had spent kissing boys. Kissing in moored boats, kissing between trees in the cool palm grove, in the chapel at school, in Dicky Herbert's airless tank, on the reef at low tide, while baby-sitting, while making *lei haku,* on horseback, on wet sand that exploded with phosphorescence every time she moved. When she thought back, she could not always remember just

who the boy had been. This was not an injustice to her partner, it was only that the sensation, the passion really, was
so strong that the boys seemed to melt into one big, delirious
boy who could kiss all night long (Gertrude used to say to
her when she scratched on the back door at four in the morning, "You look like you been smash-up, girl"). The expec-
tancy and excitement she had felt before the date, the nervous
preparation (toothpaste, mouthwash, Q-Tips, deodorant), the
lies to Mary ("Oh, we're just going to Lily Shields' to see
her father's slides of Angkor Wat"), the deep, deep comfort
and excitement of those kisses. There was even a time in the
night when both pairs of lips and two tongues and the area
all around the mouths were numb, but even though all sensation, at least in those parts of the body, was lost, the kissing did not stop. Once her boyfriend, Billy Quinn, leaned
her against a telephone pole to kiss her, and she was so moved
by this kiss that when he finally released her, she keeled over
stiffly. Little clouds of red Kaua'i dust bloomed around her.
He thought that he had killed her until he heard her moan
in happiness.

Mamie was considered a wild, bad girl by the mothers
who themselves opened back doors to dazed, chafed sons.
In fact, she was chaste. Her wildness was only the beginning, unconscious struggle for exemption from the passivity
expected of her as a girl. It was a proud, impassioned attempt
to escape the limitations she was beginning to feel as a
woman.

It was the boys of her adolescence who first experienced her
imperiousness; her sudden, irrational changes of heart; her
instability and contrariness; her high, high sense of separate-
ness. All of these things that passed for wildness in Mamie
were only signs of a disorganized resistance to combat the false
femininity that the world was forcing upon her.

If the night was about kissing, the day was about daring. The same thunderstruck boys who lay next to her on the cold sand staring up at the drifting stars while they embraced had to endure her untiring energy by day. There was not a challenge she would not accept. She provoked challenge. There was no vine footbridge she would not cross, no matter how dilapidated; no race she would not run; no tree she would not climb.

There were contests of chicken on the Kekaha highway. There was even a mysterious robbery (two jars of pigs' feet were stolen at the feed store). There were practical jokes (Lily Shields received pigs' feet for her birthday from a secret admirer). She grew famous for her recklessness, if famous is not too strong a word considering the smallness of her world.

It wasn't about sex at all. With all of her hair-flinging and teasing and kissing, Mamie was very inexperienced sexually. It was a pose. Mamie had recognized instinctively that she was not going to win (perhaps that is why she refused to go further than kissing), but there was a bravado and an exuberant sweetness about her struggle—it was not that comfortable kissing all night long in the ridged bottom of a boat.

Mamie snapped out of her reckless defiance the moment that she lost her virginity. It was during her sophomore year at college. Overnight, she became well-behaved and acquiescent, no longer demanding more than her share. The mothers who had so disapproved of her in her kissing days would have approved of her then. Stupefied by the years of their own passivity and forgetful of their own meager struggle, they would have gladly welcomed the rehabilitated Mamie into their unhappy midst.

Her old feelings did not disappear, of course, just be-

cause she finally allowed a nice, funny boy from San Diego
to force his way inside of her the night after the Rose
Bowl. Like all good resistance fighters, she simply went
underground. She stopped kissing all night long. She waited
for something to happen. She did not know it, but she
missed the feel of dry *plumeria* leaves slowly crushed to
powder on the ground beneath her, and a big-shouldered,
sweet-smelling, sweet-smiling island boy lying over her, kissing her.

"It wasn't that hard," Claire said. "I'd been fucking him
since I was thirteen."

Mamie slowly rewrapped her cheeseburger and neatly
repacked it in the bag. She rolled up the bag and set it
down on the needlepoint rug between the beds. She was
shocked.

"Why did you never tell me? I wanted to know."

"Oh, Mamie." Claire laughed. "How could you have wanted
to know if you didn't know?"

"I mean I would have helped you."

"Helped me?"

"I would have been your friend and you could have told me
things."

"I tried to tell you once. Remember the time I had to go
to the clinic because I said that I already had a Tampax in and
I put in a second one? And when the nurse was cleaning up
the room, she said, 'Next time you have sex, girly, be sure
to take it out.' I told you what she said, as a way of telling
you, and you said, 'Oh, what a mean person.' "

"I believed you."

"Mamie, you believe everybody."

"I don't really. But I believed you."

Claire could no longer pretend that Mamie was not upset.

She sighed loudly and moved over to Mamie's bed. They sat side by side.

"You didn't miss much," Claire said gently. "I used to sneak out to meet him during the summer. We did it the first time in the banyan tree."

"The banyan?"

"It was pretty uncomfortable."

"You used to say that Orval liked *me*."

"I think he did. But then he gave up."

"I do feel that I missed something. It might have been good for me if I had known."

"You were always off fording a fucking river. Or reading."

"You are this wonderful mutant, Claire," said Mamie quietly. "You have just what you need. You're not stupid and humorless like Aunt Alice and you're not dumb and serious like me. You're some genetic She-of-the-Future. You'll be all right. You'll be perfect."

"And you won't be?"

"Oh. Me. I don't know about me. I wish I could be like you."

"I always wanted to be like you. And care passionately about things. But I don't. I don't know why, but I don't. You've always had these strong feelings about things. I could feel strongly about your cheeseburger, however."

Mamie eased herself back on to her pillow, leaving her legs hanging awkwardly over the side. She moved in the careful way of someone who has been slightly injured; someone who does not yet know the extent of the damage, but is moving cautiously nonetheless.

"No, I don't want it," she said.

Claire turned over the Coleman Hawkins tape and moved back to her own bed. She ate the rest of Mamie's cold cheeseburger, using her flat stomach as a table. She kept time to "You're Blasé" with her pretty foot.

Everything that Mamie knew, she knew from books and her own watchfulness, but it seemed to her that other people, like Claire and Alysse, were more fully informed than she was about the world and how things worked. Where had they received their information? And how? Mamie was bewildered. Her mother used to say to her, "You are your own worst enemy," an observation Mamie thought neither original nor true. She had always thought it was just the opposite.

She was inhibited by her extreme notion of responsibility. It was not an exaggerated sense of omnipotence, but an expectation that the consequences of her actions would be unbearable. She had taken responsibility for Hiroshi, for McCully, for the banyan tree, for the vines ripped by Mary from the fence, for Gertrude and Sherry Alden, but she could not act on her own behalf.

The years at boarding school had been full of gaiety. Perhaps I was very busy, she thought. I was very busy and I didn't realize just how stricken I was. It was not until her last year at college that it seemed to catch up with her. When it did, she was unable to move. I am in a period of recovery, she had said to calm herself. It is grief, she had thought. This was the period when she broke up with her boyfriend, Tom Sheehan from San Diego, whom she had continued to sleep with, after losing her virginity to him, in order to justify his victory. It was not that she disliked him or had minded the relinquishing of her maidenhood. It was the disappointment of it, the commonplace loss, that had surprised and confused her. By giving Tommy Sheehan significance in her life, she gave significance to the act. She had wondered if other girls felt the same way. She had not asked them. She wrote to Lily Shields, who left the Big House for good when she was seventeen, and spent her small trust fund moving from country to country, and Lily wrote back that just as young men were sent to brothels to be introduced to the mysteries of sex, so young women should be taken in hand by practiced, older men who knew what they were about. She herself had been lucky to find such a man in Asolo, even though in her case it was a little late, as she was already the mother of a young child. She was no help to Mamie. She is in a state of amiable depression, Mamie had thought, and knows nothing. Following her advice, I should have slept with the loathsome Mr. Kipper. Mr. Kipper was a Yugoslav professor who waylaid Mamie one night as she walked back to her dorm and asked if she would show him her breasts. What is the *matter* with them? she had wondered. Do women lurk about waiting to ask men to show them their balls? Their cocks?

She stopped seeing Tom Sheehan when he asked her if she would play the part of a maid at a fraternity party. She would have to wear a very short black satin maid's costume, and high heels and fishnet stockings and a coquettish white lace cap. His request had not seemed unreasonable to Tommy and his fraternity brothers, and he was astonished when she told him that she didn't want to see him again.

When she thought back over her time with Tommy, she thought about the night she lost her virginity. What had held the most importance for her, the most humiliation, was when, the first time he put his two fingers inside of her, he did so through a hole in her cotton panties. He had been unaware of the hole, she knew, but it had mortified her, and distracted her from the astonishing rush of pleasure she had felt, the heating up of her body as he roughly pushed his fingers inside of her.

She had met Mr. Kipper once again, in the library, and he

had whispered to her in his bad accent, "In Burma, there are four things never to be trusted: rulers, thieves, the boughs of trees, and women." She had wanted to smash him over the head with the book she was reading, Volume III of *The Golden Bough,* but she'd held herself to saying wearily, "I know. I know you all hate us, but what do you want me to do?" She should have hit him with the book, rather than ask such a heartfelt question, because Mr. Kipper had grinned and answered, "Just love me a leetle." She had packed up her papers and notebooks and left the library.

It was not long after this that she stopped going to classes.

She stayed in her room for weeks, eating Butterscotch Krimpets and reading all of the Balzac she could find, listening over and over to the Bach Suites for Cello until her roommate, a nice girl from Beverly Hills, threw the cassettes out of the third-floor window. Mamie rushed out of the dormitory in her old *muumuu* to search for the tapes in the bushes. It was the first time she had been out of the dorm in a month. It was while she was on her hands and knees pawing through the pachysandra that some boys coming back from track practice stopped in curiosity to watch her and she realized that she would not be graduating that year from the University of California. She never found the tapes. She had gained fourteen pounds from the Krimpets. She figured about three books a pound. She was gone in a few days, using the plane ticket Aunt Alice had sent her as a graduation present, leaving the *muumuu* and the paperbacks under her bed.

As the weather at last turned fair and warm, Mamie began to understand more fully certain things she had once read —*Ethan Frome,* for example, and the Dylan Thomas poem

"The Force That Through the Green Fuse Drives the Flower."
As someone whose previous experience of cold was limited
to one very rainy February in 1973 when the temperature
at the Lihue airport plummeted to seventy-one degrees, and
whose idea of spring was defined by early English poetry,
Mamie was stirred and elated to discover that although the
weather did not change very much every day, as it did on
islands where there were rainstorms and drought all in one
afternoon, the weather changed in an invisible, slower and
larger way. There was winter. And then there was lovely
spring. Mamie even went back to reading Gerard Manley
Hopkins and Robert Frost. She fought the impulse, some
particularly lovely evenings when she walked home from
Deardorf's, to speak to every person she saw on the street
for she had been told many times by Alysse that the first
rule of the street was "no eye contact, darling." Mamie was
someone who, by her very nature, sought eye contact, so it
was difficult for her to practice this life-saving discipline.

As she walked home those gay, light-filled evenings, she
noticed that there were really very few ways of approach in
the city. You did not take shortcuts through backyards or
climb over fences. Distances were perfectly linear and perfectly
defined. It is not unlike society, Mamie thought. Imagination
is not required, nor originality. There seem to be clear rules
about how to get to where you want to be, whether it is to
dinner at Mrs. Gilette's or to the corner of Greenwich and
Desbrosses.

Mamie and Claire now spent every evening in Alysse's kitchen
and Mamie no longer needed to squander all of her small salary
on Reuben sandwiches and Entenmann's pound cakes. As she
had anticipated, Claire effortlessly won over the wary, lazy
Lydia, who cooked enormous dinners for them of black beans
and rice and chicken. They sat at the kitchen table and listened

to Tito Puente tapes while Lydia fed them. Claire still read aloud the want ads, Mamie still took off her shoes and stockings, and Lydia petted and spoiled them.

When Lydia cleaned the kitchen after them, she whispered to the food that she had to throw away. "Oh, poor beans. Good beans. I'm so sorry, little things, to throw you out. Do you forgive me, little ones? *Lo siento,*" she said as she scraped the food left on the plates into the garbage. Claire was quite startled the first time that it happened. Mamie had seen Lydia do it before, her favorite occasion being one afternoon when she found her apologizing to the remains of a roast leg of lamb.

"It's what intellectuals like to call magic realism," Mamie explained to Claire.

When Lydia finished, she sat with them at the table. They drank red wine and strong Puerto Rican coffee and read Alysse's fashion magazines, discussing endlessly what they should do with their hair and their lips and their eyebrows. Both girls, whose brown hair came to their shoulders, decided to grow their hair long. Lydia was thinking more along the lines of a wig.

"Lyddie," Claire said idly, studying the photograph of a nude blond woman lying across a saddle, "Do you know where my Aunt's stepchildren are?"

"*¿Quien?*"

"I've already asked Alysse," Mamie said, interrupting. "She says she has no idea what happened to them."

"She would, wouldn't she?" Claire turned the page. "Maybe *I'll* ask her."

Claire and Alysse had become special friends. Claire had charmed her. It is safe to say that Claire had charmed the entire apartment building. Claire's charm slid down the lacquered walls of Alysse's library and across the paneled hall into the elevator and right out under the canopy onto Park Avenue. Claire and Alysse had long, drunken lunches. Alysse felt more comfortable with Claire than she did with Mamie. Mamie was a little slow, in Alysse's eyes, and a little too, "I don't know," she would say, "A little too . . . bookish."

Mamie was admiring a photograph of a pair of high heels made entirely of canary feathers. They were very beautiful.

"Alysse told me she was famous for her lovely feet," Mamie said.

"She told me she was famous for her lovely blow jobs."

Mamie looked up. "Really?"

Claire nodded. "That's the difference between us."

"It's so disappointing." Mamie closed the magazine, discouraged.

"That's why I'll ask her about Courtney and Brooke."

"Ask her about Mother, too, while you're at it, will you?"

"Mother?"

"She's the only person left in the universe who knows anything about Mother. I'm so curious about her. How she came to be the way she is, so odd and so—" Mamie hesitated guiltily. "So uninteresting."

"I think Mother just *is* that way."

"She can't be," Mamie said. "It would be too devastating."

"You expect so much," Claire said.

Lydia was wiping the coffee grounds from the strainer. "*Pobrecitos!* Unlucky little coffees. Poor little things," she moaned sorrowfully.

"You think I'm bad, Lily once broke up with a boy because he said 'thank you much' to her father. To her father!" Mamie said. "Can you imagine?"

Lydia liked being with them, although she did not try to follow their talk. She sat down and tapped her big hands on the table in time to the music.

"If someone ever says to you, 'I'm a people-watcher,' start running."

"What else?" Claire asked, shaking her head in amused disapproval.

" 'Sea change.' "

"You're such a snob!" Claire said. "You do expect *so* much."

"But I get so little! I get famous feet and you get famous blow jobs. Do you think it's fair?"

"It's supposed to be good for your complexion."

"That explains my skin," Mamie said, and poured more wine for them.

They were still sitting there discussing beauty secrets (Lydia had heard from her daughter in Los Angeles that there was a cream that caused you to lose ten pounds a week for as long as you massaged it into your thighs) when they heard the front door of the apartment open and close.

Alysse was home. From the way that she whispered and giggled in the hall, they could tell she had someone with her. They heard her say, "Oh, Rod, you couldn't."

"Rod!" Mamie said with a shout. "Rod?" She put her face in her hands, laughing.

Claire whispered, "Be quiet! Be quiet!"

Mamie stood up, and Lydia motioned in fright to her. Claire shook her head in warning. Mamie had not intended to go out into the hall, only to clear away some of the many empty wine bottles, but she sat down again to make them happy. Claire was leaning forward, very still, listening to the sounds of kisses and giggles that slid under the kitchen door.

Suddenly, the door swung open and Alysse's face, flushed

and smeared, but happy, appeared in the small space between the door and the kitchen wall.

"Good news," she said. She was drunk. "I've found you an apartment. Vivi Crawford—!" She was pulled away by someone standing on the other side of the door. "I'll tell you tomorrow," she said quickly as she was tugged from view and the door closed in little jerks.

The three women in the kitchen sighed and carried their dirty glasses to the sink.

EIGHT

Alysse proposed that Mamie and Claire stay in Vivi and Whit Crawfords' apartment on Central Park West. The Crawfords were very pleased with the arrangement (Whit Crawford did not want just anyone touching his things), especially after meeting Claire, whose charm continued its steady roll through the city.

Mamie was very relieved that they would be able to leave Alysse's apartment. She noticed that Alysse was much nicer now that she knew they would be leaving in a few weeks and Mamie did not blame her. Mamie was very eager to leave. As difficult as it is to have a guest, Mamie thought, it is also very hard to be a guest. I, for one, am a nervous wreck.

Alysse had become very attached to Claire. She would miss her at morning coffee. No more drunken afternoons running up and down the escalator at Deardorf's. Alysse had bought both girls many presents, but Claire had been outfitted from head to toe during these afternoons, like a bride with a trousseau.

"You promise we'll still have lunch? And play 'Animals'?" Alysse asked Claire with a little pout. At lunch, Alysse always insisted that they play her favorite game of picking the animal they'd most like to be. It was another of Alysse's tests. She, herself, always chose to be "a deer with wings."

Claire promised.

"It's just a ying-yang kind of thing with us," Alysse said in a babyish voice.

"I think it's *yin,*" Mamie said. She had just come into the room.

"Who?" asked Alysse.

"Alysse wants to give us a farewell dinner," Claire said to change the subject.

"Not *farewell,* Claire. An introductory dinner. A launching dinner. A Claire and Mamie dinner!" The very idea excited Alysse and seemed to instantly divert her from her grief at their departure. "I'm going to make the guest list right now!"

Mamie had promised Alysse that she would return some books for her to a store on Madison Avenue. Mamie was interested in the idea of returning books ("I didn't like this Proust. Have you anything else?") and while waiting for the credit slip, she bought for Claire *Washington Square* and *The House of Mirth.* She said that they would try to find the settings of the novels on one of their walks. Claire, who was not so serious a reader as Mamie, said, "Well, let me read them first."

"Have you ever noticed," Mamie said, "that tragic heroines are allowed to live only if they have private incomes?" The ten quick minutes in the book shop had been enough to start Mamie thinking. They walked west through the Park.

Claire looked at her. "What about Alysse?"

"I would hardly call her income private. She has a public income. And she's not a heroine. She's a success. She thinks of me, however, as the poor relative, the one who's had to wear the hand-me-down shawls and become a governess, the cousin who comes in useful at the last minute when the *placement* is one woman short. As you have seen, I am always seated next to the most boring, most shallow (although I admit it's a close call), homosexual there. Usually that art critic Henry Jones's boyfriend. The one from North Africa."

"Next time don't go," Claire said. It annoyed her that Mamie had not yet learned how to decline invitations.

"I'm always caught off guard. I know that other people have little lies they know by heart: 'I'm so terribly sorry, but I'll be in Maine,' and I even know that the other person, the hostess, *knows* it's a polite fib and doesn't mind too much because she tells the same lie—it's part of the convention. But when I try it, Aunt Alice refuses to play by the rules. She asks, 'Who do *you* know in Maine?' and then I'm flustered and caught out. And end up next to the Moroccan who hates being seated next to the poor relative just as much as I dread being seated next to him. We've both said everything there is to say, ever, in the history of the world, about Paul Bowles."

"You're a heroine," said Claire.

Mamie turned to look at her. It was not like Claire to say anything kind to her. In her enthusiasm, Mamie did not see that Claire may have been teasing her.

"I have just finished the strangest, loveliest book by Sybille Bedford. Perhaps what the critics say is true, that books nowadays are small and self-absorbed, you know, how can you write about the seventies and not mention Vietnam, that argument. Well, they would approve of *A Legacy*. It is about Germany before the First World War and I had to keep reminding myself just who my metaphors were: the decline-of-the-Catholic-Church-in-the-secularized-confederacy and so on, but in the book there is a most inspiring heroine, Caroline

Trafford, and she is the one who started me thinking. *She* had a private income."

"You speak as if she were real."

"What I am trying to say is that, in books at least, a tragic heroine who happens to have money of her own will be allowed to live. If not, she dies: Lily Bart, Nastasya Barashkov. The dreaded Emma Bovary. And Tess. Think of Tess! But if she has a little private family money, like Christina Light or Ellen Olenska, she only suffers." She looked at Claire. "You see? You don't die!"

She was making Claire nervous. "Get a grip, Mamie. Get a grip."

Mamie was still too preoccupied with her heroines to be offended. "Actually, I exaggerate a little," she said. "They don't *all* die. Some become private secretaries to very mean, old, rich women."

"Perhaps you should write this down. An article for *Cosmopolitan,*" Claire said lightly. She was not feeling the pleasure she usually experienced when teasing Mamie. For whatever reason, Mamie, by insisting on taking her sister's words literally, was refusing to acknowledge her sarcasm.

"I am not a heroine," Mamie said.

Oh, no? Claire thought.

"No," Mamie said. "Definitely not."

Mamie and Claire arrived at the dark, tireless river in time to watch the city to the east of them catch fire with the light of the setting sun. On her last visit to the Hudson, Mamie had suddenly realized why it was that the city did not concern itself more with its rivers. In true American style, the rivers were too big. It was hard to imagine stone footbridges arching gracefully to Fort

Lee. These wide, dirty estuaries were for commerce, not pleasure. She did not like the rivers any less for her discovery.

Claire admired the red sky and the cold black river and this
pleased Mamie, who was worried that her long monologue
about heroines had sounded hysterical. Mamie had no one to
talk to about these things. Certainly Miss Magda, who ran
the girl ragged at work, was not interested in hearing her
theory about "Older Women in the French Novel." When
Mamie arrived at boarding school, and even when she went
on to college, she was so unused to hearing certain words
spoken that she pronounced many words incorrectly. She had
only read the word. She had never actually heard anyone in
Honolulu say "St. John Perse" or *"Weltanschauung"* or "Cu-
chulain." She had made many mistakes at college and even
now, in her rare, extended conversations, usually with startled
clerks in bookstores, she still winced preparedly before she
ventured out with "roman à clef."

On the walk back across the warm, gritty city, Claire said,
"I asked Alysse about Mother and McCully. Like you wanted
me to. She's not very interested in Mother and she didn't really
know Father very well, but she did tell me one story. It's a
little upsetting. Do you want to hear it? I don't want you to
freak out or anything."

"Are you crazy, Claire?"

"Well," said Claire slowly. "That summer when they came
on the boat, they were incredibly bored at night, not Mother
and Father, of course, who were used to quiet nights, but
Alysse and her friends were dying of boredom, especially as
we ate dinner at six o'clock, so they organized games after we
went to bed. And in one of the games a man was blindfolded
and the women lifted up their skirts and the man felt all the
legs until he identified his partner's legs."

"Mary and McCully played, too?" She was a little surprised.

"Of course. Apparently, they really began to look forward to the games each night."

"And what happened?" Mamie asked nervously.

"Well, in the leg game, which they played often because no one was very good at Dictionary, all the men were able to recognize their partner's legs by touch, except McCully. He could never do it. And the game always ended with some man pissed off when Father insisted some other woman's legs were Mother's."

Claire stopped to look at Mamie. Mamie was silent, so Claire was not certain she had understood the game. It was hard to explain.

"The men on their knees blindfolded, the men, and they had to creep along feeling all these legs until they found the right legs. You see—"

"It is the saddest thing I ever heard," said Mamie

"I *knew* I shouldn't have told you!" Claire stopped abruptly in the middle of the sidewalk, and several visibly annoyed people had to walk around her.

"It makes sense, in a way," said Mamie. She took Claire's arm and pulled her along. "Why did Alysse tell you?"

"She thought it was unbelievably funny."

Poor, dear McCully, thought Mamie. "I hate Alysse."

"It's not that Alysse doesn't like men," Claire said. "They're just not a political issue. They're jobs. Work. And if you're any good at what you do, as I suppose she is, you're promoted. You get to marry one richer and more powerful. She *thinks* that she adores men."

"I know," said Mamie. She sighed. "I don't think she likes sex much, either. I suppose it's part of the job, as you say. No speed-typing, but speed hand jobs."

"That reminds me, do you remember Mr. Hemmings at school?"

"Oh, no," said Mamie. "I'm not sure I want to hear this. I've reached my daily level of sexual humiliation with the McCully story. My *weekly* level, actually."

When Claire shrugged and was silent, Mamie looked over at her.

"Okay," Mamie said.

"He wanted me to meet him in the science lab for some experiments. Something to do with the effect of hot and cold on the male organ. Ice and—"

"I changed my mind," Mamie said quickly. Although she was laughing, she put her hands over her ears.

"Oh, Mamie! You're no fun!"

"You're my sister. My little sister. It shocks me. And it makes me sad. I don't know why it does, but it does."

"But it was funny, Mamie! How can it make you sad?"

"It's all so desperate," Mamie said. "There is something awful about McCully on his knees with those city slickers, running his hands up some grisly alcoholic leg and thinking it was Mother's. And there is something awful about a chemistry teacher in a toupee trying to get you to put ice on his balls. I *know* you say it's about pleasure and that that's what counts, it doesn't matter if Orval goes down on you, or Sherry, or Jimmy; it's only about pleasure, the body-as-machine, I understand that. It's all biological and hormonal, anyway, even for Aunt Alice. Aunt Alice is looking for a man to take care of her because she is a woman. She is helpless and she needs food and shelter. It's just not so simple for me. I told you: you're the modern woman. You're the future; I'm the past. And even though my clitoris is pumping away, as you say, it would make a difference who was going down on me, a man, a man whom I had chosen, or a mongoose." She ran into the street and stuck out her arm for a taxi.

"I told you you'd freak out," Claire yelled after her. "I *told* you!"

Mamie listened to her Hawaiian tapes on her Walkman when she walked to work. Alysse had asked that Mamie not play them in the living room. Alysse had grown quite fond of the other music, Otis Redding and Clifton Chenier and Aretha, that Claire and Mamie played for her. She did ask if the girls thought they listened to "you know, non-white" music because of their background.

"Our background?" Mamie asked in irritation. "With the slaves, you mean?"

"I loathed Hawai'i," Alysse said. "Loathed. A lot of lizards and no swimming pools. And *nothing* to buy."

Even Claire, Mamie noticed, had grown a little weary of her playing over and over in their bedroom the cassettes of old Hawaiian music and chants. Mamie tried to talk to Claire about the longing she had for the islands. "Lily has it, too," Mamie said. "She has it so much, she can't even live there."

"Oh, Mamie," Claire said, sighing. "You exaggerate everything. Lily is a very odd person."

"One day, I'm worried about the extinction of the *nene* goose, and then the next day it's the United States Army using Kaho'olawe for mortar practice. Then old Mrs. Robinson admits they're selling a thousand acres to a Texas hotel chain because of bad government sugar policies. The whole planet seems to be sliding away. Lily sees it, although she, of course, has been convinced by her father that the world has already ended."

"Then what does it matter?"

"Because of the waste of it. The carelessness of it."

Claire started to speak, but Mamie interrupted her. "I've heard the argument that it really doesn't make much difference if the last person who speaks Hawaiian dies tomorrow, but I don't believe it."

"You're just homesick, Mamie," Claire said and went back to watching "Magnum."

So, except in her letters to Lily, Mamie kept quiet about these things and listened to the sweet, intricate patterns of Gabby Pahinui's slack-key guitar in the privacy of the dingy streets.

Years earlier, on those afternoons when the other girls at school had been at cheerleading practice, she and Lily Shields were in dusty shops in Chinatown using their small allowances to make payments on old bamboo nose flutes and sharkskin hymnals. Lily's father was a collector and some of the dealers recognized Lily and gave them little things, pieces of quilt appliqué and nineteenth-century hand combs of stippled co-conut and mother-of-pearl. One summer, the girls displayed their collection in the garage at Waimea and charged a small admission. There were not many visitors, although Mamie induced some old cowboys down from the ranch to see the display of two *lau hala* hats and pheasant-feather lei. Lily's father, who was very encouraging of this sort of thing, came to their museum several times that summer and he presented them with a rare *pa-ipu heke ʻole,* a gourd dance drum, to place alongside the lone calabash of McCully's that had escaped the pull of the tsunami.

Perhaps Mamie was trying to rebuild McCully's extraordinary collection. She was ever after drawn and held by dying traditions. It suited her romanticism and her melancholy. She wondered if she had been born too late. She saw something fanciful and foolhardy in a belief in the future. The myths and music of her island, Kaua'i, disappearing so very quickly, had a strong effect on Mamie. She once begged an old, wary Hawaiian woman in Ha'ena to teach her the words to the ancient place-name chants and songs and she had written down the words in order to memorize them and in times of great loneliness, and even fear, Mamie would find these words, learned years earlier, moving through her like a stream, and the words steadied her and restored her: "If you can only see the beauty of the sparkling water. The fragrant *hala* of Mapuana seems to reach out to the restless sea. This is the end of my praise, of beautiful Kaua'i in the calm."

Mamie saw no incongruity in this. It did not seem eccentric to be walking up Fifty-sixth Street, under the shining steel frame of a new skyscraper, listening to a name-chant sung by Wahinekeaouli Pa about the moss on the beach at Polihale. She was amused by the shouts of the construction workers (it was where she first heard the request to "sit on my face") and they made her feel both desirable and guilty, as if she were beautiful *and* betraying those values of the Women's Movement that her friend Sherry Alden had explained to her when they used to talk all night long. The construction workers reminded her of the boys in the camp, even though some of these workers were white city boys. She would have been ashamed to admit it, but she often walked past the huge, clanging building site just because the men made her laugh.

She was in a dressing room at Deardorf's, shaking out a soiled jumpsuit (mustard and mayonnaise, she guessed) and she had just decided that she wasn't going to help Selena to steal any longer, when Miss Magda sternly called her to the back.

Mamie, understandably nervous, was confused to find Miss

Magda waiting for her with Mr. Felix, the designer. Mamie had first met Mr. Felix several weeks earlier when he had asked her, with great charm, to assist him before a fashion show on the third floor. He had come to the lingerie department to borrow brassieres for several of the models who had shown up without them. "My customers are not the sort to go without support," he said to Mamie as if they were old friends. He winked to make sure that she knew it was a Mr. Felix witticism. He looked at her rather curiously at the time, but Mamie, wearing away under the constant pressure of Selena's derision, thought it must have been the rare Duke Kahanamoku shirt she had on that day.

Mr. Felix, despite his name and occupation, was not effete. Mamie knew this, but it would never have occurred to her that his study of her might have been admiring. She was, therefore, as amazed as Miss Magda when Felix announced that he had asked Mr. Deardorf if Mamie could be released temporarily from the lingerie department in order to work for him.

"For you?" she asked Felix.

It seemed to be a matter already decided. Miss Magda, with a scornful expression, turned away. I will be very happy never to see another hanger, Mamie thought. Or another woman.

"Of course, my dear," Felix said. "For whom else?" He had shiny black hair and small black eyes. He had a thin, well-trimmed moustache. Mamie had noticed before that he had exceedingly good manners, in that deferential, graceful way of European men. She thought that the boys in the camp would envy the slick pomade used by Mr. Felix. It did not smell like Lilac Vegetol.

"I should like to see you in one of my dresses," he said as he took her elbow and smoothly guided her away from the lingerie department. "I have you just on the loan, you know.

Should you be unhappy, Mr. Deardorf assures you of your position here. I like to think, however, that you will be too happy to ever leave me." He smiled.

He took her down to the couture, never letting go of her arm, finding a way to touch her or brush against her whenever he could do so without making her wary or nervous. With some women, it would not matter if they noticed; in fact, it often worked to his advantage by speeding things along, but he sensed that with this girl, at least, he must move slowly.

"There is a fashion show next month in Chicago. I want you to be there."

She looked at him, startled.

"I will take care of everything. It is very, very simple. I have a special dress in mind for you. Now take this and we will see."

He picked a low-cut, black silk jersey sheath from the rack of his sample clothes and took her into a large dressing room. He closed the door behind them.

Mamie saw at once that he meant for her to remove her clothes. She had never undressed before a man, in the day, in the light. When she had made love with Tommy Sheehan in college, it had been a matter of jeans and white cotton underpants removed quickly, not from passion, but from embarrassment, in dark dormitory rooms or stuffy motel rooms. She had undressed awkwardly in closets and dirty bathrooms, reappearing shyly in a thin towel, and raced for the bed.

Felix, careful not to look her in the face and frighten her, unbuttoned the sample dress. He held it open for her, waiting.

She knew from the time when he came with his models to fit them with brassieres that the girls were not bothered by modesty. They stood expressionlessly before Felix, and even Mamie herself, a stranger, in their bikini panties, and tried on brassieres without shyness, or even interest. Mamie had been impressed. Their thin, long bodies were like the bodies of young boys, without breasts or hips, but oddly appealing in their lean, trim solidity and cleanness of line.

Mamie, whose body was not that of a young boy, did not understand that her womanliness, her full, pretty breasts and her long torso with its small sloping waist and hips, was just what made it difficult for her to show her body. Her womanliness, and sensuousness, gave her an unconscious humility. In some way, she realized the power implicit in a woman's body, in her body, and she was afraid and ashamed of that power.

She so wanted to do the right thing. She wanted to show this cultivated older man that she knew how to behave. It never occurred to her that she might simply have asked him to wait outside.

He did not let her see that he was aroused. He patiently held the weightless dress in his outstretched hand. She saw that the backs of his hands were marked with brown liver spots.

She slipped off her flat shoes. She was not wearing stockings, now that it was warm. She unbuttoned her linen skirt and stepped out of it. She folded it slowly and neatly and laid it carefully on a narrow ledge in the corner.

She looked up and saw in the large mirrors that he was looking strangely at her slip. It was Claire's slip. She had put it on that morning as she dressed quietly and quickly in the dark bedroom so as not to awaken Claire, who had been to a discotheque the night before with Alysse. She twisted her body at the waist in order to see over her shoulder.

There was a large blood stain on the back of the slip.

Felix looked away.

Mamie dropped to the floor, sitting with stiff, bare legs straight before her, hands clenched tightly in her lap.

He stood over her, the black dress dragging on the floor. "My dear," he said quietly.

She stared at his long, narrow feet in their thin brown leather shoes. There were bumps on the soles. He was wearing Italian driving slippers.

He reached down to take her hand. There was no place where she could stand that would protect her from view. The blood from the aborted birth of Claire and Orval Nalag's child was visible no matter where she put herself.

"You are so sweet," he said. "So *mignon.*"

She felt such a relief in being comforted that she didn't mind when he put his arm around her to draw her to her feet. She was so embarrassed that she was not paying close attention to him. He was very excited by her. He stroked her arms with the back of his fingers.

"I am thinking to name this dress 'Missionary's Downfall' in honor of you. But only if you promise to wear it in Chicago. Do you promise?"

He could see that as she grew more composed, she was more conscious of the intimacy with which he touched her arms and the small of her back. He touched instead each of the coconut shell buttons on her turquoise bowling shirt, and then he let her pull away from him.

"Do you promise?"

Without turning her back to him, although she knew that he could still see the bloody slip clearly in the mirror behind her, she reached out awkwardly for her skirt. "Does this mean no more Miss Magda?" She smiled. The idea of escaping from the lingerie department made her very happy.

"I saw you, months ago, on the elevator. Before we first met, before the fashion show. I have been thinking how you would look in my clothes."

"You have?" Mamie was surprised. She quickly put on her skirt.

"You belong in the world. The world should see you." He took her hand and kissed it. "The world *will* see you."

Mamie laughed. He laughed, too, and allowed her to slip shyly out of the dressing room.

It was the night of Alysse's big dinner, what the girls had come to call the Claire-and-Mamie dinner, and Mamie, still exhilarated by her change in fortune that morning, found herself standing for hours in front of the bathroom mirror. Claire's slip soaked in cold brown water in the sink before her as Mamie tried to discover just what it was that Mr. Felix had seen in her. Despite studying herself from every possible angle, she couldn't quite get it. The question is, she thought, not whether I agree with him, but whether I believe him.

It is safe to say that Mamie had never thought of herself as someone whom the world deserved to see. It was one thing to incite blue-collar compliments at construction sites ("Yo, skinny, want to go round the world?"), but it was quite another to be discovered by Felix Villanueve. It meant, too, that she no longer had to run to Eighth Avenue to pick up Miss Magda's corn removers, or to hide among the ostrich-feather bed jackets the torn, soiled clothes stolen overnight by Selena. She was astonished at her good luck.

Claire spent the morning with Lydia, who had obligingly plaited Claire's wet hair into fifty tiny braids. Claire, who had set aside an hour to unbraid her hair, was on the toilet seat, unweaving the thin, tight strands as Mamie held up yet another hand mirror to get a glimpse of herself from the side.

"Very Pre-Raphaelite," Mamie said.

"Pre-what?"

"Very pretty," Mamie said. "Your hair. Not me."

"Lydia told me about a farmer in her village in Guatemala who had an old horse that he loved. He used to make love to the horse from behind, climbing up on the flatbed of an old pickup. Lydia used to watch them."

"I'm sorry you told me this." Mamie was looking at her profile.

"It gets better."

"Not possible."

"Lydia says the horse loved it."

Mamie looked at her. The loose hair fanned out in an aureola around Claire's sweet little face.

"How did she know?" Mamie asked.

"What?"

"That the horse loved it."

Claire shrugged. "Women know these things."

Mamie laughed. Claire looked up at her, pleased. "I believe it," she said.

"You would."

"I'm happy for the farmer," Claire said.

"I'm happy for the horse," Mamie said, putting on her dress. She was wearing a lavender flocked-velvet cheongsam she had found in an antique store in downtown Los Angeles. Alysse had wanted her to borrow something of hers, but Mamie had politely refused. Alysse thought that Mamie always looked as if she were going to a costume party. Like Selena, she thought that Mamie's way of dressing was perverse. She had convinced Claire to wear one of her cocktail dresses and, in fact, it was Claire who looked like she was disguised as a middle-aged rich lady.

Alysse had gone to great trouble for the party. The apartment was filled with thousands of ruffled pink peonies and Mamie, who did not know about peonies, was delighted with the millions of rounded petals, as soft as powdered skin, and the sweet fragrance that seeped from room to room.

Four round tables had been put up in the dark green dining room. Alysse was very proud of the place settings. She had stolen the idea from Vivi Crawford. The china and silver and glasses were set on top of three or four large art books arranged on the tables before each gilt chair. Mamie, who had on her right a plump interior decorator and, on her left, a man named Alder Stoddard, had been lucky enough to draw *Monet at Giverny, Avedon* and *English Country Houses*. This stack of books in front of each guest diminished by quite a bit the distance from plate to mouth and it wasn't until the second course, a *Poitrine de Veau Farcie,* that they adjusted to this awkward foreshortening. The other difficulty was that there was nowhere on the table to place their arms, so in moments of stillness they looked like very good schoolchildren at their desks, hands folded obediently in their laps.

Mamie looked at the faces illuminated by candlelight. The women and their jewels, and the shining cloth of their dresses, shimmered with a glittering, pearly iridescence and the bare-shouldered women stood out whitely against the green walls, as if they were in a forest at night. As she looked curiously around the table, Mamie noticed for the first time that some women as they grew older, became increasingly hard, just as men became softer and more effeminate.

Mr. Stoddard was a tall man in his early thirties. He was wearing a well-cut navy blue pin-striped suit. He had dark, short hair and dark, serious eyes that flicked restlessly over the surface of things. Mamie had the sense that he was a man who was easily bored. He was frowning, with his head cocked so that he could listen to Lady Studd, who was on his other side, without having to look at her. Lady Studd ate stealthily off his plate as she told him of the time Slim Pomerantz jumped into a bonfire in Jamaica because her husband was flirting with the waitress.

"She said, 'Look, look, I'm Jeanne d'Arc!' "

Mamie turned to the man on her right. He was very famous for having recently introduced Toile de Jouy to the new world. There were very few good apartments or country houses that did not have at least one room covered in toile. Alysse's bedroom was done in a red and white toile hunting scene.

He said to Mamie, "Look at the Grand Duke. He is the exact image of the Dowager Empress, isn't he?"

Mamie allowed as how he did resemble her greatly.

"Of course, they never got on," the decorator said. "He hated his father."

"That's not so uncommon, do you think?" Mamie was trying to be a good dinner partner. "It is the classic Oedipal struggle."

"The what?" He looked at her for the first time.

"The Oedipal struggle."

He was very perplexed. With some suspicion, Mamie took it upon herself to briefly explain to him the story of Oedipus. When she finished, there was a long pause.

"That is the single most ridiculous thing I've ever heard," he said loudly. He was shocked and outraged. Mamie looked around nervously, but no one was listening to them. "Want to *kill* your father and *marry* your mother? It's ludicrous! Judas priest, girl, wherever did you hear such a thing?" he shouted.

Mamie was so taken aback that she pulled away from him and knocked Mr. Stoddard's knife from one of his art books, *Balthus,* onto the floor. She leaned down to pick it up at the same time as Mr. Stoddard bent down to find it. Mamie looked at the top of his head, and she looked at his black shoes, and then, inches apart, heads pressed against the moiré tablecloth, they looked at each other.

"She's explaining to me how she masturbates her corgis," he said solemnly to Mamie. "She says that everyone does it."

"I don't," said Mamie.

"I didn't think so," he said and they sat up.

Claire was standing behind Mamie's chair. She grinned a little drunkenly at Mr. Stoddard and leaned down to whisper to Mamie. "I'm next to someone fat from Newport who keeps talking about his 'Mummy.'" Mamie could smell whiskey and cigarette smoke in Claire's hair.

"Alysse says it's a good sign," Mamie whispered back to her. "It means he had an English nanny, remember?"

A young, handsome waiter stood behind them, impatiently waiting to pour more wine. Mamie gently nudged Claire away. The waiter, with great sulkiness, leaned around her to pour the wine.

"Is that your sister?" Alder Stoddard asked abruptly. He had given up dinner parties, especially Alysse's dinner parties, years ago.

"How did you know?"

"I met her before dinner. That gentleman over there, the man who is laughing, the Ambassador, is very sorry that the American military did not bomb Vietnam into submission. He believes it should be done now in Nicaragua and that we would regain the respect of our allies by 'standing tall.' He was describing just how Navy Seals kill village headmen when your sister interrupted him to ask a question. She wanted to know if his wife cupped his balls when he came."

Mamie, under less inhibiting conditions, would have laughed. She saw that it wouldn't do. I am now in terrible trouble on both sides, she thought. The homosexual on my right thinks I lied to him about a conspiracy to kill fathers and Claire has deliberately insulted the State Department.

Mr. Stoddard looked sternly at Mamie. She was angry

and embarrassed to be put in the position of having to defend her sister, but she knew, from the past, the futility of explanation.

"Well, does she?" Mamie asked. "Cup his balls, I mean."

He leaned toward her. "Let's get out of here."

He pushed back his chair. He pulled back Mamie's chair. She saw Alysse look up quickly. The decorator who had never heard of Oedipus did not bother to look at them.

Mamie, who was passive because she was still waiting to see what would happen in the world, and Alder, whose passivity came from having already seen what would happen and not much liking what he had seen, were unlikely conspirators. Or perhaps they only seemed unlikely. Alysse would never have insisted that he come to dinner had she known that her niece would attract his attention. Alysse would have thought Alder too jaded for Mamie—he was more her kind of man. She could never have guessed that Mamie, whom she secretly found a little too sincere, a quality she considered deadly, reminded Alder of himself before he was overwhelmed with disillusionment and the laziness that is so often the penalty for falling out of love with the world.

Mamie rose gravely from the table. Alder, with his impatience and intelligence, drew her toward him like a tidal pull. Mamie, who was never able to say exactly what she meant, or do exactly what she wanted, in fear that the whole tremendous weight of human fury would come down on her head, recognized immediately that Alder was not only unafraid of its crashing down on him, but not very interested in it. Of course she would follow him.

For a moment, she stood trapped between her chair and the precarious place setting of art books and china. She looked at him. He gently took her arm, nodded and smiled at Alysse, and led Mamie out of the still, startled room.

˅ ˅ ˅

It was a warm night, like a night in the tropics. The light breeze hit Mamie full in her smiling face as she stepped with her big, graceful stride onto the street, and she felt the soft air like an emblem of her liberation. She walked south on Park Avenue and Alder Stoddard walked beside her.

"I hope that you are someone I can talk to," she said. "I know now that this has been a problem. When Claire arrived, I thought I'd be all right. I sometimes think my reluctance to speak out is a form of acquiescence with the enemy."

"The enemy?"

"Oh, with men, or my aunt, or the ambassador who wants to kill everyone in Nicaragua. I am upset and silent; Claire is upset and goes into her karate stance."

"Most people have a punt or two in their repertoire," he said. "They kick the ball away and hope for good field position. It's just that your sister is punting all the time. That's all."

This was the most he had yet said to her and Mamie took time to consider it.

"Why were you at the party?" she asked.

"Your aunt was, for some little time, married to my uncle. Your aunt, in fact, is responsible for my having been sent to boarding school against my will."

"She was very happy about boarding schools. You must know the sisters."

"Your aunt tried to seduce me in the men's changing room of the Rowing Club in Southampton the summer I was twelve. It was on one of those very narrow benches in front of the lockers. I had never made love before, and I didn't then."

She looked across at him. He walked with his hands in his trouser pockets. He seemed all irritable joints and angles.

"She was afraid that I would tell. That's why I was sent

away. It wasn't the failed seduction that mattered, of course. Only the lack of faith."

"It's *always* that," Mamie said. She was so fervent that he looked at her and laughed and pulled his hands from his pockets.

"You mustn't mind so much on my behalf. I would have had to go to boarding school anyway."

"She didn't know that." She was completely on his side.

"She sometimes spoke of your family. It was a bit Uncle-Tom's-Cabin, as I remember."

Mamie laughed. "Now, of course, she knows better. I've often felt that she is a little embarrassed by me here in New York. Although not by Claire. When she behaves badly, I try to picture something my mother once told me. Buddy Klost took her to Paris for the first time and someone in Oklahoma had told her that the correct way to look at the Eiffel Tower was upside down, so she stood on her head, right there on the pavement, and made Buddy hold her by the ankles. She was upside-down for a long time because she really wanted to do it right."

They walked without speaking for quite a distance before Mamie said, "In a way, she's still trying to get it right."

"Are you still speaking about your aunt?" he asked in surprise.

"What would you like to talk about? The disappearance of myth? The success of disco? Don't you think it is the great loss of the twentieth century? Everyone talks about existentialism and Camus and the failure of Marxism, but really all of that is just symptomatic of something much larger and more important, don't you think?"

"You're referring to 'the success of disco'?"

"Yes," she said.

The warm, quiet night had filled her up with her best self.

She was living in the present. It was an unusual sensation for her, full of tranquillity and lightness.

"May I ask you a very intimate question?" she said. "You're the first person I've felt I could ask."

"I would be delighted," he said solemnly.

His formality stopped her only for a moment. "Do you think I'm mysterious?"

He drew her back in mid-step with his hand, and turned her so that he could see her face.

"No," he said.

She was very disappointed. She looked down at her slippers.

"You are always going to do the best thing," he said. "It makes you predictable."

He held on to her arm. She felt, incorrectly, that he was embarrassed for her, and when he wanted to say more, she quickly stopped him by putting her hand over his mouth. Her face had flushed bright pink.

"No, don't say it! You don't have to. It was a stupid question!"

They let go of each other and began to walk again. The big lighted buildings at Forty-sixth Street shimmered over them, like the outer gates of an illuminated city, locked at sundown, leaving them enclosed and encircled until the heavy doors were pulled open again at dawn.

NINE

"Alysse says she fucked him when he was a kid," Claire said.

"Yes, I'm sure she did."

They had moved that day, the day after the Claire-and-Mamie dinner, to the Crawfords' apartment on West Sixty-seventh Street.

"Said it, I mean," Mamie said. "Not fucked him."

They were sitting, a little uncomfortably, in the slippery Eames chairs in the small, crowded living room. Claire read a magazine and idly stroked a copy of a Brancusi head that was on the table next to her.

"She was *not* very happy when you left."

"I'm sure not." Mamie sighed. She had a headache. "I don't think you should be stroking that."

"You always say sculpture is a tactile art."

"No wonder you think I'm pedantic."

"I just wish you had taken me with you. I was stuck for hours and hours with Mrs. Miller who just finished decorating their plane. You can *imagine* that conversation. Alysse told me later it was a payoff."

"A payoff?"

"She caught him with two sixteen-year-old boys and he let her do the plane."

"Not much of a payoff."

"Mamie! This is just what I like to hear—a little cynicism!"

"It's my headache."

"I thought it was maybe Alder Stoddard. He was the only interesting person there. *Why* was he there, now that I think of it? Oh, this is great," Claire said, interrupting herself. "*Gentleman* magazine's idea of men is William Walker writing endlessly about his last alcoholic breakdown, but its idea of women is an article on who you'd like to sit next to at dinner. Madame Chiang Kai-shek! She'd be fun, wouldn't she? Maybe she'd let slip where they hid the gold. Or how about Mrs. Reagan? One caption is 'the sweet, siren smell of her chemise.' Not Mrs. Reagan's. Faye Dunaway's."

"He'd seen Alysse by chance at the lawyer's, the family lawyer, and she insisted that he come."

"The sweet, siren smell of his jockey shorts."

"Oh, Claire," Mamie said, standing up. She bumped her head on a Japanese kite suspended from a wooden beam. "You're such a pig."

Mamie went into the tiny library she had chosen to use as her bedroom. Mamie had quickly picked this room over the brighter bedroom down the passage. She liked its dim masculinity. In the center of the room was a steel Empire camp bed, covered with paisley shawls and bolsters. There was not a Staffordshire cow or moiré ribbon or basket of potpourri to be seen.

Vivi Crawford was the only one of Alysse's friends who had remained with her first husband. This singular fact was rare enough to be pointed out—"That's Vivi and Whit Crawford. They've only been married to each other"—like a prison record or an obscure foreign honor. Vivi and Whit were kept together by a shared loathing for the wife of Whit's guardian. She had also been the last wife of Vivi's late father. Being the wife of both men had made her very wealthy, and the sublime hatred that both Vivi and Whit bore this rather interesting older woman had bound them together for years. Whit, a composer, had inexplicably been given a grant to study in Florence. One of their first excursions, "my hajj, really," as Vivi put it, was to view the Uccellos. Vivi's other goal in life, after adoring the Uccellos, was to have a rose named after her. She had already written a book, Alysse told Mamie, a cookbook of Zen recipes. Hard to imagine, Mamie thought. "Take one bow. Let the bow shoot you into the kitchen."

Mamie lay down on the camp bed. She could hear Claire on the telephone, squealing and howling. She folded her hands behind her head. The pillows smelled of dust.

She had returned the night before to her aunt's apartment after her long walk with Alder Stoddard. He had taken her into the lobby of the building and waited for the elevator to come for her. He had shaken her hand.

He did not live in the city. His mother, a Lee from Boston, had left him a large property in Pennsylvania and he lived there alone with some animals and what he called a Katharine Hepburn housekeeper. It was not that the housekeeper resembled Katharine Hepburn, but that she was like the idealized, maternal servant in movies about spirited New England rich girls. His father, his mother's husband before she married Harry Shannon's younger brother, had been a scholarly chief justice whom his mother had tired of almost immediately after her first, and only, child had been born. She had insisted on naming him Alder Herzen after she read an article on famous lovers in the February issue of *Vogue,* the Valentine issue. She liked that Alexander Herzen's father, a Russian prince unable to give his son his real name, had called him *herzen,* "my heart."

She named him Alder after the small tree that grows on the banks of rivers.

She fell in love with the very handsome and irresponsible Teddy Shannon at about this same time, for although she was a Lee from Boston, she was one of the silly Lees. Alder grew up under the inattentive care of his mother and Teddy Shannon during the school year, and was sent each summer to his cantankerous father. It was perhaps this yearly mixture of extreme hedonism and extreme judiciousness that made Alder himself an unusual combination of languor and grimness. His mother and stepfather lived in alcoholic immorality in Sutton Place and his father, who never remarried, lived in irritable, unforgiving morality in Boston, his only pleasure the pages and pages of unpublished manuscript that littered the chairs and tables of his dark rooms. His few gentlemen friends were other academics and intellectuals. Alder could not remember ever seeing a woman in his father's chambers—and "chambers" is the word his father would have used to describe his house in Cambridge.

His father died, much honored and little loved, one Christmas when Alder was in Palm Beach with his mother and Teddy. His mother was furious when Alder insisted on flying to Boston to put his father in the ground when she had already promised Gloria McMahon that he would walk out the first debutante at the Snowflake Ball. She didn't see then, and nothing would indicate that she ever came to see, the claims of the dead over the living. When Teddy Shannon choked to death on magic mushrooms on Maui, she moved to Dublin, for the horses, and left the farm in Bucks County to her son.

Alder, with his austere luxuriousness and his sour wit, was like both his parents. If he had been asked to choose between them, to choose which one he would prefer to resemble, it would have been impossible for him to pick one over the other. Alder had disliked both of them.

"Alysse says he's married," Claire yelled from the living room.

"Did you hear me?"

Mamie did not answer.

"And there's a kid somewhere!" There was a pause as Claire waited for Mamie to say something. Mamie still did not answer and Claire, with her own odd combination of malice and good will, did not press her point, but returned happily to her conversation.

Mamie knew that Alder Stoddard was married. She knew that his wife lived with their child, a one-year-old girl named Delores, in Florida. He had tried to keep the child. His wife belonged to a powerful and vindictive Cuban family and her three brothers had fought for the child in court, and they had won her.

One of the first things that Mamie learned from Alder was the futility of questioning behavior. "But why did you marry her?" she asked at Fifty-seventh and Park. "Why did you have a child?" she asked at Fifty-ninth Street.

He had calm answers to her questions, but they were logical explanations and did not satisfy her. She did not want facts: his wife was not a good mother; she was a compulsive gambler; she lived with her father in Coconut Grove and the baby was looked after by illiterate girl maids.

"Why don't you just take the child?" Mamie asked indignantly.

All Alder said in answer to that question was a patient "Mamie . . ."

She had spoken to him on the telephone earlier that day, when Claire was at the market buying pineapples and dark rum. He was coming to the city in a few weeks and he would stay with his grandmother.

"Everyone in New York has a grandmother with an apartment on Park Avenue," Mamie had said in wonder, and he had laughed. "At home, grandmothers collect ferns. They don't wear diamonds and go out to lunch. I might as well be on Mars."

"You might as well be," he had said.

Felix Villanueve, of Spanish and French descent, claimed nobility on his mother's side ("I don't use my title in this wonderful country," he often said). He had made an enormous amount of money for years, and those least favorable to Felix said that his clothes were patterned directly from designs he stole each season from the French couture. It was of no consequence. His clothes made American women happy and he liked making women happy very much.

It appeared that he only allowed very pretty girls to work for him, not just as models, but as accountants and secretaries. The girls called him "Mr. Feel" and it was obvious that many of them were old girlfriends who remained unusually devoted to him. The staff of young, well-dressed, beautifully made-up girls caused Mamie to think that she had been inducted into a very glamorous sorority house. It took her a few days of listening quietly, looking through old copies of *Women's Wear Daily* while she waited for Felix to arrive, to understand that they were professionals, after all, and that Felix's business was run by very able women. What she had at first taken to be a girls' club now impressed her, and she realized that she had judged them by that prejudice she so hated, the distrust of her own kind.

She soon accustomed herself to the pleasant routine. She sat on the white carpet in the long, mirrored dressing room with a book, *The Diary of "Helena Morley"*, in her lap and listened to the girls. They were interesting to her. The other models accepted her without hesitation and began almost immediately to teach her some of their tricks: moustache wax smeared on the eyebrow to make each hair stand up straight; a tight, old-fashioned girdle with the crotch cut out, pulled up to flatten the breasts. The absence of rivalry made Mamie feel at ease and even happy.

When Felix did come in to look at the girls and give his approval to the shoes and gloves and jewelry that the pretty girl stylists had selected for each dress, he was polite and circumspect and did not single out Mamie for any special attention. He was very charming with her and had taken her around the first day, holding her hand, to introduce her to everyone (he called her "my hula girl"), but he was never alone with her and she did not experience again the embarrassment she had felt in the dressing room at Deardorf's.

Within a few days, she was comfortably walking through the dressing room in her brassiere and pantyhose, and although she never attained the confidence clearly achieved by the models who sat around bare-breasted in silk G-strings, she was no longer ashamed.

There was one older woman who worked for Felix. She had been his first model and he had designed his collection on her for years. She was now manager of the salon. She was just called Toni, without a surname. Her eyes, her skin, her mouth were all the color of honey. She used no makeup, not even lipstick, and her face was very wrinkled. Her blond hair was chopped in hunks and patches. She had very short, dirty fingernails. She wore the same thing every day—a beige cashmere sweater and beige unlined cashmere trousers, and leopard-skin flats. She was never without an old, enfeebled schnauzer named Pépé. She was the only one who made no effort to be nice all of the time and it was by watching Toni, cigarette held in dirty fingers, yellow eyes squinting to keep out the smoke, that Mamie realized that she preferred Toni's objective bad temper to the indiscriminate sincerity of the others.

Toni paid no attention to her. She withheld her approval from everyone and Mamie saw the power and exclusivity that this aloofness gave her. Toni had no favorites and no preferences, so her friendship had extreme value. Mamie, who made up her mind quickly to form passionate attachments and not so passionate dislikes, admired that Toni revealed nothing about herself.

Toni spoke to Mamie only once that first week when she overheard another model advise Mamie to remove the hair on her arms.

"Don't worry about it," she said abruptly to Mamie. She held an unlighted Camel cigarette between her teeth. "I never did any of that shit." She walked away, Pépé limping after her, before Mamie had time to say a word.

So Mamie left the hair on her arms, and learned how to walk up and down a runway, and how to rip off one dress and put on another in twenty-five seconds. She was busy at Felix's, and although she did not delude herself into thinking that what she did was useful or important, she had less the feeling that the world was watching her, silently and impatiently waiting for her to understand it. She read her books and wrote to Mary once a week and drank tropical rum drinks at home at night with Claire. She did not know it, but she was in a state of suspension, waiting for something to happen, waiting for it all to be made clear.

↖↑↗

After the lazy, comfortable weeks with Alysse, Claire, too, was full of energy and ready to direct the lava-flow of her charm into the business community. She answered an advertisement in the newspaper for a hostess at a Japanese *karaoke* restaurant. She was interviewed in the dark, sticky bar at ten o'clock in the morning by the proprietress, Mrs. Hadashi.

Mrs. Hadashi slowly circled Claire, studying her carefully, and Claire was surprised when the short, elderly woman did not pull apart her lips to examine her gums. Claire had already passed the inspection, but she really impressed Mrs. Hadashi when she spoke several phrases in Japanese. Claire so delighted Mrs. Hadashi with her remarks ("Good morning, it's a hot number-one day") that she wanted Claire to return that very evening. The job was not demanding: Claire must wear makeup and sexy clothes; talk to the Japanese men who came into the club every night after work; and, if requested, join the men at the microphone to sing along with the recorded music. It did not seem difficult to Claire. She explained to Mrs. Hadashi that she needed some time to get her very sexy clothes together and it was agreed that she would begin in two days. Mrs. Hadashi said to Claire as she walked her to the door that she was not expected to entertain the men anywhere but in the restaurant. She would be paid a percentage of the charm charge that was added to the customer's bill.

"Charm charge?" Claire asked.

Mrs. Hadashi nodded and said, *"Hai."*

Claire went straight from the restaurant on East Forty-fifth Street to the 92nd Street Y. She took a taxi. Unlike Mamie, she did not believe in wasting her time on social experiments like the subway. As she would not begin work until five o'clock each day, she enrolled herself in a course entitled "Car Repair and Maintenance" that met twice a week in the early afternoon. Then she walked downtown.

Claire had arranged a surprise. She was meeting Mamie at an apartment building on Gracie Square. When Mamie arrived, running from Eighty-sixth Street because her bus had been slow, Claire, who had already spoken to the doorman, took Mamie by the hand and led her into the elevator.

Still holding her hand, she waited with Mamie in front of an apartment door. Mamie was not allowed to raise her eyes from the floor lest she discover their destination, and she was able to study the mail that lay on the doormat. There were many letters from museums and opera companies and ballet troupes, and copies of *The Nation* and *The New York Review of Books*. She thought she recognized the name of an American writer. Mamie bent down to pick up the mail just as the door was opened.

She heard a woman's voice say, "Hi, Claire. Hi, Mamie."

She stood up. It was one of the sisters. It was Courtney.

"Aren't you surprised?" Claire asked, turning proudly to Mamie. "It took us months to find you, Courtney. I finally had to steal Alysse's address book."

"We're in the phone book," Courtney said, smiling apologetically, as if it were her fault that they could not find her.

As Mamie embraced her, she felt Courtney pull away, as if Mamie's hug were too enthusiastic.

"But we didn't know your married name," Claire said.

"Oh, I use my maiden name and his name. Hyphenated," she said shyly.

Mamie was thrilled to see her. She had thought about her for years, wondering what tortures she had suffered at her Swiss school and at Alysse's irresponsible hands. Mamie studied her for clues of damage, but Courtney, surprisingly, seemed rather ordinarily well. She had very blond, well-kept hair which she wore held off her smooth face with a black velvet Alice band. She wore patent leather low-heeled pumps, Pilgrims' shoes, and a plaid dirndl skirt and a white high-collared blouse.

She took Mamie and Claire into the living room and they sat on a brown velveteen sofa and drank Earl Grey tea with honey. The room had that especially neat look that no maid could ever give it. Courtney did her own housework.

"Courtney's married to a writer," Claire said to Mamie.

"I thought so," Mamie said, looking around. There were books, and black-framed caricatures of Faulkner and Hemingway. There were bottles of St. Edmund's Hall port and good sherry on a *tolle* tray on a table.

"He's in the Park. He visits the parrot tree every day for inspiration."

Mamie and Claire looked at each other.

"There is a tree in Central Park where all the escaped birds roost. Parrots and canaries and budgerigars," Courtney said quickly. "More tea?"

"I think I've read your husband's book," Mamie said. *"Highs and Lows?"*

Courtney nodded and blushed.

The book was about twenty-four hours in 1969 in the back room at Max's Kansas City. Edwin, who was admired for his ability to cover all the bases, had dedicated the book to "You Know Who You Are."

"We're very eager to see Brooke," Claire said.

"Yes," said Courtney, a little primly.

Mamie saw that she was not particularly interested in Brooke.

"Where is she?" Claire asked.

"I don't know. I mean, she works for a photographer, you may have heard of him, and they're on location somewhere. He's the one who does all the animals."

"Is he the man who takes those pictures of animals with erections? God!" Claire said, showing interest for the first time. "He's an artist, not a photographer."

"Well. Yes. I suppose." The conversation made her uncomfortable. "Edwin says not," she said timidly, as if she were afraid of both Edwin and Claire.

"Do you think at all about the time you visited us?" Mamie asked quickly. She felt sorry for Courtney as she watched her fidget with the tea strainer and the spoons. "The time the baby sharks frightened you? And the flumes?"

Courtney looked at Mamie. She hesitated. "It was the happiest I have ever been in my whole life."

"It was?" Claire asked, amazed.

Mamie thought for a moment that Courtney might cry.

"How is Jimmy?" Courtney asked.

"Jimmy died my second year at Punahou. He was buried in the palm grove. Quite a few toads showed up for his funeral."

"Claire was so distraught when Mother called to tell her, she was allowed to go home for a week. Mongoose grief." Mamie was surprised and a little ashamed by Courtney's nostalgia for the time at Waimea. Mamie was so used to being teased, or scolded, for her own attachment to the past that she had been swayed into thinking that remembrance was a weakness, rather than an act of love.

"Shut up, Mamie," Claire said. "It still makes me sad."

Courtney said, "After Waimea, I was shunned at boarding school because the other girls thought I was a liar. And when Brooke backed me up, they said she was a liar, too. They didn't believe Hawai'i was like that."

"I'm sorry," said Mamie.

Courtney smiled. She seemed more at ease, and more trustful. "When people don't believe you, you begin to think maybe they're right. At least, that's what happens to me."

"Do you have anything to drink?" Claire asked.

Courtney looked confused.

"You know, a drink drink," said Claire.

"There's port," Mamie said, trying to help.

"Oh, yes," said Courtney. "And sherry and white wine." She stood to pour Claire a small glass from one of the bottles on the tray.

"I've never had port," Claire said.

"This is Edwin's special vintage from Oxford. He brought a case back from England. He was there to lecture on the 'Lawrentian Life Force.' "

"How nice," Claire said. Mamie nudged her. "The port, I mean."

"How did you meet him?" Mamie asked.

"He was my English teacher at Vevey."

Mamie did not want to look at Claire, but she could see Claire take the tiny glass from her mouth and turn to stare at Courtney. "You know," Mamie said quickly, "this is something that has always interested me. I don't know why it doesn't happen more often in high school. So romantic."

"It wasn't really. I mean, for him it wasn't. My mother was killed in a car crash and I had all this money. He could stop teaching."

"But what about you?" Claire asked.

"Oh," Courtney said. She didn't know how to go on. She smiled in embarrassment. "I never thought anyone would ever want me without it. The money, I mean. So, in a way, I was lucky."

Mamie watched as Claire drank the port in two gulps.

"Edwin will be returning from his walk to the parrot tree and he likes to get right to work when he comes in," Courtney said.

Edwin had a very precise schedule. He headed a reading

group, of which Vivi Crawford was an enthusiastic member, and they read and discussed the Bible, which did not leave him all that much time for other worthwhile activities, such as his well-known interest in pre-Columbian glyphs. He also monitored a prestigious writing class in which the teacher, a book editor, allowed students to bring their psychiatrists. It was also said that the teacher expected certain acts of obeisance from the girl students, but Edwin was not a part of that. Edwin's novel, which he was rewriting, took place in Machu Picchu.

They embraced and Mamie gave her their telephone number at the Crawfords' and Claire wrote down Brooke's number and they all promised to have tea again soon. Courtney said that there were still many things she wanted to ask them about Waimea.

Mamie and Claire walked home across the Park, through the Ramble. The sky was flat and milky. There was a smell of musk from the umbrella flowers of the elder trees.

"I hope we don't run into Edwin," Mamie said. "Ever."

"We won't." Claire was so certain of this that Mamie turned aside to look at her.

"How do you know?"

"He's got a girl. He's not at the parrot tree, he's at the pussy tree. Alysse told me when she found I'd stolen her address book to track down Courtney. She knows the girl. She works in a rock store on Madison Avenue. You know, selling gigantic purple stalagmites to Arabs."

"Alysse shouldn't have told you."

Claire shrugged, without interest, and they took the path down to the lake. Mamie was quiet the rest of the way home, even though Claire told her about her job at the *karaoke* bar and her car class, and asked if Mamie would advance her a little money to buy a miniskirt, garter belt, and green eye shadow.

"You got it," said Mamie, meaning she would lend her the money, and they crossed Central Park West under the static white sky.

Mamie lay on her camp bed listening to Gabby Pahinui sing of the trees and coves of Kaua'i. She tried to think again about her Theory of Heroines and Private Incomes, for her tea with Courtney had left her confused. It is not that she ever thought that money alone would allow women to make their way in the world, but she hadn't fully taken into account just how much courage and luck were also needed. As was customary when she was troubled, she moved back and forth between the two disparate worlds through which she was still trying to find her way: the *mokihana* is blooming now in the rain forests of Koke'e. Their resinous, sweet smell of anise and orange leads me to them in the *maile* vines. "*I kahi 'e no ke kumu mokihana*: though the *mokihana* is at a distance, its fragrance reaches me here," lying on a French nineteenth-century bed covered with pieces of Kashmiri shawls, in a borrowed apartment full of museum reproductions, worried about a woman who once thought she was being eaten by sharks and is now being eaten by her husband. My rain forests are so lovely, Mamie thought, shimmying between West Sixty-seventh Street and the ancient footpath to the Sugi Grove. No snakes, no predators, no thorns.

Claire came into the room with a Mai Tai for Mamie. The drink was decorated with a piece of pineapple and a little paper umbrella.

"Don't you think we're drinking too much?" Mamie asked.

SUSANNA MOORE | 152

She ate the pineapple, holding it over the glass so as not to stain the antique paisleys. It upset her that the old cloth had been cut up to make covers for the bed and the pillows.

"You know, they actually bill the customers for charm at Hadashi's. We might want to do it in real life," Claire said.

"What exactly do they call 'charm'?"

"Not much. I pretend I'm Ed McMahon and announce the songs, you know, 'Mr. Yamaguchi will honor us with his version of "Feerings." ' "

"Claire," Mamie said, laughing, "are you sure this is what Alysse would call a good move?"

Claire shrugged. "I've never been particularly attracted to Japanese men. It isn't the smallness because look at Toshiro Mifune, your hero. Maybe it's the hairlessness. I definitely don't like their legs. Do you think their dicks are bowlegged?"

"I'm glad you've thought this out so clearly," Mamie said. She lay back on the bolsters and balanced her glass on her breastbone. "At least bring home some *sushi*."

What could be more secret and strange, Mamie thought, than Claire sitting cross-legged at a low table, more and more splashed with *shoyu* and Johnnie Walker Red, with a group of giggling Japanese businessmen, proudly shouting World War II American slang at her as she tried to pour hot *saké* from a little jug with her two big, pale hands?

Claire was not comporting herself in the way a girl of her background was expected to behave. While both of them had realized, almost intuitively and quite early on, that they were not like the other girls that they knew, Claire did not have a clear picture of herself, other than a romantic and indulgent idea that she was a rebel. The car repair class was only a temporary solution for Claire's unrecognized feelings of helplessness. She was unable to support herself in a way that would give her both dignity and sustenance, but she would be able, at the very least, to clean a carburetor.

With all of her insolence, Claire was struggling to hold on to her singularity. While Mamie sought comfort in books and island dreams, Claire sought it in sensation: the sensation of rum and talking dirty and petty shoplifting (she stole the eye shadow when she went out to buy a pineapple), and the sensation of physical pleasure. She explained many times to Mamie the importance of a good bathtub as a place to masturbate and she complained for days when she discovered that the Crawfords' apartment had only a shower.

"I think you'll be fine," Mamie said.

"I hope so." Claire sighed. She tilted back her glass to finish her drink and the pineapple fell onto her nose. "Do you remember McCully's desk?"

Mamie turned to look at her.

"Well, I was the one who wrote your name on it. Carved your name on it." She held the empty glass at her mouth and stared over its rim at Mamie.

"Why?" Mamie was not shocked.

"I don't know. Jealous, maybe. Neither of us had her, but you seemed to have him."

Mamie nodded. She turned away from Claire.

"Are you mad?" asked Claire.

"Sometimes, especially after he died, I used to wake in the middle of the night, wet with perspiration, thinking that I had really done it myself. I would sneak into the library to study the letters. I regretted so much that he wasn't alive so I could tell him how sorry I was that I had ruined his lovely desk."

"So like you, Mamie."

"I guess."

They sat there quietly.

"Do you want another drink?" Claire asked.

"Sure," said Mamie.

TEN

Mamie, who had never understood the moral view of time, the view whose stern adherents frowned on sleeping too long or too late, slipped into a harmless and easy routine. As she did not have to be at Mr. Felix's showrooms at set hours, and some days not at all, she was free, for the first time in many months, to do just what she wished with her time. She was not lazy or profligate. She arose each day earlier than Claire, who did not return from Hadashi's until two o'clock in the morning, and she enjoyed the new rites of her domesticity. As might have been expected, she was a good housekeeper. Claire, who veered wildly from sloth and chaos to compulsive neatness, was happy to fall, once again, under Mamie's care. Perhaps it is true that Mamie had always been like a mother to Claire. She had protected her and counseled her during the years they were at boarding school, and Claire certainly did take advantage of Mamie in that way that real mothers, wise mothers, come to expect and tolerate in their children. She did have that same subtle sense of due, not without some gratitude, as have those children who are completely confident of their mother's love. It never occurred to Claire, then or later, that it was an unfair burden on Mamie. The notion that Mamie had for years been taking on more than her share would have surprised Mamie as much as it would have surprised Claire.

If Claire's way to keep from spinning hopelessly out of control was to take a class in car maintenance, Mamie's way of keeping herself steady was her correspondence with her mother. To her own surprise, Mamie had come to look forward to her mother's letters, not because they provoked and satisfied her homesickness with their details about the breeding ground of Hawaiian monk seals and the new honeycreeper nests, but because she was, however belatedly, beginning to know her mother. In their weekly letters, there was a growing, fragile intimacy, not based on dark female mysteries (that would have been alarming to both of them), but on a simple exchange of prosaic information.

Dear Mamie,

It is hard to imagine the New York flower beds mulched with old Christmas trees, as you described them, and with their tinsel sometimes left on. You write that it is pretty. I have never been to New York, as you know, or east of Chicago. Henrietta used to take us to Chicago once a year to go to the dentist and be measured for new shoes. You had to step up onto a special machine that actually x-rayed your feet and the salesman would always say, "I think we have a perfect fit," although I never understood what he meant, as we weren't being fitted. Alice always jumped up on the machine the minute she was in the shoe store. You could look down, through a glass, and see the skeletons of your own feet. I was always frightened of it. Do you think it is possible to get cancer of the feet? Do you know? It wouldn't surprise me, all those bad rays flying into your bare feet. They didn't know about these things in the Forties.

You mention that my support for the movement to teach Hawaiian in public schools is the first political act of my life, and perhaps you are right. There is much objection to it, as its critics say the children should learn to speak English (instead of Pidgin) before they learn to speak traditional Hawaiian. You and Claire spoke both forms of English when you were children, switching back and forth constantly, depending on whether you were in the kitchen or at the table. It took me years to even understand Pidgin and I sometimes thought you used it as a kind of secret language around me, but I always admired your skill. I still can't speak it. A professor at the University, who calls it Hawaiian Creole, says it is best learned in childhood and he even writes that the "sophisticated" grammar of Pidgin was, in fact, created in one generation in the 19th century by the workers' children! It never seemed sophisticated to me, but I have come to all of this very late.

Sheridan Shields has disappeared and I hear that Lily and Tōsi are on their way home. He has probably just gone on one of his jaunts for more art. I wonder where he finds the room for it. Such an eccentric family. Always telling each other how they feel. I remember Lily as a little girl calling her mother on the telephone to tell her that she loved her.

I have been given by the University the honor of preserving the *ma'o hau hele,* the yellow hibiscus, in the garden here. It is extinct as a wild plant on Kaua'i and although there are many foreign species and hybrids, there are only a few native species left, eight, I believe. I feel that I will guard it with my life. I have already been out several times this morning just to look at it. It is like having a newborn baby you feel you must check every few minutes, you are so amazed by its very existence, and so fearful that some harm will come to it. Mrs. Kaona came to visit it, too. She says her great-aunt had many yellow hibiscus years ago in Koloa and that the leaves and buds were used to treat constipation and cleanse the blood.

I don't know how much cooking you are doing, but I have the recipe for Punahou Caramel Cuts now, so let me know if you want it.

Love,

Mother

Mamie went to Alysse's apartment to return the two very expensive suitcases Alysse had loaned to Claire to transport what Mamie called Claire's dowry—little dinner suits with shoulder pads and silk taffeta ball gowns with sleeves like big balloons—clothes that Alysse had bought for Claire. Mamie doubted if the dresses would be thought suitable by the demanding Mrs. Hadashi.

Mamie had not seen her aunt since the Claire-and-Mamie dinner, although she had written her a note to thank her. She knew, because Claire had told her so several times, that Alysse was not yet over the "humiliation" of her leaving, during the main course, with Alder Stoddard.

Lydia was very happy to see Mamie and quickly brought her, even though it was eleven o'clock in the morning and she had not been requested to do so, a cold Dos Equis beer, no glass. Alysse frowned when Lydia came rushing in with the beer, her devotion to Mamie clearly not anything Alysse had ever experienced.

Alysse was having a pedicure. Mamie had noticed before

that Alysse held certain persons to be invisible, usually some-one from outside who was paid to do something to her, as opposed to Lydia who actually lived with her and was thus in a strong position to carry out small retributive acts, such as not giving her the correct message when the Santo Domingan Ambassador to the Holy See telephoned or not canceling her session with the Scotch Hose at Arden's when she had a par-ticularly bad cocaine hangover and couldn't even get out of bed. So Mamie was not surprised when Alysse spoke as if she and her niece were alone in the room.

"Harry Shannon used to call me from wherever he was, Geneva or Monte Carlo, to tell me he'd be in New York in ten days and ask me not to bathe."

Mamie hesitated. "Really?"

"He liked must. Or is it musk? Limp, I could wrap him around my wrist."

"Your filthy wrist," Mamie said.

"Ouch!" Alysse angrily pulled her foot away from the expres-sionless manicurist and examined her toe with exaggerated concern.

"He's in a monastery now somewhere in Vermont. He's reached the second or third level of Weirdness. Alder Stoddard would know."

"I haven't seen Alder Stoddard," Mamie said calmly.

"Doesn't it bother you that you're wearing dead people's clothes?" Alysse asked suddenly.

Mamie looked down at herself. She was wearing a Mexican skirt, brightly embroidered with burros and sombreros, and a white undershirt with the sleeves rolled high on her thin arms, and silk polka-dot flats.

"Where's your pack of cigarettes?" Alysse asked, looking at the sleeves of the undershirt.

Mamie did not understand that had she told Alysse the truth

(Alysse, you just don't get it), Alysse might have admired her. She might even have left her alone. Mamie believed that it would have been rude, and even dangerous, to speak the truth, but instead of protecting Alysse from her own ignorance as she believed she was doing, she was instead justifying Alysse's secret belief in Mamie's hopelessness. The irony is that it is Alysse who would have said that Mamie didn't get it and would never get it.

If Mamie had been very candid with herself, she would have had to admit that there was another reason, too, that she did not shout out the truth to Alysse. It was the worry that once started, she would be unable to stop.

"He's had lots of girls," Alysse said carelessly.

"Has he?" Mamie said over her shoulder. She knew that her aunt was talking about Alder Stoddard.

"Scads." Alysse held her feet splayed stiffly before her. Pastel cotton balls separated each plump toe.

"I'm happy for him," Mamie said. "And the horse."

"What horse?" Alysse did not like that Mamie might know something that she did not know.

"Lydia's friend's horse in Guatemala. Hasn't she told you?"

"What *are* you talking about?"

Her pedicure was almost finished. The manicurist dried each pink nail with a gold Japanese fan. Mamie finished her beer, holding the bottle by the neck, and asked the woman which way she was going, they could walk together. Startled to be acknowledged, the manicurist admitted cautiously that she was headed downtown. She quickly packed her things.

Mamie burped contentedly, politely covering her mouth with her hand. She hoped that Alysse would not offer to walk with them, to take the air, as she put it. Mamie had walked with Alysse on Madison Avenue, Alysse's favorite street, and she had been exhausted by the effort within six short blocks. Alysse was thorough. She did Madison Avenue as if she were doing the Nile.

"Give 'Feel' my love," Alysse said as she hobbled into the bedroom. "Tell him I'm coming in for a preview and I want a discount." Alysse was late for a luncheon meeting to plan the Library's new fund-raising theme, "Befriend a Book."

Mamie didn't answer and Ruda, the manicurist, was not certain whether Mamie licked her lips or stuck out her tongue.

They walked together as far as Ruda's next appointment, a lady from Colombia who had taken the twentieth floor of a hotel on Fifth Avenue. Ruda was booked to do sixteen hands, presumably belonging to Senora Campos's many sisters and cousins.

Ruda thought Mamie a little odd at first, maybe even eccentric, but by the time they reached the hotel, she had offered to do Mamie's plain hands for half-price whenever Mamie wanted a good manicure. Mamie looked at her short nails and wondered aloud at how it might be just another thing to worry about. Ruda went through the revolving door into the hotel and Mamie went serenely on her way, the roar of the city all around her.

Mamie had found once or twice before that just when she was beginning to lose hope, something unexpected and fortuitous appeared before her to fortify her and give her the interest to begin all over again. She thought this about Alder Stoddard and she thought this about two dead chickens she came across on a big rock in the Park. Their skinny legs were bound with white rags. There was no blood and the animals did not look as if their throats had been ceremoniously slashed to propitiate the *loa*. They did not frighten Mamie at all. She was used to seeing chickens in far worse degrees of butchery after the cockfights in the workers' camp.

The chickens reminded her of the homemade wire coops, full of small animals and poinsettias, in the little back yards of Waimea. Over the years, Mamie had come to be taken for granted in the houses of the servants and field workers and they did not bother to conceal from her their rites and passions. For quite a while, when she was young, she had believed that people who were white did not have sexual intercourse, or at least did not have it like Mr. and Mrs. Buddy Mendoza, who were always fighting violently and then making love so hastily and exuberantly that they did not bother to close their front door. She knew, too, that the workers' lives were secret because they were able to magically transform themselves into timid laborers and laundresses whenever her mother was around. The moment that Mary was gone, they again became noisy, funny men and women, full of opinion.

While the local people were superstitious, and saw nature as an animated force that could be rewarding or vindictive at will, Mamie knew that her mother did not pray to her plants, or use them in healing or in sacrifice. There was for Mary no animistic, spiritual connection to the plants and hills and trees, and certainly no chant or legend passed down through generations of Clarkes. The Mitsudas, however, tied pieces of inscribed paper and trinkets to the pine tree in front of the Hongwanji temple and the Kaonas refused to pick litchi at the abandoned Gay estate because the old house, built on Hawaiian burial ground, was full of malevolent *mana*.

Mamie learned many things in the camp. She liked having her fortune told with bones and she heeded the warning of Mrs. Kaona, who scolded her for disturbing the tree of the *pueo*, the owl totem of the Kaona family. These superstitions and taboos were good for Mamie because they implied order and reason, cause and effect, and this made her feel less isolated and less helpless.

So when she saw the voodoo chickens laid on the rock in Central Park, she was reassured. It meant that someone, somewhere in the exhausting city, still believed in the Spirits.

Mamie walked to Mr. Felix's salon. It was the last week of fittings before Felix took the collection and two models to the big department stores in Chicago and Dallas and Los Angeles. It was how he best sold his clothes, making a personal appearance tour, standing on the floor with his models, flattering the customers. The women who came to see the collection preened and fluttered and spent a great deal of money when he made one of his trim bows and kissed their hand. Mamie and another model, a blonde, were going with him.

The dresses, although they were more formal and more mature than Mamie's own clothes, looked very well on her. She was sometimes surprised to catch sight of herself in the mirror wearing Mr. Felix's clothes. She did not like them. Mr. Felix was equally surprised at the way Mamie looked when he happened to catch her coming or going, in her old khakis and gold flats. Once or twice, he stopped her and made her spin around for him as he watched her with squinting eyes, and she noticed the appearance of a few new details in the collection, like appliquéd skirts and more fully cut trousers.

Toni did not speak again to Mamie after telling her not to shave her arms, but Mamie continued to watch her and to admire her. She was very surprised when she arrived one afternoon and settled with her book on her usual spot on the floor to be told that Toni wanted to see her.

Toni was in her office. None of the models had ever been

inside the office and there were rumors that Toni actually lived there. They said she hadn't left the building for the last twelve years and that Pépé, who came and went on the elevator by himself, brought her what she needed from the outside.

She was sitting at a long table. She was eating raw vegetables and *sashimi*, and Pépé, seated across from her, was doing the same. She gestured with her napkin to Mamie to sit down. She did not suggest that Mamie share her lunch, nor did she stop eating. Her hands, as always, looked dirty and ragged.

"You seem like a sensible girl," she said. "You *seem* like."

Mamie had been hoping, especially since meeting Alder Stoddard, that she did not seem sensible. She did not say anything. She moved a swatch of pink crepe de chine and sat down in one of the lemon wood Biedermeier chairs. Everything in the room was the same amber color.

"At least you read books," Toni said. She held a piece of fish in the air with her yellowed ivory chopsticks.

"Yes," Mamie said. "Maybe too much."

Toni opened her eyes wide and looked at her.

"I am sometimes confused and I can't remember what came from which book. It all becomes lost in one endless book."

"Are you really from an island?"

Mamie smiled at the question.

"You never can tell with Felix. He gets carried away. He used to introduce me as his little 'princess' and the twats believed him."

Mamie looked at her and wondered if Toni, too, was one of those floating ghost-women without grandparents, or a piece of land, somewhere, to which she felt she belonged.

As if she could read her mind, Toni said, "I was born in Bakersfield. I've sometimes wondered if that's why I like the color of dust-in-the-sun so much. Felix went to the Shah's Birthday in Teheran, along with Dr. Peele, the plastic surgeon.

Felix did the clothes and Peele did the faces. Felix brought back an album of photographs given to him by the Empress and it all looked like Bakersfield. Such a disappointment, and yet . . ."

Toni took a bottle of Evian from a drawer and poured herself a glass of water and one for Pépé.

For someone whose hands look so dirty, she is a very clean eater, thought Mamie. She liked that Toni was not very polite. There was no condescension. Mamie realized that if she wanted a glass of water, she was expected to ask for it.

"Do you go out?" Toni asked abruptly.

"Out?"

Toni nodded.

"I don't know very many people here. My younger sister is here now and that changes things. She goes out."

Toni laughed.

Mamie wanted to look at Toni's room, but she did not want Toni to see her looking at it. There was a paneled, gold leaf Japanese screen. There was a copper vase, of the Arts and Crafts Movement, full of brown fritillaries.

"There is a temporary air about you," Toni said. She touched the end of her napkin to the water and cleaned her mouth very carefully, then wiped Pépé's mouth.

"Temporary?"

There was a knock at the door and Felix pushed it open a tiny bit and sidled inside. He looked slyly from Toni to Mamie and back again. "I am disturbing you?"

"Hardly," Toni said calmly.

"I need Mamie for the finale."

He held out his hand to Mamie, as though he were going to lead her in a quadrille.

Mamie stood up and Pépé, noticing her for the first time, growled.

Toni laughed at him. "You're just like Felix," she said to the dog.

In the corridor, as Felix walked with Mamie to the dressing room, he said to her carelessly, "Be careful, *niña,* or you will have both of us madly in love with you."

Mamie frowned. She did not understand him. He smoothed the wrinkles on her forehead with his long fingers.

"Madly," he said again, drawing his hand away reluctantly.

She backed away from him. He took her hand and patted it. "So sweet. So *mignon.*"

"Like a filet?" He made her uncomfortable. She was not sure of the meaning of his words, in English or in French.

"My dear. So funny you are!"

With the help of three dressers, she put on a silk brocade wedding gown. It was trimmed at the hem and bodice and cuffs with bands of white mink. She wore a headpiece of fur and tulle, and white brocade Russian boots. When she stepped awkwardly onto the rehearsal runway, Felix applauded daintily and the seamstresses and other models began to clap, too.

Mamie was embarrassed. She could see Toni standing at the far end of the room, nonchalantly leaning against the wall. As Mamie came slowly down the runway, Toni smiled and bent down to lift up old Pépé so that he, too, could see the beautiful bride. Mamie, who had flushed bright pink when Felix began to applaud, felt foolish until she saw Toni smiling up at her. If Toni approved of her, then Mamie knew that she would be all right, even with the mink toque wavering precariously on her head, and the twelve-foot train, mink roses on tulle, dragging heavily behind her.

ELEVEN

Claire spent only four weeks at Hadashi's before she told Mrs. Hadashi that she would not be coming back the next evening. Claire was a popular hostess and Mrs. Hadashi reluctantly offered her more money. It wasn't the money, Claire explained, or the customers who regularly fell into her lap toward the end of the evening, or even the young banker from Osaka who vomited a giant clam on the marabou pom-poms of her new black satin mules.

She did not even mind accompanying the men to the dressing room where the presumably heterosexual customers dressed up in traditional bridal kimonos or nurses' uniforms. Claire particularly enjoyed squeezing the businessmen into the Playboy Bunny costumes that Mrs. Hadashi provided for them. The pin-on bunny tails were old, soiled powder puffs. Claire was helpful in the dressing room (it was sometimes difficult to conceal the dark hair on their chins), and Mrs. Hadashi had complimented her on her facility with pancake makeup by pressing five crumpled dollar bills into Claire's hand one night when Claire was leaving.

It was just that the men were too silly. She could no longer smile politely at the bad puns in English; the bad attempted puns such as "mini-mouse skirt." She thought she was being clever by telling Mrs. Hadashi that she was going to be married in two days. Mrs. Hadashi, however, was very relieved to hear this and generously offered her a night off for her honeymoon. She saw no reason why marriage would interfere with Claire's work. Finally, Claire just had to walk out, Mrs. Hadashi tripping furiously behind her, cursing in Japanese and shaking her fist.

So Claire was there when Alder Stoddard arrived at the Crawfords' to pick up Mamie. It had been Mamie's idea to go to the theater when he asked her what she would most like to do, and although he no longer went to the theater, he was very happy to take Mamie.

Claire was going to Alysse's for the evening. Alysse was giving a small dinner for the former dictator of a Central American country and she wanted as many young, pretty girls at the table as possible. Mamie disapproved of Claire's going, reminding her that the guest of honor was personally responsible for the beheading of a young union organizer (he borrowed a machete from a bystander), but Claire told Mamie to mind her own business. Alysse had promised to seat Claire next to a former Secretary of State, a particularly rapacious man, and Claire was looking forward to meeting him. Mamie, who suspected that Claire was trying to provoke her, was able to control herself and say nothing more, even though it upset her that Alysse would pander in this way, and that Claire would go along with it.

The play was a disappointment. Mamie was surprised. She apologized to Alder.

"It's not always disappointing," he said.

"But you don't go to the theater."

"No."

He had brought her two paperback books. It had been very difficult finding the right books because he knew how much she read. He was wearing a dark gray pin-striped suit and navy blue tennis shoes. Naturally enough, Mamie was curious about the shoes, but she did not mention them.

He took her to a restaurant in the Fifties, on the East Side. Mamie had noticed that each section of the city had its own very specific residents. To Mamie, the side streets of the East Fifties seemed populated with discarded mistresses and former wives. The women who lived on these side streets wore tan poplin raincoats and printed silk scarves on their heads, and dark glasses. They looked as if they had just awakened. They did not bother to put on makeup, and it was easy to see that they had once been handsome. Mamie could discern the evidence of high cheekbones and good legs. These women, too, had a look about them that suggested they had been left behind, some by men and others just by time. They did not have that sense of rush about them, as did the women farther north in the city, who were always on their way somewhere, often with a child. They did not carry full grocery bags, either, like other women. They were not feeding families. Their plastic I LOVE NEW YORK bags contained a few cartons of yoghurt and a quart of vodka and freshly squeezed grapefruit juice. These women were more interesting to Mamie; less officious, more tender, than the women farther uptown who nearly exploded with intention. Mamie often tried to imagine what their lives were like, or more precisely, she tried to imagine what their lives had been like, when men looked after them.

Jerry, the bartender at the restaurant, was very happy to see Alder. When Alder introduced Mamie, Jerry was oddly uninterested and did not speak to her. Alder took no notice, but guided her with his hand in the small of her back to the table that he was always given. Mamie felt his hand there, but not with the shock of intimacy that she had hoped to feel when she had imagined him touching her again. Perhaps it is too soon for that, she thought.

He gave her the first two books of *A Dance to the Music of Time*. He was relieved when she said she hadn't read them. He ordered two martinis for them. "This is a restaurant for martinis—banquettes, rare steaks, and bad tips on Knicks games."

"My first martini," she said.

The bartender brought the martinis and Mamie was sure that he looked at her with disgust when he put her drink on the plate in front of her. He squeezed Alder on the shoulder as he went past. The martini smelled like rubbing alcohol.

"I realize now that the bad thing about living far from home is that you can never make yourself completely understood," Mamie said.

He looked at her. She saw that he was waiting for her to go on.

"All of the things that I know are secrets. Claire knows, but I can't keep Claire next to me my whole life just so I will have someone nearby who knows what it smells like in the *keawe* forest at Polihale or what a litchi really tastes like. When someone in New York, anyone, says 'Mallomars,' everyone screams, 'Oh, yes, oh, yes'—there are 'oh-yesses' ricocheting around the room. The solution, I know, is to stay among your own kind, clustered in a large group, but I can't do that, either."

"This is why you are an exile, Mamie. You should hear the poet Repovitchsky talk about his beloved steppes. The only difference between you is that he can't go back. You both love the place you have come from, but think of all the people who are relieved not to be in their hometowns, relieved and saved. Some people would die if they stayed at home. You are the other extreme. You're going to die if you don't go back."

She laughed. "Not really, of course."

"No, not really," he said in his cool way. "All of the reasons that people give for living in New York—the opera, the art, the food, the conversation—are not very interesting to me anymore. I think New York is an aesthetic affectation as a city, but no one will admit it. My European friends adore New York, although they don't for a minute understand it. They are profoundly moved by the white steam blasting up from manholes. That seems to them unbearably metaphoric. The French, especially. They also love those little plastic bears with honey inside. I thought one of my friends from Paris was going to cry one night when we walked past a homeless man sitting on a grate in front of Rockefeller Center—not out of pity, but because the symbolism was too much for him. That's a little how I feel about the whole city—it's full of sentimental self-congratulation. I wouldn't mind so much, I suppose, if they'd just admit that it's about money, not art. I like that about New York, that it's about money.

"I remember the first time I was allowed to mail a letter alone on a New York street, without my governess or my mother. I went out onto York Avenue to the mailbox on the corner and I slipped the letter inside and turned to look up at the apartment and my mother and Teddy Shannon were standing at the window watching me, silently clapping their hands."

Mamie laughed. "I must have covered thirty miles a day on my bike."

"You see," he said.

"But it's very different there. Everyone is either related to you or works for you." She paused for a moment before she said, "No one would ever hurt you."

"We went to East Hampton on the weekend," Alder said, "and I was sometimes taken on long car trips with my grandmother and her spinster friend. I sat in the front of an old black Buick sedan with the chauffeur, Mr. Ulysses de Beaupré, and my grandmother and Miss Endicott sat in the back. Every fifty miles, Mr. de Beaupré would ease the car off the road, he wasn't allowed to use highways or go faster than forty miles an hour, and the two ladies would get out and toss a beanbag back and forth in the grass by the side of the road while Mr. de Beaupré sat beneath a tree and had a nice, quiet smoke. Then we all climbed back into the Buick and went the next fifty miles. My grandmother would hold an orange in a handkerchief and peel it with a little knife and pass the slices up front to me. We went to Newport or Saratoga. Sometimes south to Pawley's Island. Then I went to boarding school and those trips ended for me. Other things became important. You know, girls and lacrosse."

The bartender handed them two enormous plastic menus. He leaned against the empty table alongside and asked Alder if he had seen the fight last week from Vegas. Alder had, and they talked about it while Mamie listened from behind her menu. The man still refused to recognize her presence.

"Why is he like that?" Mamie asked when he left. "Why is he so rude?"

"I used to come here with my wife. He liked her. He thinks you're my girlfriend."

Mamie was shocked. "Well, tell him I'm not."

He looked at her in surprise. "Does it matter that much what he thinks?"

She hesitated. She didn't think it did matter that much,

and she did not expect Alder to explain to the bartender the story of his marriage, but she did not like to be treated unjustly either. There was a middle way if Alder would explain to him that Mamie was his friend.

"He wouldn't believe me. There's no need to justify it, Mamie." He made a gesture to Jerry to indicate that they would have two more martinis.

Mamie was confused. She was not going to insist that Alder clarify her position, but she blushed when the man brought the drinks to the table. The gin made her feel self-conscious, as if her movements were clumsy and exaggerated. She imagined that Jerry would think she was drunk.

Alder laid the stiff menu on the floor next to his chair. "I'm hungry," he said. "Shall I order for you?"

She nodded.

Alder ordered steaks and home-fried potatoes and creamed spinach.

She kept her eyes on her plate until Jerry was gone, then she said, "The strange thing is that he blames me and not you. After all, you're the one who is married. You're the one with the wife. But I'm the one who is bad. He gives me too much power. No wonder you hate us. He's just like Mr. Kipper."

"Mr. Kipper?"

She did not want to be distracted by Mr. Kipper and his list of Burmese anxieties. "Jerry thinks you're just great. Girls and steak tartare and boxing matches in Las Vegas. But I'm bad." She laughed. "I am very, very relieved to have figured this out. You confused me. You both made me feel as if I really *had* done something wrong."

"I don't think you're wicked. My guess is that you're not wicked enough."

"Oh, I can be convinced," she said. "To think that I am."

Her tone was so wistful and weary that he smiled and took

her hand. It may have been the martinis and it may have been a dim intimation of the trouble that lay patiently in wait for her, trouble bestirred by the suspicion that, as a woman, she was born wicked and deserved everything that was coming to her, but she kept her hand inside of Alder's hand and allowed herself to feel, for the moment, good and safe.

Alder took Mamie to his grandmother's house. Mrs. Lee lived in a very handsome brownstone on Seventy-first Street. From the street, the dark house looked as if it were empty. Curtains were drawn across the windows of the rooms on the second floor and the only light in the house came from a small dormer window on the top floor.

Alder held Mamie by the elbow as he opened the front door. It was a glass door, protected by intricate, leafy vines of ornamental ironwork, and it reminded Mamie of the thorn hedge in *Sleeping Beauty*. Alder pushed her gently into the entrance hall. It was cold and damp on the ground floor and Alder took her by the hand and led her up the marble staircase. In the darkness, the white stairs were the cool, thin color of moonlight. There was a landing on the second floor between two large, dark rooms. The furniture was covered in faded blue-and-white-striped dustcovers. On the faded walls, dark paintings waited vainly for someone to gaze at them. There were no ornaments of any kind. The leggy French table that had proudly held Mrs. Lee's famous collection of eighteenth-century gold seals was bare. The clocks, no longer ticking, were nestled deep in their felt pouches, alone on the Gibbons mantelpieces. The light in the rooms came from the back garden, reflected from an old magnolia tree whose branches pressed against the glass panels of a french door.

Mamie held on to the bannister. The house was cool and silent.

"My grandmother is confined to her room." He startled her when he spoke in a conversational tone. She would have whispered. "These rooms have been this way since 1949. She won't let anything be touched, although Mr. de Beaupré has put away all of the small things. Or stolen them. I hope he's stolen them. He deserves all the Fabergé eggs he can get his hands on."

Alder took her into the back reception room, the one facing the old garden, and when she sat down in the draped *bergère* that had once been in Madame's apartment at Versailles, little puffs of powdery dust rose from the cushion. She could smell mold and floor wax. He turned on a small pink-shaded lamp on a buhl chest in the corner and opened a red lacquered cabinet. There was a small refrigerator inside, and he took out a bottle of champagne and opened it.

"My grandmother was very vain. The lamps in these rooms were chosen especially to bring out the fineness of her lavender-colored skin."

Mamie knew better than to ask if her skin really had been the color of lavender. Perhaps it had been. She looked at the paintings. They were all portraits of a high-nosed, stout woman in strands of pearls.

"Now she's lying upstairs, tyrannized by de Beaupré. He bathes her and feeds her and dresses her. There is a day nurse and a night nurse but she refuses to allow them inside her room."

"De Beaupré was the chauffeur who smoked under the tree?"

"Yes. She was in love with him."

He was looking for something in the bottom half of the lacquered cabinet. He finally found it, a record of King Pleasure, and he put it on the record player and brought Mamie a glass of champagne.

"I don't know this music," Mamie said. She had been talkative and excited at dinner, but now she felt heavy in her bones, languid and tranquil, perhaps because of the martinis, the still house, and the picture she had made in her mind of the old woman and the old black man somewhere above them in the big, dark house.

He asked her if she would dance. King Pleasure sang his flirtatious, breezy version of "I'm in the Mood for Love" and Mamie took off her shoes and went into Alder's embrace as if they had done this many times before, at senior proms and coming-out parties and summer weddings, and she felt that she had been wrong before about the feel of his hand on the small of her back. They danced on the landing.

King Pleasure sang "This Is Always." The old parquet floor was uneven and Mamie did not like the feel of the warped wood through her stockings, so she bent over and took them off with one hand, while Alder held her steadily by the other hand. They did not talk.

"I knew it on that night we met, never will forget, you tied a string around my heart, darling, tell me how can I, how can I forget I met you? How can I?" King Pleasure sang.

She held herself erect so that their eyes and noses and mouths met at the same place and when she turned her face away from his shoulder, her lips might have been his lips, her lost breath his given breath. He kissed her. Oh, she thought, I remember what it is like now. He opened her mouth with his own mouth. He did not try to swallow her with his mouth, and when he did not, she began to wonder whether he was, after all, making love to her, then it went quickly through her mind that this was a man who knew exactly what he was doing to her. The idea that he might be experienced did not offend or worry her. There was such relief and pleasure in her willingness to finally give up everything, and to give it all up to him, that she felt as if her spine were melting down her back, and dripping like candle wax onto his grandmother's French floor.

He took her up to the third floor. It was not his room, but a guest room. There were two narrow beds stripped of linen.

He laid her back on one of the beds and went to the window and opened it. There was the sudden smell of magnolia, and the room was warmer. Mamie watched him. She knew instinctively that she was not to move, not to touch herself, not to speak. He undressed in front of the window. She thought about his shoes. He came to her and she sat up silently so that he could undress her. He touched her so deliberately and so slowly that she began to feel as if different parts of her body were being lighted with a torch. For a moment, she saw the burning torches of the men fishing on the reef, the flames sparking and guttering in the darkness as the wind came back off the shore-break. When he had undressed her, he lay on top of her. He held her wrists in his hands, stretched above her head, pushed hard against the frame of the bed, and when she was just about to cry out that she could not stand it an instant longer, he, too, reached the limits of denial and with a low moan, descended into her.

He wanted to see her face. He raised her head, his hands spread in her damp hair, so that the light from the garden shone on her glittering face. She did not want him to look at her. She was too open to him, too new and unused, and she struggled to turn her face away from the light, to hide herself, but he would not let her and he held her face before him until he had seen all that he needed to see.

˅ ˅ ˅

Mamie woke up because she was cold. The guest room in Mrs. Lee's townhouse was full of watery light and the air was full of dust. Mamie was alone. Her panties and old Chanel skirt and blouse were on the floor between the beds. A yellowed damask tablecloth had been spread over her while she slept. She noticed a little tag that was stitched into the hand-rolled hem of the tablecloth, L. P. R. LEE—THE GROVE.

She also noticed, standing in the bathroom doorway, an elderly black man. His white hair curled up around a red fez that sat far back on his head. He had a white, pencil-line moustache and he wore a quilted silk paisley dressing gown.

"Won't you come in?"

He was holding a demitasse. The cup was so delicate that Mamie could see the dark coffee through the transparent china.

"This isn't for you," he said, nodding at the cup. He took a sip. "I don't do that anymore."

"No," she said. She pulled the tablecloth closer around her, not out of modesty, but because she was cold. She looked across to the window, but it had been closed. Above the big, waxy tree and the row houses opposite, the sky was cloudless and pale.

"I didn't see Mr. Alder this morning. He was gone before I came down. I don't come down unless I have to, you understand what I'm saying?"

He handed her the cup and saucer, after all, and Mamie raised herself up against the wall so that she could drink the coffee. It was warm and very strong.

He sat on the other bed. There was a thump on the ceiling as if a solid, small object had been dropped on the floor above them.

"She's echo-locating," he said. "She doesn't see too good anymore. I am her eyes. And her hands and her nose. Always was, if you want to know." He spoke to Mamie in that familiar manner sometimes assumed by old people, as if he shared a past with her or, more likely, as if he could not be bothered to fill in the empty spaces. That would be up to Mamie to do.

He crossed his legs. He wore yellow leather Turkish slippers with upturned toes. There were dry, light patches of skin on his thin, hairless legs.

"Too much chicory?" He nodded again at the demitasse. Mamie had finished the coffee and wanted more.

"No. Perfect, I'd say."

"You know, one time I drove them up to North East Harbor, Mr. Lee was alive then and we were young, the three of us, inside that Buick for two days. I often think about it. She was just about the age you are now. The actual length of a life is always an interesting question." His eyes filled with tears. Mamie raised the cup to her mouth even though it was empty.

"Buenos dias," he said and pushed himself up off the bed. He thinks I'm Alder's wife, Mamie thought. He went through the bathroom, and Mamie listened to his Ali Baba slippers slap across the cold bathroom tiles.

There was a note for her on the bedside table. "Sick horse. I'll be back." It was written on his grandmother's gray stationery. Mamie folded it in small squares and put it in the pocket of her skirt.

She walked home across the Park. It was not until she reached the pond at Belvedere Castle that she finally began to feel warm. The King Pleasure song wound through her like a silk thread.

She let herself into the apartment on West Sixty-seventh

Street. The curtains were drawn and it was very dark. She felt her way, hand over hand, across the room. She smelled apples and cigarette ash. She turned on a light.

There were two empty bottles of Whit Crawford's good Calvados lying on the floor of the entrance hall. The Brancusi head was wrapped in with what looked like a nylon hair net. Red wine had been spilled on the beige linen sofa and the antique kite had been yanked down from the beam and lay torn and splintered under the piano bench. A fire had been started in the artificial fireplace with torn-up magazines, and bits of flying paper had burned holes in the Portuguese needle-point rug.

There was a hash pipe on the dining room table. Under the dining room table was a naked girl. She was asleep. She had the sturdy overarched body of someone who has done too much amateur gymnastics. Mamie could not see her face. It was covered with long light brown hair. The hair suddenly fell from around the girl's mouth, and Mamie could see that she was smiling in her sleep.

"Hi," Claire said.

Mamie, to her own irritation, jumped at the sound of her sister's voice. Claire had just taken a shower and her wet hair was held back in big plastic clips. She looked young and clean.

"You missed Sean. He really wanted to meet you."

"Why would he want to do that?" Mamie asked. She tried to brush some of the ash and burnt wool of the rug into the shallow fireplace with her foot.

"I think he read your letters. I'm not sure. I can't remember. Anyway, he thinks you're interesting."

"My letters?"

"He's great, Mamie. He says he only likes thin people."

Mamie bent down to brush the ruined rug with her fingers. There was a strong, bitter smell of singed hair.

"Is he still taking pictures of little dogs with hard-ons?"

"He has another project now. It's so brilliant. He's doing this whole series on famous accidents, like the truck driver who decapitated Jayne Mansfield. He's already done the boy who delivered the sandwich that choked Mama Cass to death."

"Are you all right, Claire?" Mamie said.

The girl under the table mumbled in her sleep. Claire, who was wearing underpants and a LET'S GO, METS! T-shirt, looked at Mamie in amazement.

"I suppose *you* spent the night at an all-night library," she said. She took a big plastic bottle of Coke from the refrigerator, what Alysse called "a maid's bottle," and drank from it.

The girl under the table said, "Fix me one, too. I'm so thirsty." She crawled out on her stomach, expertly using her elbows to pull herself forward. Urban Special Forces, Mamie thought.

Claire said, "Mamie, say good morning to Brooke."

"Hi, Mamie!" said Brooke. Her top lip pulled up over her big front teeth. She had very small breasts. She went to Mamie and put her arms around her. Mamie could smell the smoke from the fire in her lank hair.

"Don't you remember me?" Brooke stepped back to let Mamie look at her.

"I've thought about you so many times," Mamie said. "Are you all right?"

"You keep asking that," Claire said.

Brooke yawned and shook herself like a dog who has just come out of the water. Mamie had noticed that the girls at Felix's salon, in their harmless narcissism, watched themselves in the mirror at every possible opportunity. Brooke's nudity was very different. She behaved as if she did not have a body at all.

"I'm real sorry you weren't here last night," Brooke said.

She dropped sleepily onto the stained sofa. She yawned again and smiled. "Though I'm not sure how Sean'd feel about three girls."

Mamie picked up the ruined kite. It had flown a hundred years ago, traveling one day from a small farm village in Japan, across the Pacific, across the country, to hang from a hollow wood beam in Whit and Vivi Crawford's apartment. It managed to hold on for another entire two weeks after we moved in, thought Mamie.

Brooke was rolling a joint on the coffee table. She emptied the loose marijuana from a small plastic bag into a silver bowl commemorating Whit Crawford's victory the year before as Over-Forty Doubles Champion. She saw Mamie staring at her.

"It's easier to clean this way." She sifted and separated the twigs and seeds.

Mamie sat down wearily on the piano bench with the kite hanging over her knees.

"Where were you?" Claire called from the kitchen. There was the loud sound of the blender. Claire was making the morning Mai Tais. Mamie didn't answer.

Brooke asked if Mamie minded if she turned on the portable television. "It's like cartoons," she said when the tiny screen lighted and the images jumped jerkily one after another. Claire brought in a tray with three big Mai Tais.

"How did he read my letters?" Mamie asked her.

Claire shrugged. "He was in your room for hours."

"He tried some of your clothes on," Brooke said. "He looked real cute. Oh!" She turned suddenly from the television set to ask Claire, "Do you think he was telling the truth about . . ." She looked at Mamie. "You know . . ." she said slyly to Claire.

Mamie carefully laid the kite on top of the piano. Claire held out a Mai Tai to her. Mamie shook her head.

"I don't know about Mamie. She's hard to please," Claire said.

Mamie looked at her.

"Do you remember that boy you met at UCLA?" Claire asked. "He showed up on Kaua'i wearing a terry-cloth beach jacket that matched his bathing suit and beach sandals and Mamie took one look at him and went into the water and stayed in. She body-surfed for six hours rather than come out. I thought she was going to drown from exhaustion. He kept calling to her to come out, the waves were too big for most people to even go in, and she pretended that she didn't see him and caught another wave. He finally went back to his hotel and Glenwood, a two-hundred-pound Hawaiian boy, had to go in to help Mamie out. She was so tired she literally could not get out of the water."

"I was an asshole," Mamie said.

"Well, Sean said that was how everyone did sex," Brooke said with a pout to Claire.

"Let's ask Mamie," Claire said.

"Let's not," Mamie said quickly. "I don't want to know what he said or how everyone does it. I especially don't want anyone in my room again. Ever. And that includes both of you."

"God," said Brooke. She looked at Mamie with exaggerated fear and Mamie did not know whether she was making fun of her or if she really was frightened.

Claire sat calmly in one of the Eames chairs and sipped her drink. "Where were you last night?"

"With Alder." Mamie stood up and stepped around the bottles and cushions on the floor.

"Don't tell A-ly-eese," Claire sang.

"Fuck you," said Mamie and walked out of the room.

˅ ˅ ˅

Mamie pulled Whit Crawford's favorite leather chair, the one from his happy years at Yale, over to the small window of the library and sat in it. It was not easy to get the chair through the books and clothes that had been dropped on to the floor and just left there, but Mamie did not have the heart to begin cleaning the room. She had been looking forward to having a few hours in which she could think about Alder. She had a queasy and tremulous feeling in her stomach. It was not unpleasant and Mamie, of all people, would never complain about a symptom that might be taken as the first sign of lovesickness. She looked over her shoulder at the bed. The silver Deardorf's hatbox full of her mother's and Lily Shields's letters had been opened and the letters and postcards were scattered across the bed. Lily Shields always sent funny cards, nude men diving from the cliffs of Capri, and her cards, spread out on the bed, looked as if they had been arranged there for a photograph. Mamie slipped off her shoes and put her feet up on the windowsill.

She could suddenly smell her body. Gertrude had once told her that if you had sex with the wrong man, you would smell bad. Gertrude even claimed that she could tell how long it had been since her own man had last come by the way she smelled after making love with him. That was her way of knowing if he had been true to her. Mamie smiled. She had not known that she remembered these love-tricks whispered to her so many years before. Her vagina did not smell bad. She had not made love with the wrong man.

Gertrude worked as a cashier in the Big Save in Waimea. Mary found her the job when Gertrude's pretty brown belly had grown so big that even Mary, who was not particularly observant of people, had to admit that Gertrude was going to have a baby. Gertrude wanted the baby even though she was not married to Benjie. Mamie and Claire had tried to convince Mary to let her stay, but Mary thought that Gertrude was a very bad example to the girls and the other servants. It had never occurred to her, of course, that Gertrude was the primary influence in the lives of her daughters.

Gertrude had moved to a tiny house near the river and Mamie and Claire stopped at the Big Save almost every day when they were home from school and stood alongside the cash register and talked to Gertrude as she worked, pulling the fish and *taro* and cases of beer along the rubber conveyor belt. Mamie and Claire threw the groceries into brown paper bags while Gertrude gave orders to everyone. "Janine, how much da root beer? Mamie, you look too white, girl. Try check da price root beer, Claire." Gertrude had three children now and Benjie was one of the most feared police officers in Lihue.

Mamie wondered if Gertrude would teach her own girls the secrets she had passed on to her and Claire. Mamie thought that she might not, that she and Claire might be the last repositories of such significant information as how to prepare a love potion from red sugar cane, and sensible advice like "always leave 'em steef." Mamie had limited herself to kissing, and any deliberate attempt to leave them stiff so that they would come back to her would have seemed to her, at sixteen, dishonest. Her admirers were to like her for herself. Given what she now knew about Claire, it was clear that Claire had profited early from Gertrude's sensible counsels. Mamie, when she thought about these things, had been prepared to admit that perhaps Claire, despite Orval Nalag, had got it right and that she had done it all wrong.

She no longer thought that way, however; certainly not after

her night with Alder. She was so agitated, in fact, by her
night with Alder that in the short time she sat that morning
before the window, she convinced herself that she had been,
until twelve hours earlier, a virgin. And, in a way, she had
been.

Mamie, perhaps because of the novels she had read, believed
that there could be little that was more erotic than longing;
to be a young woman at a ball, with the formal restrictions
of mothers and dance cards, as well as one's own glittering
inexperience; to be raced across a spinning, warm room to the
moon-pull of a Strauss waltz; to fall in love at the ball, perhaps
unwisely, had always seemed to Mamie to promise a kind of
sexual yearning that modern love could not provide. Given
this nineteenth-century ideal, it is not surprising that Mamie
should have found Tommy Sheehan from San Diego a little
disappointing. Mamie might have lived on for years, an excited
Natasha awaiting her first invitation to dance, if Lady Studd
had not taken the trouble to explain to Alder Stoddard how
she masturbated her dogs.

She did not fully understand it until much later, but she
believed that Alder Stoddard, too, knew the possibilities of
longing. Because he was a man, he was able to exploit it by
the way that he used his body and her body; and because she
was a woman, she was able to draw him to her and hold him
inside of her. With any luck, and without having to resort to
any of Gertrude's tricks, she could keep him there.

In honor of her good fortune, she put on the waltz in A
Flat Major by Chopin, the one written for the Countess Bron-
itska. It would not have been Gertrude's way of celebrating,
but then Mamie was far from home. It was perhaps a sign of
Mamie's increasing willingness to live in the twentieth century, her own century, that she admitted to herself for the
first time, that no one, not even Prince Andrey himself, could

have danced to the Chopin waltzes. They were too fast or too slow; they were meant to be performed in salons. Mamie smiled at herself and changed the record. She did not put on Gabby Pahinui, which was another promising sign. She did put on Billie Holiday, but that was only to be expected.

TWELVE

Claire and Mamie were on the subway. It was a concession Claire had made to Mamie when Mamie said that they did not have the money to take a taxi to Greenwich Village and home again. Claire, who was not working, but who had enrolled in another class, lifesaving, and who was dependent on Mamie, had to agree. They had been invited to dinner by Toni. Or rather, Mamie had been invited and, as an afterthought, Toni had said, "And bring your sister, if you like. The one who goes out."

"It's that people look at you," Claire said on the subway. "That man over there has been staring at us since Fifty-seventh Street. And, what's worse, it makes me stare at him."

"Well, in taxis they *talk* to you," Mamie said in her ear. "The other day a Chinese man turned around and asked me, 'Good for suck?' Chinese, can you imagine? So unlike them."

"Suck?"

"Yes."

"I think it's your sweet voice, Mamie."

"You mean it's my fault?"

"Not your fault. Just your voice."

"I wanted to ask you, was it my imagination or did Brooke really train her pubic hair to grow in the shape of a heart?" Mamie looked around to make sure that no one was listening to them. "You know, like topiary."

"She had it waxed for Valentine's Day and everyone liked it so much, she kept it that way. Isn't it cool?"

"This was the girl who wouldn't go down a flume."

"She'll go down just about anything now."

They sat quietly for a few stops. Mamie liked the graffiti in the subway cars and she stared at it while she thought about Brooke and Courtney.

"I thought you were with the Butcher of Santo Cristo last night," Mamie said as she suddenly remembered that Claire was supposed to have been at their aunt's for dinner.

"Brooke telephoned just as I was getting ready to leave. Gosh, Alysse was really, really mad this morning. At the last minute, she had to put Mrs. Crooker next to General Barrios instead of me and Mrs. Crooker told the general that she admired his country's handicrafts. She was just trying to make dinner conversation, poor thing, but he thought she was making fun of him since there aren't any hand-embroidered tablecloths left after fourteen years of civil war."

"He's very sensitive. I suppose dictators are."

"He told Mrs. Crooker that as far as he was concerned she could suck out his asshole. In perfect English. Alysse said I ruined the party and hung up."

"I had no idea you figured so prominently in her social plans."

"Not any more," said Claire. "Look, that guy over there, the Italian guy, he wants you, Mamie."

"Me?"

"You think he has permanently chapped lips? Or maybe it's just a nervous habit. He's trying to tell you something."

Mamie turned sideways in her narrow seat so that she could not see the man lifting his eyebrows in invitation and sensuously flicking his big tongue at her. His tongue was green.

"Poor man just ate a whole box of Tic Tacs," Mamie said.

"He reminds me of Orval."

"Maybe it's you he wants." Mamie sat awkwardly in her seat, her knees sticking out into the aisle.

"I think he's coming over," Claire said, starting to laugh and now she, too, looked away.

Mamie giggled, unable to help herself, furious at Claire for encouraging the stranger.

They were both very relieved when the car stopped and he swung out the open doors like a trapeze artist. Mamie looked up. He gave her a big wink and she couldn't help but smile back at him.

Toni lived in an old clapboard row house off a gloomy brick courtyard overgrown with dusty ivy and ailanthus trees. The little courtyard was entered through a small wrought-iron gate and the low shuttered houses that enclosed the courtyard were painted red with white doors and window boxes.

Toni opened the little crooked door and Mamie had to shout to introduce Claire over the loud barking of dogs. Schnauzers leaped and nipped around them. The ground floor of the house was a dog-grooming salon. Toni took them upstairs, carrying Pépé in her arms.

There was a woman in the tiny kitchen taking a meat loaf out of the oven with a big fireproof mitt that looked like a lobster. Toni introduced her. It was difficult for them to shake hands because of the mitt. The kitchen smelled of parsley and garlic.

Her name was Jean. She had a small, pale face, made smaller

by the huge amount of thick black hair that seemed to stand straight out from her head. She had a space between her front teeth.

Toni handed them each a glass of red wine and they sat down to eat at a table in the front room.

Toni, who was not given to random conversation, spoke very little, although she was an attentive hostess and jumped up to open a bottle of wine when she saw Claire looking for wine on the table.

Jean spoke one soft command to the hysterical terriers and they lined up, as if in a drill, and sat down, and quietly stayed that way for the rest of the evening. It was Jean who had the dog-grooming business. She washed and trimmed dogs and sometimes, when it was requested, painted their nails. Mamie noticed ribbons and cups from dog shows on a shelf of the bookcase.

Claire ate voraciously. "Did you go to the Puerto Rican Day parade?" she asked.

Jean and Toni admitted that they had missed it.

"There were thousands of people on Fifth Avenue, with lawn chairs and Eskimo coolers and little cooking stoves. It was if they had just moved in, with all of their relatives and all of their belongings. There were even a few people with beds. That's what New York is like in the summer. Businessmen; and then hundreds of thousands of nice brown people. Where are all those big white women in Ferragamo Shoes and all those blond children with book bags?"

Toni laughed and lit a cigarette. She had not eaten very much.

"When do you go to Chicago?" she asked Mamie.

"Two weeks from Wednesday."

"Felix may surprise you," Toni said. She squinted to keep the smoke from her eyes and waved the smoke away with her hand so that it would not disturb Claire, who was having more mashed potatoes. Jean rose to clear the table and Toni stood up to help her. Mamie noticed that they were very solicitous of each other. It had never occurred to her that Toni was homosexual, but now that she understood, it did not shock her.

"He's had great success with women," Jean said.

Mamie did not feel the sexual attraction of Felix, but she had seen enough at the salon to know that the women like Alysse who came to buy their clothes wholesale, and many of the girls who worked for Felix, were very, very fond of him. They trusted him. Unlike other men, he paid attention to the things that interested them. It was his business, after all. When a woman asked Felix if he liked her shoes or her breast implants, he told her the truth. In Felix, a woman had someone who would make love to her and then spend hours discussing the kind of neckline that best suited her. It was no wonder that he was a success.

"I don't like him," Jean said. She brought a lemon meringue pie to the table.

Toni laughed. "Jean hates his clothes. She says that like all bad designers, it's about the sleeves. Too much shoulder."

Mamie watched Jean cut the pie. She had not thought about Felix's sleeves, but she could see that Jean was right.

Claire said, "Our stepcousin—is she our stepcousin, Mamie?—told me that she broke up with her last boyfriend because he complained that she ruined his Hermès ties when she tied him up." She held out her hand to pass the dessert plates.

Mamie held her breath. She hoped that the lemon meringue pie would stop Claire.

"She sounds smart to me," Toni said calmly.

Jean asked, "Will you have coffee?"

"I've been thinking about it all day," Claire went on. "*Is there a way to do it so the ties won't be ruined? A slip-knot? What is an Hermès tie, anyway? Perhaps this relationship could have been saved.*"

"I'll have coffee, please," Mamie said to Jean.

"Maybe this would be a perfect use for Velcro," Claire said thoughtfully, as if she were considering rushing down to the Patent Office in the morning.

She looked up and finally saw that Mamie was embarrassed. To be fair to Claire, it was almost never true that she set out to offend or shock. She was spontaneous and these things interested her. Even the night when she'd asked the Ambassador if his wife cupped his balls when he came, she had spoken in temper, not from a desire to titillate.

"People say the most extraordinary things to me," she said, trying to make it up to Mamie. "If you're a girl, they think you can't be too smart, so they tell you anything. Even other girls. They think you won't remember."

Mamie looked at Toni. She was holding Pépé in her lap and she was smiling. Mamie was relieved.

"You know," Toni said, "I told Jean that you are always in museums, Mamie, and that she should go with you sometime. She has only just recently started to visit them again."

Jean put down her fork. "I had to stop going because I had this strange idea that the museum guards knew something about the paintings. They stood there day after day, year after year, looking at them, and I just knew that they would have, well, certain thoughts about them." She stopped. She was blushing.

"She made the mistake of asking one or two of them about certain paintings," Toni said. She looked at Jean fondly.

"They thought I was crazy, of course. They didn't even know what paintings I was talking about."

Mamie laughed.

After Claire finished the pie, the sisters offered to carry in the dishes, but their help was refused. Toni lit another Camel and said that she had to take out the dogs. She would walk Mamie and Claire to the corner. They thanked Jean and shook hands in the kitchen, Jean wiping her wet hand on an apron.

Toni took them down the narrow staircase and out into the warm, quiet night. The courtyard was very dark and the weedy ailanthus hid the gray sky and the reflected glare of the huge, lighted city.

They walked slowly up Grove Street, stopping at each mottled sycamore tree for the dogs. The tree bark reminded Mamie of the white patches on Mr. de Beaupré's legs.

"I wanted to tell you something," Toni said to Mamie as they waited for Pépé. "You needn't do anything you don't want to."

Mamie looked at her. She couldn't see her expression in the shadow of the trees.

"Don't be afraid to be difficult. If something doesn't feel right, don't do it. Your instinct will always be better than theirs. The difficult ones are always the most interesting, anyway."

Pépé was entangled in the leash and his old, spindly legs were bound together. Mamie bent down to free him. When she stood up, Toni reached out and held Mamie's chin gently in her hand.

Mamie smiled at her. "Were you one of the difficult ones?"

"Not difficult enough," Toni said quietly and took her hand away.

In the subway on the way home, Mamie was grateful that Claire was quiet. She said nothing about the two women and their domestic arrangement. Perhaps she was too full from dinner, and still a little tired from her night with Brooke and Sean. She said only that Jean was a wonderful cook, and that she liked the little house. She said, too, that she thought Toni should have the old dog put to sleep immediately, he was so decrepit, but Mamie didn't answer her and they sat in comfortable silence until Seventy-second Street.

The phone was ringing as they came into the apartment. It was Alder. He had been trying to reach Mamie for hours.

"How is the horse?" she asked.

"I'm afraid she died."

Mamie knew that he wasn't being funny. Danny Harrington at the ranch in Hanalei had a cutting horse that had foundered.

"I'm sorry," she said.

"She ate too much."

"Just like Claire. She ate too much tonight."

"Shut up, Mamie," Claire said from the sofa.

He laughed. "She's not dead, though."

"Not yet," Mamie said.

Alder and Mamie went to the movies. She sat in the dark next to him, so conscious of his body there beside her that she had to keep herself from brushing against him too many times as if by accident. She had a hollow, airy feeling in her stomach, a little like stage fright. She had not eaten very much since the night she stayed at his grandmother's house. He saw that she was staring at him, so he turned from time to time and leaned forward to look at her in the dark to reassure her.

They walked after the movie. There was a light rainfall and it felt sharp and fresh on Mamie's warm face. There was the smell of black tar from the steaming streets. Alder was not hungry, either, and they decided to keep walking, east along the edge of the Park.

It never occurred to Mamie in the movie theater or at any time after, that Alder Stoddard might be experiencing any of the tortures of love that she herself was undergoing. Even when he yawned, and said apologetically that he had not been sleeping well, she did not suspect, even for an instant, that it might have anything to do with her. Mamie was simply following her heart.

Alder, who, as Alysse had said, had known many women, was caught by surprise by Mamie. He was fascinated by her individuality, and without pitying her, he saw clearly that she was troubled by her inability to set things right. He saw that she could not do it, and, worst of all, that she could not get used to it. Alder believed that you were given your life on the understanding that to the very end, you tried to set it all right, so he understood Mamie's struggle, even if she did not understand it herself. He recognized in her the anxiety and guilt of someone who fears that something has been left undone. He was able to recognize her distress because he, too, had the sense that he had forgotten something very important. The difference between them, as well as age and sex, was that Alder took the distress as something good.

"I liked the movie," she said.

"Yes."

"Do you think we like the same things?"

He looked at her. "You mean a shared passion for Jacobean furniture and *The Duchess of Malfi?*"

"Is that how you pronounce it? I don't personally admire Jacobean furniture, so perhaps I am all wrong."

They walked to the crooning of the traffic. The car tires in the wet street made a stream of hissing sound and Mamie could smell the horse dung lying at the curb where the horse-drawn carriages waited for customers.

"Alysse has been trying to reach me," he said.

"She doesn't like that I see you. I had to drop off a ball gown from Mr. Felix and she wouldn't allow me in the library. Once a week, she and Mrs. Washburn have a French lesson and tea with an assistant professor from Columbia and they aren't allowed to speak English the entire two hours. I knocked on the library door and she yelled, '*Attention! Attention!*' "

Alder laughed. "Are you coming home with me?" he asked.

They went again to the guest room on the third floor and she saw that someone, perhaps Alder, had made the beds with fresh linen and put piqué blanket covers on them, and pillows, and had taken the dust-sheet from the Louis XV chaise longue in the corner. The window to the garden was open and there was the smell of old, wet leaves. It was a feminine, formal room, with little grisaille panels between the *boiserie*. How funny, Mamie thought when she saw it, I liked it better the other way.

"Mr. de Beaupré was worried that you were cold the other morning."

"Did he do this?"

Alder nodded. He turned out a silver lamp on a desk, but left a small lamp glowing on a table in the corner, like a child's night light.

She sat on one of the beds and looked at the light.

"Do you want me to turn it out?"

She shook her head.

Just his simple, strong gesture of loosening his tie and unbuttoning his cuffs was enough to excite her. She turned away from him, surprised by the pleasure she already felt. She was fascinated by his masculinity. It aroused her, but it also moved her and made her feel protective toward him. She watched him. She was hypnotized by his maleness, not only in a phallic sense but in the more superficial ways that he differed from her; the very tie and shirt even, the brown hair on his arms, his brusqueness of movement and speech, his fastidious coordination. He did not bother to fold his tie, nor did he drop it to the floor in seduction, but tossed it deftly across the room to the chaise. He is different from me, she thought. He is without affect, without self-awareness.

He sat on the bed beside her. He watched quietly as she undressed, standing between the two beds, his knees touching her as she reached down to lift the hem of her silk slip to pull it over her head. She stood between him and the light, so he saw her body only in its dark, slender outline. He put his hands around her waist and drew her close to him, between his legs. He kissed her hips slowly.

"I am sore from the other night," she said quietly. "It's been a long time since I've made love." She wanted him to know this in case she had disappointed him.

"Has it?"

"Yes."

"A few months?" He held her hands behind her back and traced a stream down her neck, between her breasts, across her ribs.

"Day. A few days."

"There goes the erection," he said and fell back on the bed, pulling her down on top of him.

She said, laughing, "It's a lie, it's a lie."

He suddenly turned her so that she was kneeling on the bed before him, her hands grasping the pillow, and he was on his knees behind her, holding on to her hair. He encircled her waist with one arm and pulled her hips back to him in a movement so quick that it seemed as if she took him in, rather than his entering her. He did not let go of her hair, or her waist, and it seemed to him that, even had he wanted to, he could not have separated himself from her, so neatly and tightly were they bound together.

It was painful for her at first, the arch of her back, his bending over her and pushing into her again and again. She could hear him, but she could not see him. She was dizzy. If she looked between her own legs, she could see his legs pressing against her legs, entrapping them and holding them and she could see his testicles, and the base of his penis as it moved in and out of her. With each thrust into her, he pulled her hips back onto him, and her damp skin made his hands wet.

She shoved the pillow off the bed and reached behind with her hand to touch him.

He took her hand and pushed it under her so that she was able to hold him.

"Like the Ambassador," she said.

She heard him laugh, out of breath. His arm, the one she had stared at with such desire, with its wristwatch and brown hair and pink shirtsleeve, bare now, and the brown hair flattened with perspiration, reached around her. He put his fingers inside of her.

"Protect me," he said.

Exhausted and blinded by pleasure, she gave herself to him and did everything that he wanted her to do, not thinking, without shame or even consciousness, and she protected him.

` ` `

Alder returned with two cold bottles of beer.

Mamie leaned against the bedframe like a pin-up girl, arms folded boldly and luxuriously behind her head, and said, "I liked it better before."

"Oh, great." He handed her a beer and took off his trousers and lay down on the other bed.

"The room. I mean the room."

"You're lucky Mr. de Beaupré didn't climb in with you. He was confused and thought you were my grandmother thirty years ago."

"Perhaps they used to come to this room."

They lay there on top of their separate beds, not looking at each other, but exhilarated and intimate. At that moment, it would have been impossible for either of them to imagine ever leaving the room.

He stood to open the window and as he stepped over the clothes that had been left on the floor between the beds, he put his hand on her vagina and said, "You're very prettily made, Mamie."

"Do you think so?" she asked in quiet surprise. "My friend, Lily, and I used to have what she called Cooze Seminars. Her theory was that, in the end, the world wins. You start out thinking that your vagina is all right, harmless even, and then something happens when you're about thirteen, actually happens, and it all changes. It's as if it's turned inside out and suddenly it seems ugly and shameful and not at all harmless."

He started to speak, but she interrupted him. "I've read all the theories about concavity and *vagina dentata* and the darkness. I have even considered it from the point of view of aesthetics. Lily and I used to study sex magazines. Obviously, *someone* thinks they're attractive, but isn't it interesting that women themselves don't like their own vaginas? That is what Lily means: the world wins. Something happens along the way and we become ashamed."

"I think," he said slowly and carefully, "I think that you can get it back again, the lack of shame. You must try to get it back. It gives men too much power if you don't."

"Alysse told Claire that when she belonged to a 'conscience-raising' group, as she put it, they would sit in a big circle and show their vaginas all at the same time to overcome their self-loathing."

He laughed, and she smiled.

She sat on her bed facing him, the pillow held in front of her. "Men suffer the Fall from Grace as well and they aren't ashamed."

"No," he said. "But they're something else; they're afraid."

"My sister is neither ashamed nor afraid. Claire would have refused the fig leaf: 'No, thank you, I'm perfectly happy this way.' Claire likes her vagina. She says so all the time."

She lifted herself to pull down the blanket. He turned out the little lamp in the corner, and the room was filled once more with the cream-colored light reflected from the magnolia in the garden. There was the faint, intermittent sound of car horns and sirens, as if the city were falling away from them. She lifted an edge of the blanket and he slid in beside her, opening her legs, both of them wondering if he could perhaps change her mind, if he could convince her that the world had not won, after all.

"What was her name?"

"Baby."

"Mrs. Baby Stoddard?"

"I'm afraid so."

It was their second day in the guest room. From time to time, Alder left for a few minutes and always returned with some little thing: a cassette player and tapes (Roy Orbison, *Il Trovatore*); clean blue-striped shirts for each of them; baked potatoes with sour cream; towels and a toothbrush. Mamie had called to tell Claire that she was with Alder, but there was no answer at the Crawfords'. Sometimes when they slept, Mamie was awakened by the sound of footsteps as the restless man above them paced slowly back and forth.

"Why did you marry her?"

"Her family. They were very charming. You know what South Americans are like. Irresistible."

"I presume you mean rich South Americans."

He looked at her. He was stretched out on the chaise in his clean shirt and boxer shorts.

"I hate the sloppiness of it," she said. "The carelessness. I don't mean you so much because you would take your child if they'd let you, but look at your mother and look at Alysse, and Brooke and Courtney's parents. It's so second-rate. My sister says that I am a snob and I'm contemptuous because I feel I've been let down by the world, but she's wrong. Besides, it's not that it's second-rate for me, it's second-rate for everybody. For your daughter. For Baby even."

"I'm afraid that Baby is deliriously happy." He lighted a cigar.

She looked at him, thinking. He shook out the match and looked at the tip of the cigar.

"In boarding school," he said, putting the match in a drawer next to him, "there was a boy whom all the parents admired.

My father thought he was the most promising new boy since Learned Hand. He was the president of our class. He worked as a Senate page each summer. He even had the *Washington Post* delivered to the dorm. My mother, who was never particularly interested in my school friends, was angry with me for not inviting him home at Thanksgiving. I couldn't stand him. Then one term, at the urging of his friends, the Joint Chiefs of Staff, he fried his pet parakeet on the hot plate in his room."

"What happened to him?"

"He went to work in the White House for Nixon. And then he did a little time."

"They almost always get it wrong, don't they? My mother did. It bothered her when I read too much, so she would send us off to the ranch and one of the cowboys, Daniel Alohikea, taught us a chant that we used to sing when we jumped rope and all the *paniolos* would fall in the dirt laughing. It always seemed a little odd to me. Then in an anthology years later, I read that it was a famous sex chant: '*He'e ana, i ka muku la, Ho'i ana, i ka lala, 'ea 'ea.*' "

"Perhaps in English, Mamie," he said, hidden in cigar smoke. "It's not working."

" 'Surfing to the left, surfing to the right, it was I who rode into that shore. I thought that she was there in my arms. This ends my praise of *Halala*, the bird's beak.' " She blushed. "We'd have been better off with *Hans Brinker*."

"Not necessarily," he said. "*Halala?*"

She came over to him and sat on the edge of the chaise and he started to unbutton her shirt, the cigar held deep in the fork of his fingers.

"Isn't it my turn to do something to you?" she asked solemnly.

"Is this feminism or desire?"

"Feminism."

"All right, then," he said and crossed his arms above his head and rested them against the faded silk damask.

"May I smoke my cigar?"

"If you can," she said.

THIRTEEN

Mamie finally went home because she was worried about Claire. Alder offered to go to the Crawfords' to leave a note for her. He wanted Mamie to come with him to the farm, but she had been with him in the gray and white room at Mrs. Lee's for two and a half days and she wanted to be alone, not because she was tired of him, but to have the luxury of thinking about him.

Claire was lying on the sofa when Mamie came home. There was a Mai Tai, with its paper parasol, on the table next to her. A damp washcloth lay across her eyes.

Mamie, who would be away for a week showing the collection with Mr. Felix, was anxious about leaving Claire alone in the apartment. They did not have much money. Mamie was paid three hundred dollars a week by Mr. Felix when she was working, and each sister received two hundred dollars a month from Mary. The Crawfords would be back in two months and Mamie and Claire would have to find someplace to live. There was also the question of the ruined kite, Mamie explained to Claire, and the stained sofa and other broken and damaged things that would have to be replaced. Claire had shrugged and told her to forget about the kite.

"I've quit the new lifesaving class," Claire said. "I wasn't learning anything." She held the washcloth to her head with her hand. "It was *very* upsetting."

Mamie sat on the arm of the sofa. She rubbed Claire's bare toes.

"It was taught by this really cute policeman, you know, with a moustache and muscles, and he kept calling me up to be the volunteer. He made slings for both of my arms, and a stretcher out of two poles and a blanket, emergency equipment we usually have with us, and I had a broken neck and two sprained ankles. Of course, he was touching me all the time, flipping me over and wrapping me in gauze. Everyone else in the class was seventy years old. The final insult came during the resuscitation demonstration when he pretended to pull me from a lake." She lifted the washcloth from her eyes and looked at Mamie. "Saved by a thousand French kisses."

Mamie laughed. She massaged Claire's feet, and then her calves. She noticed a dark bruise and welts on Claire's legs. "Did he do this?"

Claire sat up and threw the wet cloth onto the table. She looked down at her legs.

"No," she said with a tired sigh. "That was Sean. You should see my ass." She began to unbutton her jeans.

Mamie jumped up. "Don't! Don't, Claire. I don't want to see it."

Claire shrugged, a little disappointed. "If I don't mind, why should you mind?"

Mamie hesitated. She was confused as to why she should mind, especially since Claire had spent years trying to convert her to the belief that, as Claire put it, "if it doesn't hurt anyone, it's okay."

"I'm not sure that it doesn't harm you," Mamie said. "You say that you don't mind, and I even believe you don't mind, but I'm not sure that it doesn't cause you harm anyway." She slid into a leather chair. "We've had this conversation many times."

Claire nodded and lay back on the sofa.

"Where were you?" Mamie asked.

"With Sean and Brooke. I went to the Frick with Brooke yesterday and it was incredibly interesting. She believes she's had earlier lives, she's reincarnated, you know, so she kept recognizing paintings that once belonged to her. Do you know that Ingres painting of the countess in the blue silk dress?"

Mamie nodded.

"That was hers."

Mamie smiled.

"No, really." Claire finished her Mai Tai and played with the tiny parasol, opening and closing it on its little stick. "I think I might try to get into that writing class, you know, the one where you have to fuck the teacher. Only I'm hoping Edwin will get me in without that. Courtney says she'll introduce me to him and—"

"What does he do to you?" Mamie asked quietly. The very thought of what Sean might do to Claire made her sad.

Claire looked at her. "Belts and things. He takes—"

"Don't tell me! I'm sorry," Mamie said quickly, interrupting her. "I love you."

Claire smiled. "There's mail for you. *And* I didn't open it. Aren't you proud? Alysse has a new boyfriend. Well, *she* calls him a beau. A German art dealer who wears green crocodile shoes. He buys all the paintings for the Bressen-Bach collection. And all the girls, I'd imagine."

Despite the pain behind her eyes, Claire carefully made her way to the record player to put on Billie Holiday. She sang along with Billie, and Mamie noticed, as she had before, that Claire always gave the words of the song the same pronunciation as the singer: "Our few-cha togetha . . ."

There was a letter from Vivi Crawford asking that Mamie not allow anyone to touch the piano. It had belonged to her father and Oscar Hammerstein had once played the score from *South Pacific* on it. Mamie looked at the piano. It had a cigarette burn on it. Brooke had left a lighted joint the size of a hot dog on top of it.

There was also a letter from her mother.

Dear Mamie,

The canoe race from O'ahu to the beach at Nawiliwili was yesterday. It was on the television live, all through the night, the pictures taken from an escort boat. There was a full moon and I stood on the beach looking south-southeast, even though I knew they were still fifty miles offshore, thinking about them paddling across the rough channel, like Kamehameha's warriors, hoping to subdue the chiefs of Kaua'i, the only island never to be conquered. I have always thought how frightening it must have been to look up one afternoon from mending your nets or planting *taro* to see the long, ominous war canoes coming in fast, the men in gourd helmets with ivory nosepieces and human hair bristles. I have often thought I felt the presence of those ancient Hawaiians. Once I went to the Gay Estate to pick litchi, you were with me, but wading in the stream, and to this day I can feel the chill presence of the ghosts there. Later Daldo Fortunato told me the place is abandoned for that reason. Anyway, not so many people as in the past showed up for the race, and everyone is blaming the TV.

Old Mr. Bingham at Lawai has finally broken down and given me twelve specimens of the rare native lobelia he has been hoarding for twenty years. They were from Queen Emma's garden there.

The prickly *wiliwili* are flowering. Do you remember when Mothers used to keep their children out of the water when the red *wiliwili* were blooming? The young sea-birds, trying their wings, bring the sharks close to shore. I never paid any attention, but McCully used to say there was a good reason behind every one of their superstitions. I wish that I had listened to the women more when they used to say these things. You don't hear it so much anymore.

I miss you, especially when I stay alone up in the cabin at Koke'e. I remember you in the mornings, you were so sweet, rushing out to bring in the stalks of wet, yellow ginger to scent the rooms, and some sticks of eucalyptus to add to the fire. It was so cold in the early mornings, wasn't it, dear?

Love,
Mother

The letter surprised Mamie and made her happy. She had tears in her eyes. She put the letter back in its envelope. "Tell me one thing, Claire, and I won't bother you anymore."

Claire moaned.

"Do you think of it at all?" Mamie asked.

Claire studied her sister for a moment to see whether or not she could answer truthfully. Neither of them thought it necessary to clarify just what it was that "it" represented, that impersonal pronoun that could only mean the island, and home.

"I'm not like you, if that's what you want to know. I don't walk around in some flora-and-fauna hallucination with tears in my eyes."

Mamie looked down at the envelope in her hand.

"I do have a few, very specific things I *sometimes* think about," Claire said quickly. She paused. "Not too often, though. *Sometimes.*"

"Like what?"

"Well, the taste of a Duane's Ono-Burger. Or the time we were caught on the Hanakapiai cliff trail during that storm and it took us four hours to crawl a half-mile in the mud on our hands and knees."

"I don't remember that," Mamie said, frowning.

"Mamie!"

"Just teasing. Just teasing." Her voice was full of melancholy, and even sorrow, not for the constant island in her heart, but for her sister. It had nothing to do with islands. Claire, who was in the kitchen making two new drinks, did not see the regret in Mamie's face, nor hear it in her voice, and even if she had, it would not have made any difference.

The morning that Mamie was to go to Chicago to do the first show of Mr. Felix's collection, she was awakened by the telephone. The telephone was in Claire's bedroom. The ringing went on for so long that Mamie, even in her sleep, realized that it must be an important call.

Claire's room was such a tribute to the vernacular, filled with tequila bottles and empty tins of Almond Roca and packets of vitamins and filaments of dental floss and jars of pink Dippity-do and disposable douche containers, that Mamie could not make out at first if Claire was in her bed. She had not made the bed for the eight weeks they'd lived there.

It was Alysse on the telephone.

"Where were you?" Alysse asked irritably.

"I'm going to Chicago," Mamie said.

"I want you to take that gown back to Felix. It's too big. You'd think he'd remember how big around I am. That's the only thing I remember my mother ever saying, 'Big feet; small foundation.' "

"I thought your feet were small." Mamie yawned. Claire was not in the bed. She looked around the room in admiration and amazement. There was a small dead animal in the corner.

"How's Alder Stoddard?"

"Limp, I can wrap him around my neck."

"What?"

"He's fine." The animal in the corner trembled. Perhaps it's not dead, Mamie thought. She waited for it to move again, but it was still. She wondered if Claire had had Jimmy exhumed and sent to her.

"She left him, you know."

"Who?"

"Baby."

"Oh. Baby. Yes, I did know."

"Do you know why?"

"Yes," Mamie lied. She yawned again loudly. "Excuse me, I was asleep when you called."

"She told him he could have all the girls he wanted, she didn't care about that. He was just so boring. Always reading the newspaper."

"That *is* tiresome," Mamie said.

Alysse did not say anything. Mamie closed her eyes tightly and willed herself not to speak.

Alysse said, "His mother, Laura Lee Shannon (she was older than me, of course, but she was crazy about me), had her face scraped and peeled the same time as me, and she invited me to The Grove, old Mrs. Lee's house in Connecticut, to recover. On the way out of town, we saw an ice cream store on First Avenue and we made that good-looking black chauffeur stop the car. He didn't want to. We were so hot under all the gauze. He wouldn't get out, so we jumped out and bought ice cream sodas to sip through the bandages. Speaking of bandages, I'm just on my way to the hospital to see Dodo. She finally had her baby. Born without a stomach or a lung or something, but she still gets the money."

"I've been thinking about Dodo," said Mamie. "She used to do these shows for Felix, didn't she?"

"He was crazy about her. Fucked her during the first fitting."

"You said once that Dodo didn't get where she was just on her looks."

"Did I?"

"And I've been wondering what it was then, what it was that got Dodo where she is—?" Mamie really had been wondering about this. "And where *is* she exactly?"

"Oh, didn't you know?"

"No, I don't know anything."

"She was the last girl with that congressman, you know, Congressman Guardini, the night he was assassinated."

I really don't know anything, Mamie thought; I wasn't kidding.

"Give 'Feel' my love," Alysse said. "You can pick up the dress when you get back."

"Yes," said Mamie and she put the phone down between a bag of barbecue-flavored potato chips and an open jar of petroleum jelly. Under the jar was a linen dinner napkin with the name of the former Secretary of State and his office telephone number (he was married) written on it in lipstick.

Mamie went to the corner where the animal lay huddled.

She touched it timidly with her bare toe. When it did not stir, frightened and curled in its tense, defensive coil, she bent down and cautiously picked it up. It was a brown fur brassiere. It looked like something a buxom cave-woman might wear in a movie. It was clumsily made, possibly of mouse or shrew fur. It made Mamie laugh. She threw it on the flea market that had once been Vivi and Whit Crawford's prized eighteenth-century marriage bed, and went to Chicago.

Thanks to Bones Washburn, Mamie was not altogether unprepared for the splendor of the hotel suite that Felix Villanueve had reserved for her in Chicago. Perhaps she thought all good hotel rooms looked that way. It was not done in the very special style of Mrs. Washburn, who was given to elephant tusks and antelope-hoofed chairs, but it was padded and swathed, from floor to ceiling, in pale yellow silk. The white furniture, in the style of Louis XV, was covered in yellow-and-white striped silk and the big, raised bed was draped in swags of yellow silk. There were silver baskets of grapes and a bottle of champagne in an ice bucket in the sitting room. Next to the bed was a bowl of gardenias. There was also a note from Mr. Felix. He hoped that Mamie would be able to dine with him that evening.

He was early. She had just stepped out of the bath and put on her old blue-and-white cotton *yukata* to open the door and he smiled when he saw her, barefoot, in the elegant room, in the girlhood kimono that was too small for her.

She said that she would dress quickly, but he told her not to—he had just ordered dinner for her. She must be in bed early in order to look beautiful the next day. Did she mind if he sat with her and nibbled a little something? When she wondered where Jacline, the other model, might be, Felix explained that he had changed his mind at the last minute. He only needed Mamie.

He looked around the room. "You haven't opened your champagne." He peeked into the lovely bedroom. In the closed room, the smell of the gardenias was very strong. He opened the champagne and brought her a glass. He sat down on the striped silk sofa and patted the seat next to him.

"Are you sure I shouldn't change? I'd really rather change."

"My dear," he said. "It is so unnecessary."

The room service waiter arrived to prepare the table. Felix had ordered with care: a vegetable consommé, a small, neat piece of grilled fish and a timbale of carrot and turnip—all for Mamie's good nutrition. He asked for another bottle of champagne. The waiter treated them with knowing deference. He never spoke and never looked at them and it was clear from the satisfied precision with which he set the table that he was delighted by his own tact.

"There is a wonderful exhibit at the museum here. Late Picasso. I should like very much to take you. Perhaps after the morning show. I must lunch with Mrs. Green *mañana*, I do it every year, it is particularly, particularly dull, but she buys the entire collection and they tell me I must give her lunch."

He chatted on amiably, alertly filling the champagne glasses, making Mamie smile with his deliberately awkward American slang, taking his time with her, attentive and polite.

"I should like, I should like very much," he said, holding up his glass to her, "if I could think of this as the beginning of our special friendship."

Mamie lifted her glass and blushed.

"In all my years of admiring beautiful women, you are the

first I have spoken to like this. I will train you. I will groom you, guide your every step, dress you."

Mamie did not say anything. She did not want him to dress her. Or guide her every step. She was uncomfortable sitting there in the splendid room, with Mr. Felix watching her every gesture with shrewd, exultant eyes. He daintily wiped the wet corners of his mouth with his fingers.

"You must put yourself in my care. You must do everything I say. For example, my dear, you must finish your vegetables."

She picked up her fork. She was not very hungry. She did not know if he was teasing her. His talk about Marbella and backgammon and the pretender to the throne of Spain and the firmness of Mamie's skin was both fatherly and effeminate, and it confused her. She had no experience of a father, so she was not to be blamed for mistaking his interest in her as kindness. Alder, who would never have spoken to Mamie in this falsely intimate way, was, to Mamie, a mature man, while Felix was a bewildering combination of girlfriend and uncle.

"No pudding, of course," Felix said, smiling and pushing his chair back from the table. "We must get you into bed early-early."

Mamie wanted dessert. She wanted an espresso, but she was paralyzed by her discomfort and embarrassment. She wanted to ask him to leave, but she did not know how to do it. She stayed at the table. She finished her glass of champagne. She had drunk a little too much, out of nervousness and a wish to seem sophisticated.

"Put on your nightdress and get into your pretty bed and I will tuck you in with my blessing."

He sat in one of the small chairs and picked up the book

she had brought with her, *The Journal of Eugène Delacroix,* a present from Alder, and calmly looked at the illustrations. "I warned you, after all, that if you want to become the great beauty I promise you can, and will, become, you must do as I say, my dear."

She had the uneasy feeling that he was presuming on her inexperience and taking advantage of both her helplessness as a woman and her dependence as his model. She had always suspected that the mistake of feminism was its refusal to admit the superior, undeniably superior, strength of men— not economic or political strength, that was another thing altogether—but the simple fact that at any moment, Felix, for all of his idle, silly talk about princes and princesses, could lay Alder's Delacroix book on the little French table, reach over and snap her narrow wrist in two.

She went into the bathroom and locked the door. She brushed her teeth and washed her face and hands and changed into her modest cotton nightdress that buttoned to the neck. She came out of the bathroom and waited by the side of the bed as Felix deftly stood the French bolsters on end in the corner, and folded the heavy quilted silk bedspread at the foot of the bed, and pulled down the blanket and top sheet.

She climbed into bed. He sat on the edge of the bed. She was unable to pull the blanket up over herself because he was sitting on it. She held her hands on her chest, as if she were saying her prayers.

"Goodnight," she said. "Thank you for the gardenias." Their night smell was dizzyingly sweet.

"May I give you a goodnight kiss?"

Before she could answer, he took her by the shoulders and held her back against the pillows. Without her ever knowing how he did it, it was done so smoothly and quickly, he lay on top of her, stretched toe to toe, hip to hip and mouth to mouth, fitting her perfectly. He had no time to remove his Italian driving shoes and they rubbed against Mamie's bare feet.

She pulled her hands out from under him and grabbed him by the shoulders to push him away. He rubbed against her, eyes closed, moaning softly. He had unzipped his trousers. His movement, up and down, caused her nightdress to raise up around her hips. He pushed the small, wet tip of his penis up and down, through her pubic hair, as if he were fruitlessly plowing a furrow, over and over. It had happened so easily, his pressing himself on top of her, his assumption and his arousal, that it was as if Mamie were not there. He did not even look at her.

He came on her stomach. She looked down at him. He was panting. His eyes were still closed. He rolled over onto the bed, one leg still across her, and she saw his semen on her stomach. She had never seen it on her own body before. It ran into her navel and slid down her side. She lifted her arms high in the air as if she disdained even touching him with her hands, disdained touching herself.

He reached over and grunted as he stretched to turn out the lamp on the bedside table. She listened in the dark as he lifted his leg from her and, tucking in his tight silk shirt, went into the sitting room to find his suit jacket.

He let himself out.

She left her beautiful rooms without ever unpacking her bag. She left the cotton nightdress on the marble floor of the bathroom and she left a note for Mr. Felix.

She was at the airport too early. She sat in an orange molded-plastic chair that was bolted to the floor. Too distracted to read, she waited quietly as the airport filled up around her. She went over each meeting with Felix, from the happy day when he had saved her from Miss Magda and Selena to the last view she had of him from the bed, silhouetted in the yellow light of the sitting room as he wiggled his polka-dot tie up under his chin to make a knot. There was no knowing whom he might meet in the hall.

All that she could see, as she went over it again and again, were warnings and hints. She especially questioned her presumption, given Felix's reputation, that she would be the exception; that because she was an island girl, Felix would treat her differently.

On the plane, in the first class seat that Felix had bought for her, grateful to have a round-trip ticket, she was calmer and more logical. Her habitual fair-mindedness was bound to lead her eventually to Felix himself and, somewhere over Ohio, she finally caught up with him. Felix, who had not behaved in any way untrue to himself, would be rather surprised, and certainly inconvenienced, by Mamie's note (in which she simply wrote that she was returning to New York). She knew that he would be disgusted by her inability to understand that the world worked in a certain practical, self-serving way and that, as far as these things went, she was fortunate to have caught his attention. Many girls considered themselves very lucky to have been discovered by Felix Villanueve, girls who went on to become famous, including a girl from Wisconsin who was eventually beaten to death by her pimp and a girl from Finland who married the Duke of Savoy's cousin. Mamie knew all of this. She knew that she might have had a far more dangerous mentor than Mr. Felix, and because she was not without ambition, she knew, too, that she might have had a more vulgar Mr. Felix. She did not want to sell underpants at Deardorf's. She understood that her Mr. Felix was at least marked with a little glamour and prestige. She might have been rescued by the Mr. Felix of frozen fish. It happened all the time. Mamie knew that there were girls in Des Moines, at that very moment, on business trips with their employers, being rubbed up against at machine-parts conventions. She did not see herself as a special victim.

She was ashamed of her naïveté, and she was ashamed of her physical helplessness. It was not that she couldn't have tumbled him onto the floor, or poked his eyes with her fingers or bitten him—it was that she had not. It is true that there would have been the risk of being hurt had she injured him, or even embarrassed him, but she had not even tried to defend herself. Worse, she had not even asked him to leave her room.

She did not understand that her silence had come from a falsely guilty sense of her own complicity, and from a confused wish to be liked by him, to hold onto his admiration and, most compromising of all, to hold onto her job. What worried her was that she had allowed herself to be caught beneath the writhing, heaving man because it had been easier than asking him to leave.

That a woman might be wise enough to say just what it was that she wanted, and at the same time protect her own body from harm; that she might spare the feelings of the man, so that if he were denied or rejected, the humiliation would not cause him to hate her or do violence to her, was an idea that only came to Mamie later. She was too young.

It must be said, too, that, for the first time, Mamie had come up against the powerful force of sexual impulse. Felix had been in a masturbatory trance, his mind and body unified and drawn forward by one thing only, sexual gratification, and it would have been very difficult to stop him from having what he not only wanted, but what he assumed was his right. Mamie, in her humility and shame, suspected that once she had allowed him to get to that stage of willful delirium, she had relinquished her ability, if not *her* right, to insist that he turn back.

It would have been impossible for Mamie to have behaved otherwise, but all through her journey, and in the taxi into Manhattan, as she worried if she'd have enough money to pay the talkative driver, and up in the slow elevator, and into the quiet safety of her own dusty bedroom, she was unable to forgive herself.

After taking another shower, she put on a record of Marlene Sai singing "Nanakuli." It was very like Mamie to find solace in the Hawaiian music.

She telephoned Alder in the country. He was very surprised that she had returned so soon and she said that Felix had decided to use only one model, after all. She did not tell him what had happened in the hotel room.

He hoped that she was not too disappointed. Oh, not at all, she said. She was drying her hair with a towel, as if doing many things at once—rubbing, talking, keeping time with her foot to the fast hula—would scramble her thoughts, like jamming an enemy's radio waves. He invited her to the farm. She was pleased to be asked. He'd be there in three hours.

"I'll take you to the Barnes," he said.

"I like cows."

"No, baby, not cows. Pictures. Pictures of cows."

"I like those, too," she said.

She made herself one of Claire's Morning Mai Tais, which

had more rum in it than juice. She played the Marlene Sai record again and sat back on the wine-stained sofa and listened to the lovely voice sing, "Oh, the Boston girls will love you for your money, singing Honolulu hula hula heigh, but the Honolulu girls will be your honey, Honolulu hula hula heigh."

FOURTEEN

The big farmhouse was built in 1740, and while it remained untouched in structure and line, it contained the distinctive mark of generations of Lee women. His grandmother had used it only a few times a year when she went there to hunt, early in her marriage. She always thought it too small and too American. She left behind a few good quilts and some pieces of country furniture and Philadelphia silver when her decorator, in 1932, introduced her to the ancien régime.

His mother, however, had made the place her own. She often came with her friends to search in the small towns nearby for antiques and to swim in the freezing river and to use a few drugs. She named her son after the round-leaved trees that grew along the river that ran through the farm.

Alder had never changed the rooms, or his name, and her belongings—sculptures of the Egyptian goddess, Isis, and Tiffany lamps and big batik pillows—filled the old house. There were even a few relics of the woman and the child who had come after her—a high chair in the pantry and a pair of pearl earrings in the drawer of a hall table. Alder came across his wife's earrings while looking for the keys to a shed. Mamie was embarrassed for a moment, afraid that he might regret these souvenirs.

"She didn't like it here," he said. "I think we only came a few weekends, at the end, when I thought the answer was to spend more time together. She found a snake on the tennis court and that was it." He smiled.

It was a house full of women, and even the housekeeper, Mrs. Bellows, amiable and competent, with her kitchen garden bordered by hollyhocks and pale delphiniums, glazed the house, like one of her famous doughnuts, with the sweetness of her temperament. Full of things left behind by other women, the house, thanks to Mrs. Bellows, was also full of their ghost-smells—Connecticut peonies in old red glass jars; oily black tea still shipped by Mrs. Lee's merchant in London; lavender sachets, made late each summer from flowers planted in 1952 by Alder's mother's college roommate, and tied each September to bed posts in the guest rooms; even the cooking smell of roast chicken, made from Mrs. Lee's grandmother's recipe. Alder was surrounded and protected by all of this. It was no wonder that he chose to live at the farm. What was interesting about Alder, despite his withdrawal from the world and his safe enclosure within the embrace of all these women, was that it did not deprive him of his own strong mark—to the contrary, it offset his individuality. The piles of books, the Weegee photographs, the Francis Bacon, the cigars, the pamphlets from the Department of Agriculture on grafting and duck raising—were his own.

Alder, who did not frequently invite people to the farm, having had enough of house parties when he lived with Teddy Shannon and his mother, was happy to have Mamie there.

She was astonished by the greenness. It was not just a color. She could hear it and smell it. It was a dense, buzzing leafiness, fragrant of lilac and river grasses. The garden was airless and still, except for the black gnats that swarmed at twilight. It was not like the gardens of her childhood whose charm came from the gay coming and going of gardeners in straw hats, and bare-legged boys carrying transplanted royal palms like rolled-up carpets. The garden in Pennsylvania did not smell like her colorful tropical gardens, either, with their thick, sweet smells of ginger and *plumeria*. In Alder's garden, listless with humidity, there were sassafras trees, once favored by Indians for their fragrant dugout canoes.

The gray fieldstones of the house, the oak trees, the cobbled stream, the cool stone roof of the icehouse had born witness to hundreds of years of greenness, and to silent Delaware braves and to young, tired Union soldiers and even, in the last half of the twentieth century, to Mrs. Shannon's nude scavenger hunts. The greenness held its peace.

When Mamie said vaguely that she did not think that she would be working any longer for Mr. Felix, Alder did not question her, but said instead that she should come with him to Paris. "Travel as longing for the past—you should be good at it, Mamie," he said, teasing her. He held her hand as they waded across a cold, clear brook. He was taking her to the small experimental hatchery where his manager was restocking a chalk stream with brown trout.

"What about Claire?" Mamie asked.

"Claire will have to take care of herself."

"I don't think she can."

"It is always very interesting when someone is left on his own—for years, my stepcousin begged her husband to have children. He refused, she finally left, and he married a woman with five daughters."

"I go to Paris, Claire becomes head of the UN?"

"Exactly."

"I don't think so," she said.

` ` `

Although there were many examples to the contrary in his own family, Alder would have said that a gentleman did not divorce his wife. He did say so, in fact, to Mamie, her first night there, as he sat in a Windsor chair in the bathroom upstairs and talked to her while she had a bath. Mrs. Bellows had made a pitcher of Rum Collins and they had cocktails while Mamie bathed.

Mamie, lying in the hot, soapy water, wondering if the Foaming Bath Petals were left behind by Baby, did not know whether this idea of how a gentleman behaved was honorable or pompous. She was confused. She wanted to ask him where it left her, or some other woman he might come to love, but they had never spoken of love and she would not allow herself to ask him. She had vowed, the second time they had gone to Mrs. Lee's, that she would not tell him that she loved him, and although there had been moments, especially when he was inside her, when she longed to admit it, she never broke down and confessed. That it was unnatural not to tell someone whom you loved that it was so was a refinement overwhelmed by the unfortunate suspicion that she had a better chance of holding onto him if he were a little unsure of her devotion. Gertrude would have approved of this subtlety, even if it were a technique that she herself had never used.

"I never expected," he said, "that it would happen this way, or that my daughter would be taken away from me. And taken from me in order to punish me. Of course, now that it has happened, it seems predictable and inevitable. The only mystery is how I didn't see it."

"I had a friend who told me when she was drunk that there was a terrible secret in her family. I tried for years to get it out of her, imagining all sorts of things. She finally broke down and admitted that her father had been married before."

"Harry Shannon, my uncle, your uncle, too, our stepuncle, left his first wife the morning of the honeymoon."

"I'm sorry," she said. She leaned forward to turn on the hot water and she held the soap bubbles modestly around her breasts.

"He was madly in love with her. He came downstairs the morning after the wedding, they were staying in Nantucket, and she was sitting naked on the toilet eating a big bowl of Rice Krispies. She greeted him happily and he was so appalled he went out the front door and took the first plane back to New York."

Mamie laughed. She didn't know if he was teasing her.

"I always thought it was a little harsh of him," he said.

He was looking out the old sash windows as the blue darkness fell slowly across his fields and woods. Ribbons of mist threaded through the horse chestnut trees, laden with white flowers like candles. "There is a vixen that sometimes sits in that meadow at nightfall," he said quietly, as if the shy fox might hear him. He watched for the fox, but she did not come.

"I'll leave you some time alone," he said. She had been given her own bedroom. "We'll meet at eight."

She rose in the bathtub, the water streaming from her, puffs of soap bubbles, like clouds, clinging to her body.

He was at the door. He turned back into the room and took a towel and began to dry her back and waist, and the tops of her legs. When he reached the backs of her knees, the end of the towel fell into the water, so he gave her his hand, the second time that day over water, and she stepped out of the tub.

"This is going to be very interesting," he said, not looking at her, intent on drying her shoulders and stomach.

"What?"

"This. From now on."

He sat her down in the chair and took one of her feet in the towel to dry it. He was very thorough, drying between the toes and rubbing the heel. He dried the other foot. It was only when he finished and had put the towel aside on the wood floor where he was kneeling, that he looked at her face. She was the color of a pink rose, and her skin was porous and faintly swollen from the heat and the moisture.

He slowly pulled her knees apart so that her thighs were against the sides of the chair. He opened her gently with his fingers and looked at her.

She tried to close her legs, but he took her knees in both his hands and held them against the chair. She tried again to conceal herself, but this time he pushed her legs open with sudden, even impatient, firmness and he bent over her and put his mouth on her.

She did not want to watch him, even though she knew that what he was doing to her and what he was giving her were the very things that she and Lily Shields used to wonder about when they studied their vaginas, each in a separate room.

The sensation that began in her clitoris, of frustration and tension and startling pleasure, spread quickly through her body. She could feel the blood moving through her arteries, away from her strong heart, straight to his mouth. She could feel the electricity gathering slowly in every eager nerve. She could feel the slide of liquid between her buttocks and she did not know if it had come from her or if it was his saliva.

She made herself watch him. He took her hips in his hands, her knees splayed now in slack submission, and he tilted her hips so that she was more exposed to him and more open. He moved her hips back and forth in the chair.

"Do this," he said. "Slowly."

"I don't know what to do," she whispered.

"I'll tell you. I'll show you." He moved her with his hands until she caught the motion and began to move herself. She closed her eyes, afraid to let him see her.

"Breathe," he said. "You aren't breathing."

She didn't answer, pressing herself against him as if she could not draw him deep enough inside of her. She put her hands on his head and held him to her.

Later, when he kissed her on the mouth, she could taste and smell herself on him, and to her surprise and delight, it tasted and smelled like the sea.

Mamie would not swim in the pond with him. It was not the opaque brown water; the ocean at Hanalei, after a storm, was no more limpid. Mamie needed running streams, a tidal change, and, despite the muddy rainwaters of lovely Hanalei Bay, she liked to be able to see the bottom.

"It is very like you," he said, floating on the pond. He was sorry that she would not come into the water. "The need for clarity. It will cause you to miss some things, Mamie. Such as this swim."

Mamie did not defend herself. As someone who had seen as a child that the consequences of one's actions could induce a terror and despair never implicit in the act itself, Mamie did desire clarity. While Alder, too, had the temperament of some-one who wants to diminish, as much as is practical, the pos-sibility of surprise, Mamie had gone far beyond that rather fundamental wish. Mamie knew there would be surprises; it was inevitable. What she hoped for, and it is why she sought clarity, was the relief in knowing that the surprise had not been occasioned by herself. Mamie, who embraced every kind of responsibility, real and contrived, may have been, in truth, avoiding responsibility by taking it on so eagerly, but she would never be accused of neglect or carelessness.

Of course, Alder was right, too. She would miss some things. She would have to fight in herself a certain rigidity and impatience. She would grow tired, sooner than others, from the unflagging concentration needed just to make out the bottom through the muddy water. Her watchfulness would exhaust her.

Ever since her adolescence, when she had so eagerly begun the long lesson of discovering what it was that she was going to be allowed to have, she had, in the trusting, concave way of her sex, accepted everything that she was given. Even the boys she picked were chosen with the idea of wanting to know what she would be allowed. If she was allowed kissing, what else was she allowed? Even if she was given only a little, it was better, at fifteen, than having nothing at all. It would only be when she was older, older even than she was now with Alder, that she would begin to understand that she had only two choices: if she could figure out what it was that she was permitted, she could take the risk and ask for it, or she could find safety and comfort, and even a kind of rigorous, intellectual pleasure, in having nothing at all.

What was so sweetly ironic was that the lack of clarity, so thankfully absent in most things, not only country ponds, was just what drew Mamie on, what lured her forward and kept her interested. The secrets of all things enticed her and ensnared her and saved her.

"Are there water snakes?"

"You sound like Baby."

"They don't have snakes in Hawai'i."

"So you've said."

"Many times?"

He nodded.

She took off her T-shirt. She took off her jeans. Although it was very hot, her pale body, in her brassiere and underpants, was pricked with goose pimples. She stepped into the pond. Her toes sank slowly into the cloudy layers of silt and came to rest at last on the slippery clay bottom. Alder watched her.

"This is because of Baby and the snake?"

She shook her head. "If Pal Kaleihao ever knew that I was afraid to go into a little mud hole—"

He swam to her, making his way through the clotted weeds. He stood up and took her hand and pulled her back up the muddy bank.

"Mamie, he won't know. I promise." He looked at her. "It's not all a test." He handed her her clothes.

"It isn't?"

"I don't think so. I can't be certain, but I don't think so."

"I know that I seem to refer everything back to my childhood, but may I tell you one more story? Then I won't ever say the words 'palm tree' again. I *know* it's tedious. Even Claire is bored and she had the same childhood. Perhaps that's why. I promise."

"Tell me, Mamie." He was laughing at her.

"There was a girl named Gwenda Tanaka at the local school. She was Japanese and she was particularly responsible and tidy and organized, the way Japanese girls are, and we elected her class treasurer. It was her job to collect the class dues, little sweaty piles of quarters and nickels, which were set aside for the dreaded Seventh Grade Picnic. Well, she lost the money one day, perhaps someone stole it, but it disappeared forever, and she never came back to school. They moved to another island." Mamie looked at him. "Everyone in Waimea thought it was very honorable."

Alder was amused, as much with Mamie's odd little story, as by her choosing to tell it. "Why have you told me this?"

"It can't have been that much money. Eight dollars maybe."

"Mamie, is this all about the pond?"

"I do think, in the end, that it's often a test." She laughed at herself. "They all thought Gwenda Tanaka did the right thing. But I never thought so. That's all." She smiled up at him. He was standing over her, holding on to the low bough of a flowering pear tree. The white petals, like torn tissue paper, dropped onto his wet head and bare feet.

"Are there snakes in the pond?" she asked, pulling on her jeans.

"Yes."

She put on her T-shirt.

"Did I pass?" he asked, watching her.

"That wasn't a test," she said in surprise. "I was afraid and I hate being afraid. Gwenda was afraid, not honorable. It is what I dread most."

He took her hand and they walked home through the fox's meadow.

It had been some time since Mamie had what she called in childhood "the white-bone fantasy." Perhaps it was that, her body having completed its metamorphosis, she no longer felt the disgust and fear she had suffered at twelve when startling patches of new leaves and bark began to appear on her body. That transformation, and the discovery of shame that had so interested her and Lily Shields that they held meetings just to discuss it, lost some of its immediacy the moment both girls discovered that boys rather liked the seedlings and nests on the girls' bodies, and while they had not turned these strange physical manifestations to account, the way Gertrude or Alysse might have done, they tried, at least, not to despise themselves. Their girl friends, too, had the same wild grasses growing under their arms and between their legs.

It was not until Mr. Felix ejaculated on her stomach that Mamie had cause to remember the old longing, that old seeking for purification. In her fairness, she admitted that Felix had not asked for that much. If her part had been to discover how much the world would allow her, Mr. Felix's part had been to see how much he could take. In his own way, he, too, had been passive.

Mamie was tired.

To be a castaway, sheared and stripped of the world; to teach, through the long, silent days, cats how to dance as the abandoned sailor, Mr. Selkirk, had done, was a way of starting fresh. She would be cleansed of the semen running down her hips, and cleansed of the city.

Her sister had exhausted her, too. Claire's determination to be gratified; her assumption that the world was lucky to be just like her ("Everyone I know is masochistic"); and her contempt for the ineffectual, the damaged, the frail had left Mamie encrusted in chalky secretions of plankton and calcified shell. Mamie did not know how to scrape herself clean except by casting herself away. Like Aphrodite in Cythera, another island girl, she would rise from the foam and start anew, as smooth and as white as a bone.

She was not so sure, however, just what she would do once she had stepped ashore. She knew that she would not work for Mr. Felix. The Crawfords would be returning soon from Florence. Claire did not have a job, and even had she seen the need for one, her idea of employment was to take the test for the Fire Department. Mamie did not want to live in other people's rooms, worried all the time that she had forgotten to rinse out the sink. She didn't know what she was going to do.

Mamie walked with Alder to the walled orchard. He was trying to grow miniature peaches against the warm, mossy bricks of the old walls. It was very like him to be growing a few dozen small, perfect fruits at great expense and care. He planned to eat the peaches himself.

"Why did Baby go away?" she asked, pinching a dried leaf from one of the delicate, espaliered branches. The trees reminded Mamie of the eighteenth-century prints that Lily's father brought from Japan. He had given her a print of a gray monkey in a cherry tree for her thirteenth birthday. The peaches were not yet ripe on their tiny stems.

"A friend of mine sent her some letters."

Mamie looked at him.

"A girl I was seeing sent her letters I had written to her." He spoke deliberately so as not to seem evasive.

"Alysse said Baby didn't mind about the girls."

"She didn't mind. She grew up with two of her father's natural children. I think that she was lonely. She comes from a big, chaotic family. Everything is a crisis—a death, a lost bracelet, a missing section of the newspaper—it's all the same. She thought I was interesting because I didn't mind when the maid forgot to warm the maple syrup."

Mamie smiled. She watched him bind a pale, wavering shoot to a trellis. She looked at his hands and the clean black dirt beneath his nails and the slender turn of his bare wrists.

"I once saw her father stuff an overcooked pork roast down the front of the cook's apron. No one, including the cook, seemed to think he behaved unreasonably. Later, when she was pissed off and bored, she used to tell me what her brother would have done had, oh, the doorman forgotten to put *his* tennis rackets in the station wagon."

"What would her brother have done?"

"Killed the doorman, I'm afraid."

She helped him pull the fragile weeds from the curly white alyssum.

"What is so hypnotizing about love," he said suddenly, absentmindedly putting the weeds in his pocket, "is that you are given a reflection of yourself in the eyes of the beloved. You love the self that is imagined by the other, and you are encouraged to do so. It's as if you are given another chance, to become your best self, your loved self. It's like a mirror."

"Baby was your mirror?" She was hurt by his explanation of the irresistible narcissism of love, as if she were forever excluded from his experience by having met him too late. She was jealous.

"Baby? I don't think so."

She patted the black earth around the roots of a climbing purple clematis. The flowers with their spiked yellow centers were like the *liliko'i* on the grove veranda at Waimea. There was the steady praise of bees, flattering the peaches, teasing the clematis. Mamie watched the bees, soothed and warmed by their sunny hum.

She wondered about him. In his solitude, he was not unlike her mother. Although it was not difficult for her to imagine him when he was younger and more in the world, it was difficult to think of him now, on the farm, with his trout fry and tiny fruit, in his still green woods. He lived like an old man. Mamie could see why Baby had fled back to the conviviality of Palm Beach.

To apologize for Baby, as well as for herself, she said, "You didn't stand beneath the swaying cane, humming sambas. It was the saddest thing, the longing to be gone and the grief at leaving behind something so loved."

"No," he said. "I never have. I am just beginning to feel, after all this time, that this is where I live—not where I belong necessarily, but where I live. That's probably why I've never changed the house. I hate that fucking furniture from the sixties, don't you? Why don't we get rid of it? We can go back and throw it all out. The Indian bedspreads. And the stained glass."

Mamie laughed. He was excited.

"I thought we should be putting up jam or something. As Lily Shields would say, 'Too, too Rousseau.' "

"Perhaps we should go away," he said. He had already forgotten about the Indian bedspreads. He went to turn on the water.

Mamie went back to the hot, fretting city with a hamper of lilacs, eight jars of Mrs. Bellows's apple butter, and Alder. She hadn't expected him to return with her. The country, too, was frayed with humidity, but there was relief to be had there in the brown pond, or stretched out on old Mrs. Lee's double wedding ring quilt with a fan and a block of ice in the open window.

To Mamie's surprise, the apartment was very clean. Too clean, really, and there was a strong odor of Pine Sol. Claire was not there. The sitting room was just the way the unsuspecting Crawfords had left it, except for the burned rug and the broken kite and the sofa, which looked as if someone had been murdered on it. And, of course, the handcuffs that Alder idly picked up from the top of the piano.

"These yours, baby?" He was trying to figure out how to unlock them.

Mamie was in the kitchen.

"That's baby with a small *b?*" She came into the sitting room with two Mai Tais. Claire now kept the drinks in glasses in the refrigerator, so that no time would be lost with the blender or cutting pineapples and oranges.

He held up the handcuffs, still fiddling intently with the lock.

"They must be my sister's." She blushed.

She knew that while Alder was not averse to the endless physical manifestations of love, he had a rather formal view of sexuality, including his own infidelity. He'd told Mamie that it had always been rather difficult to cheat on his wife when they were in the same city. Mamie had laughed at him. It was not unlike his opinion that men did not divorce their wives. He thought, in both instances, that he was being cavalier. Mamie thought he was being dishonest. Nonetheless, she did not think that Alder was ready, at this point in their romance, to come up against her sister's philosophy of the free spirit. Alder, she suspected, would not readily accept Claire's notion that it did not matter what you did, so long as it didn't hurt anyone. It was a little too simple for him. Besides, he tended to enjoy the possibilities of risk.

Mamie herself had only just begun to understand what it was that was false in Claire's philosophy. The assumption that there would be no harm done was reckless, especially as Claire was attracted to men who spent their time taking photographs of the erect penises of animals. That Claire seemed to have more fun than Mamie, a truth that had bothered Mamie, did not trouble her as much as it once had done, and after meeting Alder, she had not worried about it at all. She was happy that they were alone in the apartment.

He tossed the handcuffs to her and went into the kitchen to look in the refrigerator. He stood there like a teenager, bent at the waist, not bothering with anything that was wrapped in aluminum foil or stored in a plastic box.

"Everything in here is from a fucking island. Coconut milk, very practical; pickled kim shee? kim chee? looks disgusting; pineapples, of course; cold rice; oh, good, just what I wanted, dried squid . . ."

"Don't open it!" she yelled, running into the kitchen. She grabbed the package from him.

"Gertrude sends it to me. It smells bad."

"What smells bad?" a voice said behind them.

They turned around, startled.

It was Claire.

Her eyes were so dilated they had lost their color. Her lips were white and split with tiny cracks that she kept licking. She took Mamie's Mai Tai from her and drank it down.

"Hi, Alder," she said. Mamie noticed red welts around Claire's wrists.

They followed Claire into the living room. Alder sat on the piano bench and watched Claire curiously as she ran her fingers, over and over again, through her hair. She jumped up to put on a Fred Astaire record.

"Mamie, I hate to worry you about these things, but I have a date with Sean tonight and I just turned over all the money you loaned me to a man sleeping in a tunnel in the park . . ."

Alder put his hand in his pocket.

Mamie said, "Here, here it is," and she quickly gave her sister the loose dollars that were in her handbag. She didn't want Alder to give Claire money and she minded that Claire had asked for it in front of him.

"Are you coming to Mamie's birthday?" Claire asked him. "I've found this, well, really Brooke found it, great nightclub that Mamie will love. I can't tell you the name because I want to surprise her."

The bright, romantic music—"Every night at seven, you walk in as fresh as clover and I begin to sigh all over again" —was making Mamie brittle with irritability.

Claire shouted, "I WANT TO SURPRISE HER!" because Alder had been unable to hear her.

Claire was not herself. Mamie realized that Alder had seen it immediately. Claire let the last drops of Mamie's Mai Tai roll into her mouth. She went into the kitchen.

"We're running low," she called. "I told you, Mamie, if you drink them, make new ones to replace them!"

She came back with a drink for herself and one for Mamie. "Why don't you guys come tonight? You'd really like Sean. He's incredibly unpretentious. You'd like him just for that, Mamie. I said someone was neurasthenic this morning and he got really mad and said, 'Don't ever use big words around me again.' "

"Neurasthenic?"

"He's the opposite of Alysse and her friends and even Mother's friends at home with their depressed good manners. God!" She pushed her fingers exultantly along her scalp. "He asked me one night in a Mexican restaurant what the green stuff was called." She laughed. "You know what I was thinking, Mamie, because we got a package from Gertrude with *see-moi* and *limu* and some mountain apple bark, just in case, you know, we need it—that Gertrude is like a Garden Isle version of Alysse. Not as mean and not as selfish, of course, but just as practical . . ." She lost interest in her own thought.

"I think I've figured something else out, too," Mamie said angrily, "if you're interested in hearing. Alysse and Apollonia and Bones Washburn and all of those women have become men. Maybe it was their only chance, the only way they could survive, but it's what they've become. Worse, they've become *their* version of men. The men they know and despise."

She turned off the music. She felt as if she were about to burst with bad temper. She wanted Alder to say something, but at the same time she was grateful for his tolerant silence. He turned around on the piano bench so that he was facing the keys. He played the first sixteen bars of "Satin Doll."

"Just like Duke Ellington," Claire said, leaping up and clapping her hands.

"I had Mr. de Beaupré teach me this one song. When I was at Harvard, I would reluctantly sit at the piano to play it, then refuse to continue out of modesty and shyness. Everyone thought I was this brilliant jazz pianist. Which, of course, I wasn't."

"How great," Claire said flirtatiously.

"Not great," Mamie said.

Mamie was suddenly tired of both of them. Alder closed the piano and stood up, his hands in his pockets. There was no air-conditioning and the small room smelled of black rum and pine disinfectant and lilac.

"I think I'll have a shower," Claire said brightly, her swollen face twitching and winking. Mamie looked at her, and her anger flooded from her in a long, silent draining and she wanted only to go to Claire to take her bruised, trembling body in her safe embrace to comfort her and calm her.

As Claire stooped to gather her sunglasses and her shoes, she farted loudly.

She stood up quickly. "Oh," she said. "I'm sorry, but I just got fucked in the ass." She gave them a satisfied, insolent smile and went to her room.

Mamie stood very still in the center of the room.

Alder said, "Perhaps I should go."

She wanted him to go. She wanted him to stay. It didn't matter if he stayed. She knew very well that if she followed

Claire to her bedroom, Claire would only say, "What would you prefer? Anus?" and laugh at her.

"Perhaps you should," she said.

"When is your birthday?"

"Oh, soon. A few days."

"Maybe we should go away," he said again. "I have a little house in Positano."

"Maybe."

"I'll be at my grandmother's tonight." He kissed her on the cheek and she let him out. She stood in the hall, waiting until she heard the tin hum of the water in the shower, before she let herself breathe again.

He came back that evening. Claire had hurried out in a rush, unable really to talk to Mamie, she was going to be so late in meeting Sean. She did pause long enough, however, to ask Mamie for more money, and then she was gone.

Mamie, when the doorman called up, was in the unfortunate position of having handcuffed herself to a copy of a Mackintosh chair, out of curiosity, so she had to drag herself and the tall chair to the intercom, and in her nervousness at hearing that Alder was on his way upstairs, she was unable to work the little key in the lock. She opened the door still handcuffed to the chair.

"I'm so glad I came back," he said, looking at the handcuffs. He kissed her, aroused. "You sure you want to take them off?"

"I think so," she said into his chest.

"Do you mind if I keep them?"

She smiled, despite herself, and he opened the lock on the handcuffs and released her. He put the handcuffs in his pocket and they went, very happy, to the movies.

⌄⌄⌄

The Japanese pagoda trees were blooming on West Sixty-seventh Street and Mamie took in their strange, voluptuary scent, as it made its way through the tremendous reflected heat of the city, up the streaming walls of the building, and rolled through the window. She was waiting for Claire. She had tried to read the Anthony Powell book that Alder had given her, but she had read the same paragraph eight times and had finally put the book aside.

Claire had not come home the night before. Mamie, despite Alder's suggestion that they go away, knew that she and Claire were in trouble. They had no work and, in a few weeks, they would have no place to live. That Mamie would be able to find work that would be interesting to her was a hope she had abandoned. With all of her diligence and imagination, she might be back selling bedroom slippers. She would try, at the very least, to work in a bookstore.

But Claire, that tireless and inventive tormentor, what was to become of her? Perhaps we should go home, Mamie thought. At least, there are boundaries there—the Pacific Ocean, for example—and the chances of Claire harming herself might be less. Or of dying. Claire is trying to die.

With her need to be comforted and her resolve not to be comforted, Claire may have already been beyond the reach of Mamie's care, beyond the encircling, protective arms that had taken her in so many years before, but Mamie, feeling fierce and determined, was not yet ready to abandon her.

Claire came in noisily. Her face was less swollen, and the lovely flower-color had faded from her bruise. She was happy to see Mamie, and Mamie realized that Claire did not regret her behavior of the day before. It had not even occurred to her that she might have embarrassed Mamie in front of Alder.

"I have a present for you." She handed her a book of the paintings of Watteau. Perhaps she is sorry, thought Mamie, and then she felt ashamed because she suspected that Claire might have stolen the beautiful book. She looked at Claire.

"Where did you get it?"

"I didn't steal it, if that's what you mean. Brooke has this friend who owns an art gallery downtown and he gave it to me." She sat down. "He sells bad paintings and good drugs to rich people."

Mamie didn't know if she was telling the truth but she decided, with both resignation and relief, that it was of little importance how Claire came to have the book.

"Did I tell you I quit the lifesaving class? He kept bandaging my tits. I think it was love."

"Yes, you told me."

Claire was exhausted and restless at the same time. "Brooke is auditioning for a soca band from Trinidad today."

"What about you?"

"Me?" She sounded surprised.

"You have to work. *I* have to work."

"Oh. That. The guy who has the gallery said he might need an assistant, well, a receptionist really, someone to answer the phones, I guess . . ." She was distracted. "I thought you liked Watteau. Courtly love and all that . . ." She lay her head back on the chair and stared at the ceiling. "Are you going to Sicily or wherever it is he wants to go?"

"No."

"Why not?"

Mamie heard in Claire's tone that she didn't much care whether Mamie went away or not.

"Because I don't want to leave you, for one thing."

"Oh, please," said Claire. She jumped up, knocking the

heavy Watteau book off the arm of the chair as she went to put on a record.

It was Frank Sinatra, and when he sang "Violets for Your Furs," the music instantly filled Mamie with longing for a different kind of New York. It was the New York she had seen, over and over again, in faded prints of Suzy Parker movies at the mill theater. She had seen *The Best of Everything* five Saturday mornings in a row.

"Don't use me as an excuse," Claire said.

It was so cruel of her, so gratuitous, that it was as if she had hit Mamie in the face. It was another example, a bitter one, of Mamie's lovely notion that memory was so individualistic as to make it unreliable.

"You mean, then," Mamie said slowly, "that it's all been for nothing?"

"Oh, Christ, should we make up a bill? Twenty dollars for gym shoes in tenth grade; Mamie writes Claire's book reports, another twenty; abortion, seven hundred." She sat heavily in the chair, as if her calculations had exasperated and tired her.

"I never thought of it like that."

Claire looked at her lazily. "Gosh, Mamie, this isn't like you."

"You're in trouble," Mamie said quietly. The violence of her feelings had caused her to calm herself. "You've been in trouble for some time. Can't you see it, Claire? Who is this asshole who's never seen guacamole? And Brooke, who could be more pathetic? What do you think you're doing? This absurd health-food idea that none of it matters as long as you stay stoned and happy—just who says you aren't hurt? What would you look like if he hurt you?"

"You still don't get it, do you? It's my choice. Mine. I love him."

"Oh, fuck!" Mamie yelled. "Fuck that! It's not that simple. Where did you even learn this shit, anyway? You're like some moronic hold-out from the seventies. Your choice? Is masochism a choice? Selfishness? Get out! Get out of here!" Mamie stood up. She was shaking.

Claire looked at her calmly.

"Get a grip, Mamie. I'll pay you back, if that's what's bothering you." She stretched with her arms over her head.

Mamie only knew that it was impossible for her to remain in the same room with Claire, breathing the same mean, metallic air, with Sinatra's sexuality and "I've Got You Under My Skin" careening all around her.

Claire watched her defiantly, slouched lazily in her chair.

Mamie left the apartment. Claire lay down to have a little nap.

Mamie went into the Park. The sky was white and heavy and her anger gave her a determined liveliness. A woman with two children coming toward her on the path stepped nervously out of her way. Mamie did not even see them.

Although she had a deep sense of the insult done her, as well as the danger in which Claire stood, she did not think that Claire was stained with vice. It wasn't about sex. Mamie didn't mind who made love to Claire, or where, in the ass, in the mouth, but she was frightened by the willful desecration that Claire so boldly revealed. Mamie could not bear that Claire had relinquished herself. She had meant to tell her that.

She sat on the greasy grass. The tentative but hopeful answers she had tried to make for all those years seemed worthless to her, and her secret attempts to make sense of her answers seemed meaningless, and even a little embarrassing.

That she could not protect Claire, that she would not be

allowed to do so by Claire herself, even were she willing to devote her life to it, was a discovery that Mamie would have had to make some day. It came a little sooner than she might have wished. It made her feel foolish. Perhaps Claire will be famous and I'll be the nun, she thought. It would be better.

She used the pay phone outside the Delacorte Theater to call Toni. A man in a black leather jacket was using one of the other telephones and he turned to face her when he heard her pick up the receiver and he smiled and stared at her, even though he was speaking to someone. She turned away from him.

Toni said, "I've been trying to reach you for two weeks."

"I was in the country," Mamie said.

"Felix said you walked out on him."

"No," Mamie said. She sighed. "Not quite."

"He said you wanted him to marry you and when he refused, well, as he put it, you left him holding the shit. Actually, he said 'sheet.' "

"I wanted to marry him?" Mamie said loudly. She remembered the man next to her, using the other telephone, and she blushed.

"I know he's a liar, Mamie," Toni said calmly.

"I think you tried to tell me. The night Claire and I came to dinner."

"Did I?"

"Well, I wasn't difficult. I left, but I wasn't particularly difficult."

Toni did not say anything.

"But I'm trying to learn," Mamie said. "My sister is having a birthday party for me in a bar she's discovered. Will you come? And Jean?"

"I don't know," Toni said. "I'll let you know."

"I'll be twenty-one," Mamie said.

They said good-bye. The man on the telephone alongside had disappeared. Mamie slowly walked home, without her fury, without her liveliness, under the pale northern sky.

In the days that followed, Claire and Mamie found ways to avoid each other in the small apartment. Claire was going to Atlantic City for two days with Sean and Brooke. Brooke had decided to become a performance artist and she was hoping to do her first concept on the boardwalk in front of the casinos. Wearing a shower cap and a wet suit loaned to her by Claire (Mary had mailed it to her), she would drench herself with water from a large zinc bucket. She said it was symbolic of the artistic drought in the city.

Mamie stopped Claire in the hall as she left to meet Sean and Brooke in the lobby downstairs. They did not come to the apartment when Mamie was there. Mamie held Claire in the open doorway.

"I love you," she said. "You're an island girl, remember."

Claire laughed and patted Mamie gently on the face and said, "You don't understand. I'm all right. You always exaggerate, Mamie. Such a sensitivo." She wiggled her way past Mamie and rushed to catch the elevator.

Mamie went to her little room. The room was lighted only by a small bronze desk lamp, and with the hanging tapestries and the paisleys and the steel bed, Mamie, as she lay on the bed, clothed and sleepless, might have been a general waiting in her tent for the battle at dawn, and in a way, she was waiting.

She tried to collect herself. Haunted, she thought. I have been haunted for so long. How strange it was for her to feel the natural lightness of the ghost, to remain suspended ever so tantalizingly over the lovely earth, and to feel the constant longing to fling herself onto its comforting, maternal surface. But she had reached out for the world's solace long enough to know that it was not to be had simply for the yearning.

FIFTEEN

It was the night of Mamie's birthday. Claire had arranged everything and even managed, despite her tendency to tell, ("Secrets are for telling, that's why they're called secrets"), to keep the details of the party from Mamie. Alder would meet them at the nightclub. Toni and Brooke were going to be there, but not Alysse, who had bought a table at a benefit to raise money to restore opera costumes damaged by warehouse rats. Sean was not able to come, as he was in the South, taking a series of nude portraits of Cubans in deportation camps. Claire was relieved that he would not be at the party. He had accused her of purposefully keeping him away from Mamie and perhaps she had kept him away, but it was not for the reason he suspected, that she was ashamed of him, but because Claire did not want Sean to like Mamie better than herself. She was convinced that, given the choice, anyone would always choose Mamie. She could make a list, beginning with McCully.

The party was at the Aloha Kai, a bar on Tenth Avenue at Fifty-third Street. Claire was proud to have found the club and she was very pleased to see her sister's surprise when Mamie found herself submerged in bright turquoise light, under dusty fishing nets and giant clam shells—the Aloha Kai's attempt to reproduce the effect of being underwater. A big balsa-wood Polynesian god, a tiki, stood behind the bar. The waitresses wore sarongs and plastic flowers.

Toni had waited on the street for them. They were late because Claire had forgotten Mamie's present in the apartment and had insisted on going back for it.

"So this is what Hawai'i is like," Toni said to Mamie as Claire chose a table. They sat in front of the raised stage. There was a row of drums on the stage.

Claire ordered Mai Tais for all of them, but Toni stopped the Puerto Rican waitress as she passed behind her and changed her order to a vodka. There was music, the soundtrack of the Elvis Presley movie *Blue Hawaii*. Claire shouted that she had only ordered pupus for them—egg rolls and chicken wings and fried wonton.

Mamie kept looking toward the door to see if Alder had arrived. Claire and Brooke ordered more drinks. There were rubber orchids in the rum drinks and Brooke lined them up in a row on the sticky tabletop. There were fat ceramic tikis on the table for salt and pepper, and dirty cruets of soy sauce.

Toni leaned forward and asked Mamie, "What are you going to do?"

Mamie, who was not sure of her meaning, hesitated.

"Felix asked me to tell you he would be very happy to have you back. He is doing the winter collection." Toni shrugged and smiled. "So I have told you."

Mamie shook her head. The loudness of the music forced them to exaggerate their pronunciation and their gestures. Mamie, who was astonished by the Aloha Kai, had worried at first that Toni, with her dirty nails and her fastidiousness, would be bored, but of all the women at the birthday table, she was the most at ease. There were not many customers in the bar, although it was almost eleven o'clock. Claire promised that it grew very crowded after midnight.

A black man and two white men ambled nonchalantly to the bandstand from different corners of the room. Mamie had noticed the black man sitting at the bar when he had turned on his stool to look at them when they came into the club. One of the white men, a thin man with long arms, said lazily, "Good evening, ladies, how you doin'?" as he moved around their table to step up onto the platform. Even in the white light of the stage, he had the gray skin of a night worker. His face was the color of papier-mâché.

The black man played the marimba. The thin man was on the congas. The last musician, an older, effeminate man with a hairpiece, was the vocalist. While their repertoire could not be called Hawaiian, even if Mamie's strict standards were relaxed, they did limit their selections to songs about islands. They played "Yellow Bird" and "Jamaica Farewell" and "Little Brown Gal." Claire wanted Mamie to dance the hula to "Little Brown Gal," but Mamie refused. She was still looking over her shoulder every few minutes, hoping that Alder would be there every time she turned to look for him in the darkness. It was not like him to be late.

The man playing the congas seemed to have taken an interest in their table. Claire smiled up at him. Brooke yelled out a request, "Light My Fire," and the man nodded and held up his fist in a power salute. Toni sat quietly, sipping her vodka. When the band listlessly finished the short set, the black man hopped stiffly from the platform and went back to the bar at the front, and the drummer brushed past the table and said, "Can I buy you ladies a drink?"

Mamie shook her head and Claire smiled and said, "I'm afraid this is girls' night. It's my sister's birthday." She shrugged apologetically.

"Well, many happys," he said slowly. Although he spoke with a lazy deliberateness, his eyes were tense and unsteady. He looked down at Toni, who smiled up at him, a little cynically, but not rudely; just enough to let him know that while it was nothing personal, it was just not working on her. He shrewdly let his gaze jump over to Brooke, who handed him one of the orchids. She was already a little drunk. Mamie thought for a minute, when he turned aside, that he was going to pick up an empty chair and sit down, but he was only looking for someone in the watery blue light. He took the orchid and walked into the darkness outside the glare of the spotlights.

Toni said goodnight. She gave Mamie a little box wrapped in tissue paper. Mamie stood up and they kissed on the cheek. "Happy Birthday," she said. She shook hands with Brooke and Claire. Mamie watched her make her way calmly past the men now standing at the bar, and the women sitting cross-legged on the high bar stools, blue cigarette smoke hanging over them. Claire was right, the bar did become crowded.

"We'll be right back," Claire said to Mamie. "I wonder what happened to Alder?"

As she stood up, Brooke knocked over the card listing the special drinks and cover charge. Claire and Brooke went toward the back of the club, where a black corridor led to the toilets.

Mamie opened the present from Toni, holding it under the table. Don Ho was singing "I Will Return." His voice, slurred with false sexuality, reminded Mamie of stewardesses and the smell of Coppertone.

Toni had given her one of her ivory bracelets. Mamie had seen her wearing it. It was the color of wood, stained with betel oil by the African woman who had once worn it. The inside of the bracelet was almost black with the old color of the oil. Mamie pushed it on, over her knuckles, and held out her arm to look at it. It will be my good-luck amulet, she thought.

She waited for Claire and Brooke. She finished her drink. It was not as good as the Mai Tais that Claire made, but then Claire used fresh fruit and sugar syrup that she boiled down herself.

The band did not return to play, although Mamie saw the marimba player sitting at the end of the bar. He was laughing with a man in a nylon windbreaker who looked like an undercover policeman. The black man seemed to know everyone at the bar.

Mamie went to the bathroom. Claire and Brooke were not there. She walked down the corridor to a little office. A man in a baseball cap sitting behind a cheap wooden desk looked up quickly when she appeared in the open doorway. He slowly opened the top drawer of the desk so that it pressed into his big stomach. He laid his hands, fingers outspread, on top of the receipts he had been checking.

Mamie walked back to the front. She stopped one of the waitresses to ask her if she had seen the two girls, and the woman shrugged and pointed overhead. "I seen two go up with Vinnie," she said without interest.

"Vinnie?"

"Yeah, he's got a room upstairs." She pointed to a back staircase. "But they all use it, those guys."

Mamie went up the dirty stairway. There was a strong smell of marijuana. At the top of the stairs was a landing and three doors. One of the doors was open to a messy storeroom with cartons of canned maraschino cherries and toilet paper stacked against the walls and blacked-out windows. Behind the next door, Mamie heard music and a girl's laughter.

She knocked on the door. There was no answer. She knocked again, harder, and this time, before she had taken away her hand, the door was pulled opened and Vinnie said, "C'mon in."

He was the man who played the congas. She could not see around him into the brightly lighted room. As if to prove he had nothing to hide, he stepped aside, and with a big smile, gestured to her to come inside.

It was a small room with a red Formica and chrome dining table and two matching chairs and a sofa bed and a leatherette reclining chair. One wall was mirrored, and glass shelves held dusty brandy glasses and some empty miniature liquor bottles and a bottle of Kahlúa. There was a stereo with big, professional speakers. Vinnie was playing Van Morrison. Brooke was in the recliner, her legs stretched out in front of her on the hinged footrest. She was speaking to her, Mamie thought, until Mamie realized that Brooke was talking pleasantly to herself.

Claire was on the sofa, in the corner. She was barefoot. Her head lay back against the water-stained wall, and her eyes, big and flat, stared at the shaded light that swung on its cord over the table.

Vinnie closed the door behind Mamie. He rolled down his sleeves.

"We were just talking about you," he said familiarly, "wondering if you might want to join us. You really from Maui?" He jerked his head forward on his neck rhythmically.

Mamie looked over at Brooke, slipping into unconsciousness. She was struggling against the drowsiness, not out of any interest in the party, but instinctively fighting it as she blinked and rattled her head. There was a syringe on the folding television tray table next to her.

"What can I do you for?" Vinnie asked sarcastically.

"I think I'll be taking my sister downstairs now," she said cautiously. "They're bringing the birthday cake now."

"Is that so?" He laughed at her.

Mamie went to Claire. She bent over to pull her onto her feet, but Claire was leaden and heavy. She did not see Mamie, although she looked at her.

"She don't want anymore sweets," Vinnie said, taking Mamie by the arm. She took his hand from her arm.

"I'm going downstairs to get someone."

With a sigh, Vinnie poured himself a shot from an open bottle of Wild Turkey that was on the Formica table and drank it with an exaggerated growl of pleasure.

Brooke had lost consciousness.

Claire lifted her cumbersome head and stared at Mamie.

Vinnie lazily stretched out one of his long arms and squeezed Mamie's breast. He did not let go, smiling at her, daring her to object as he squeezed harder and harder.

She pulled away from him and ran to the door.

With a sigh of great weariness, he came up behind her just as she opened the door. He slammed the door shut with his open palm and gently turned her around by her shoulders and slapped her across the face.

"Now quiet down, cunt, or I'll get bossy."

Jerking Mamie after him by the wrist, Toni's ivory bracelet caught under his thin fingers, he sat down and pulled her onto his lap. He held her wrist tightly and took her other hand and pressed it down on his penis. He was already hard and when Mamie tried to free her hand from his grasp, he effortlessly turned her over onto the floor and, yanking up her dress, straddled her from above. His one hand pressed around her throat. His knees held her tightly, as he unzipped his trousers and shoved himself into her mouth.

Mamie was afraid that he would kill her, and Claire and Brooke. She knew that she must do what he wanted until she was able to kill him herself. She knew that they would not hear her downstairs if she screamed.

Her instinct to survive was so strong that she was able to keep her loathing, and even her terror, from overcoming her. Her brain raced as if she, too, had been shot up, but with some electrifying, generous chemical, not the stupefying narcotic that was flooding the blood of Brooke and her sister.

While Vinnie rocked back and forth inside Mamie's mouth, he reached up and took from the table one of the ceramic tikis from the Aloha Kai. Pulling himself from her mouth, he swung his leg over her so that he was turned away from her, sitting on her. Without removing her panties, he ripped them open at the leg and shoved the tiki inside of her.

Sobbing with the effort, Mamie struggled to sit up and push him off her chest.

He spun around angrily and jerked her head back and again pushed his penis into her bruised mouth. She tried to hold her lips closed, but his hand, encircling her neck, quickly tightened around her throat when she refused him. She opened her mouth.

Claire watched them.

Mamie's mind began to wander as she protected herself, shielding herself from her own sight. The words to an old chant, a body-slapping dance, came to her and she repeated the words over and over as other words formed and clotted behind her burning eyes. Claire has lost her shoes, who will pay the bill downstairs? "*A'e pahu i ka moku, ua ho'ohiolo ka 'aha:* push out to the ship, whose sails have been let down; behind stand the Sacred Images that fill me with terror, I yearn to flee to the ship, the tall-masted ship of the white man . . ." This is my fault, she thought, this is my penance for the time I rode my bike too slowly past the boys in the workers' camp, and walked too slowly past the construction workers on Fifty-fifth Street, and because I wasn't smart enough to understand about the hotel room in Chicago. I thought I'd be allowed to sleep alone, peacefully, in the yellow silk room. It is because I was not able to stop Sherry Alden from presenting me with her first menstrual blood, and it is because I kissed Cecil Furtado in the vegetable garden, rubbing against the rough, fragrant tomato leaves, driving him to such desire that he would shove my chafed and surprised face (yes, surprised, I promise) into his jeans, Cecil smelling like cheese and motor oil, *"e ku i ka hoe 'uli:* I stop the boat with the steering paddle, and press it against the side of the boat, I make fast the rope to the coral, and circle my rope around and round. Yes, you're someone now. Yes, you're someone now." Because of dear, beloved Hiroshi, whose cracked, sweetly soiled fingers rested on my pale, plump vagina for a few bewildering moments. It is for my McCully, most of all, my McCully, and because, really, as Hiroshi understood, I am a woman and I deserve no better. I forgive you, Hiroshi, and I forgive you, McCully. Yes, you're someone now.

It was an hour before the drugs began to work on the man, but eventually, like Brooke and Claire, he, too, began to show signs of stupefaction. He slumped on top of Mamie, his chest on her crushed face, his legs still grasping her in their boney embrace.

She opened her eyes. It was difficult for her to breathe. The smell of the damp shag carpet, the smell of dirt and piss, and the acrid, oily smell of the man on top of her made her gag.

She waited a long time to make sure that he was not just asleep. Her vagina burned sharply and she shook with fear and rage. She could see through the one small window that the sun had risen. To her surprise, she heard a bird outside.

She slowly slid herself out from under him, realizing as she did so that she need not fear his awakening. His head fell heavily onto the floor as she pulled away from him. She sat up. She could see the thick legs of the yellow tiki emerging from her vagina. She pulled it out slowly. She was bleeding.

Claire stirred uncomfortably, eyes finally, mercifully, closed. Mamie shook her awake. Claire wanted to speak, but Mamie quickly put her hand over her mouth. Claire tried to push aside Mamie's trembling hand, but then she saw the blood on Mamie's dress and the man sprawled on the floor, his mustard yellow trousers around his thin, white ankles and for once, for once, she succumbed to Mamie. Mamie held her finger to her own swollen lips, signifying silence.

Brooke, in deep, drugged sleep, could not be fully wakened, so Mamie took her by one flapping arm and Claire took the other, and they carried her suspended between them to the door and into the hallway and down the stairway.

They had to stop halfway down the stairs for Claire to vomit, noisily, but there was no one in the back corridor or the bar downstairs and no one to stop them from pulling open the heavy brass-studded door and falling out into the clear early light of Tenth Avenue.

The moment they were outside, Mamie let go of Brooke, and Claire had to struggle to keep Brooke from falling to the ground. Mamie sat on the curb and put her head on her knees. She was shaking.

"What happened to Toni?" Brooke asked, squinting and rubbing her eyes like a sleepy child. Mamie lifted her head to look at her. She lay her head back on her knees.

"What are you doing, Mamie? Are you all right?" Claire

was barefoot. She felt in her pockets. "I forgot to give you your present and now I can't find it."

Mamie, at the curb, looked up at them again. Her jaw ached and the membrane inside her mouth was ripped where she had bitten herself. She could taste her own blood and worst of all, most sickening of all, she imagined that she could taste the semen.

"I'm hungry," said Brooke, looking around. She did not know where she was.

Mamie stood up slowly and deliberately and calmly smoothed down her ruined dress and pushed back her damp, matted hair. Then she began to walk uptown, not looking back, not wanting to see them, dangerous, dangerous babes in the woods. She would not take care of Claire any longer.

"Mamie! Mamie, wait!" she heard Claire call, but she did not turn back, and she did not wait.

Mamie walked to Mrs. Lee's house. There was no answer at the front door, but she was patient, knowing now that the house was not as deserted as it appeared to be. Mr. de Beaupré opened the door. He showed no surprise at seeing her, even in her torn dress, and he led her without question into the back garden. He was having breakfast under the magnolia tree. The table was set with a lace cloth. There was a German silver coffee pot and thin toast, its crusts trimmed, in a silver rack wrapped in an ivory damask cloth, and a bowl of peaches lying in their dark green leaves. Mamie noticed different jams and marmalades in small turquoise blue Sèvres pots. The little spoons and knives were of mother-of-pearl and vermeil.

He asked her if she would like something. She said no, thank you. He was not disappointed. He ate slowly and meticulously. There was a boiled brown egg in a gold cup. He whacked it deftly, lightly, and removed its little cracked skull.

He did not notice when she went back inside the house. She crept to the bedroom on the third floor. She had imagined as she walked across the city that the only thing she wanted was to clean herself. Now that she was in the room with its clean beds in their crisp piqué covers, she only wanted to lie down. She did not feel that she could go so far as to get under the covers, her despoiled, filthy body soiling Mrs. Lee's linen sheets. The body that used to be her body was thankful to rest. She had been foolish to think that she had ever earned it back. She had assumed too much.

Mr. de Beaupré came in with a tray of coffee and milk. He set the tray down on the other bed and poured the coffee and held it out to her. His quivering hand made the cup jump noisily in its saucer, and coffee spilled into the dish.

"She never cared much for her own people. Take young Miss Laura, she had no interest in her whatsoever. I saw the girl try with her mother, the way children do, but it didn't matter. You know, sometimes it is the fault of the man and the woman. They are so taken up with each other, they don't have no time for the children, you see what I mean? But this does not apply here. She says it was because she was so crazy for me, but the fact is, she just didn't like her children." He laughed and rubbed his knees. He was wearing a navy blue jumpsuit and a captain's hat with a black patent brim.

Mamie thought of her own mother.

"Why didn't she like them?" she asked. She was shivering and he took the blanket from the chaise and put it over her. Mamie was grateful for his odd lack of interest in her. He had not asked why she was there, or why she was trembling.

"She was too smart and restless. They couldn't hold her

attention and, to tell you the truth, she didn't know how to talk to them. Miss Laura would bring a picture home from school for her mother, and Leonora would say, 'Thank you, lamby, but shouldn't the house be bigger than the pigs?' You know, she just didn't know how to talk to them nice."

She handed him the cup and saucer and he poured more coffee and gave it back to her.

"What about her husband?"

"What about him?" Mr. de Beaupré linked his fingers and cracked his knuckles.

"Where is he?"

"He is dead and buried. Two years ago, three years ago this October. He died in this very room. I picked out the clothes he wore in his coffin. His good gray suit, that he used for meetings with his banker; a dark blue, navy blue, not your royal blue, tie. He looked sharp."

It did not bother Mamie that Mr. Lee had died in the room that she now thought of as her room, perhaps even in the same bed. What she had not imagined was that Mr. Lee had lived in the house with the two of them all those years.

Mamie had only lately begun to congratulate herself on being able to locate that tenuous line of balance between protecting herself and accommodating society. She had begun to form a theory, not about older women in the French novel, that seemed a little academic to her now, but a theory to explain the sexual aggression that seemed to track her all through her life. It was an aggression that manifested itself in many ways, harmless as well as violent. The Chinese driver who politely asked if she was good for sucking; the boys in the camp, innocents still themselves, who turned a shortcut through the camp into a ritualistic hazing; Mr. Felix, who believed in a good diet and moderation in all things, even ejaculation; the men who whispered to her in the street. It is necessary for a woman, Mamie thought, to be very, very careful. Always ready to run.

She had blamed herself for being naïve about Felix Villa-nueve, but she did not blame herself for Vinnie. She knew that there was nothing more she could have done. I was only looking for Claire, only looking for Claire, she thought over and over. Only looking for Claire.

It is conceivable that a woman might never be able to relax her vigilance, and, neither, she realized, could some men. Who could trust Alysse? Alysse could not break a man's neck with a flick of her hand, but Alysse had found, both in her defense and in her ambition, other ways in which to use her strength. That her goals were materialistic and greedy, rather than sexual and licentious, did not make her any the less capable of injury. The difference, and it was of great impor-tance, Mamie knew, was that Alysse did not subject her victims to physical harm, and death. It was not an equal struggle.

"He was my best friend," de Beaupré said.

There does not seem to have been sexual aggression in this house, Mamie thought in confusion, but how am I to really know? She was tired. It is impossible to know, she thought as she felt her eyes closing in exhaustion.

The last thing she heard him say was, "And I think I may say I was his."

She was there for four days. Mr. de Beaupré took care of her, bringing her sweet sherry, crackers and butter and Stilton cheese, and books. She began to read *Jane Eyre* on the second day, even though she had read it before. It was a bound library book, full of pale insects' wings, from a girls' private school. It was due back the twenty-sixth of April, 1957.

She telephoned Claire on the third day. Alysse answered the

telephone. She was helping Claire to pack. Alysse, who went to India every year for a month and returned looking astonishingly refreshed and years younger, had asked Claire to stay in her house in Portugal—that way the tweenies won't steal me blind, she said. Bones Washburn always believed that Alysse never went to India at all, but boarded a direct flight to Zurich where she went straight to the clinic on the mountain, and Bones was right.

"Claire will be such a help," Alysse said. "Isn't it wonderful? And we'll do some shopping."

"Shopping?" asked Mamie. "Is there anything left? I thought you and your friends had already bought everything on the planet."

"Teddy Pugh-Page is doing the apartment while I'm away. Completely country English, with a little room off the front hall for muddy Wellingtons and fishing rods and those straw basket things they put the dead fish in after they've caught them, and tweed caps. Maybe the walls in my personal tartan. You won't even know you're in New York. I'm *sick* of New York. And Claire says she's sick of New York, too. I tell you, no one has manners anymore. The way people behave at table chills the soul. I've had black cleaning ladies who had better manners. And, frankly, I'm shattered by the number of people who don't send flowers, or notes at least, after a party. Shattered. Here, Claire wants to speak to you."

"Mamie?"

Mamie took a breath.

"Mamie, where are you?"

"I'm at Alder's grandmother's house."

"I was so worried about you. You seemed so weird the other morning."

"Are you really going away? You've decided so quickly."

"Yes, well, I hope you don't mind. Alysse just asked me

yesterday and it seemed like such a fun thing to do. There's some duke she wants me to meet. Actually, she wants me to marry him. I'll water the garden and open the mail while she's in India."

"We talked about this one day by the river, do you remember? Heroines with private incomes."

"I don't remember. It must have been someone else."

"No," Mamie said. "It was you."

"You sound funny. Are you sick?"

"How's Brooke?"

"Don't mention her name! This whole time, she was going out with Sean, too. Just by themselves."

"She didn't look it." Mamie couldn't help herself.

"Exactly!" Claire was furious. "That's just the point. I get tied up and slapped and she gets earrings and chocolate."

"Well, I'm sorry," Mamie said.

There was a long pause as neither of them spoke.

"There's something I have to tell you," Mamie said at last.

"We leave in the morning," Claire said. "I'll be back at the end of summer. Alysse has to be here in September for the Antiques Show."

"You're going to become another Alysse, if you're not careful."

"Oh, Mamie, I wish you were coming with us."

"Maybe you won't become Alysse. You believe that everything is permissible. She's only interested in what advances her. I think I finally figured out what's wrong with your idea that it doesn't matter what you do so long as no one is hurt against their will—I even take into account your argument that it's a matter of choice. It's just not that personal, Claire."

"What isn't?" Mamie could hear Claire yawn.

"All of it. It can't be. The soul needs more. The soul asks for more. A certain amount of transcendence is necessary. And responsibility. Remember when Mrs. Nagata would scold us for disturbing her silkworms and tell us that the Buddha was in us *and* the worms, so how could we be so thoughtless? I'm not sure she was right about the godhead, it's nice to think she was, but you could start there, start small, and work up. Reverence for your own body. And his body. Your regard might grow until you encompassed whole countries, whole nationalities."

"You think so?" Claire said something to Alysse that sounded to Mamie like "pinch the cat."

"That's not what I wanted to tell you, though," said Mamie. "It's about the other night. At the birthday."

"Do you know what happened to my shoes? I can't find them anywhere and I want to take them."

"Vinnie has them."

"Who's Vinnie?"

Mamie had anticipated some resistance from Claire, but it had never occurred to her that Claire would not remember anything. She did not know what to say for a moment. "Your friend. The man who held me down and came in my mouth."

"Oh, Mamie. *Such* a sensitivo." Claire laughed. "The last thing I remember is taking a toke of something unbelievable through a rubber tube. I don't even know what it was. You weren't even there, Mamie!"

"I'm afraid I was. You're going to get yourself killed, Claire."

"Brooke had diarrhea for days. I'll never do that again."

"Good." Mamie took a big breath, and then she gave up. "Neither will I." I'll tell her another time, she thought, and maybe she really would.

"Well, hundreds of kisses, Mamie."

Mamie hesitated. "Six or seven kisses, Claire."

"Oh, I *am* going to miss you!"

Alder came on the fifth day. He had been calling the Crawfords' apartment and he was very worried, even though he had spoken twice to Alysse and had asked her to give Mamie the message that he had called and the number where Mamie could find him. He had been in Palm Beach, Baby having summoned him to discuss, at last, the terms of their separation. He had been asking to see her for weeks and she had always refused, only to call suddenly, drunkenly, to say that if he could be there in six hours she would listen, alone and without her brothers, to what he had to offer her. He had tried to reach Mamie, but she had already left for the birthday party. He had even sent a telegram to the Crawfords.

"I thought you were dead," she said. She was in bed in the gray room, wearing a faded blue satin nightgown made for Mrs. Lee's trousseau by Poiret. Mr. de Beaupré had brought it down to her, with a pair of swansdown slippers, yellow with age.

Alder sat on the edge of the bed. He held her hand. "I wouldn't die without telling you," he said.

"Hiroshi did. McCully did."

"Who?"

She told him about the birthday and what had happened in the room above the Aloha Kai, what the man had done to her, with Claire watching. She told it to him very simply, without trying to explain what she had felt, because she was afraid that he would be repulsed by her violation and unable to love her, and because she was afraid that he would be so infuriated, in the way that men have of appropriating the woman's outrage and making it about their own assaulted honor, that he would call the police or go after the man himself. She explained, without unnecessarily betraying her sister, that there had been drugs in the room, perhaps heroin, and that Claire and Brooke had been there for quite a while before she'd found them.

When he was so stricken and sad for her, when he did not jump up and threaten to kill the man, when he held her to him and stroked her hair and face, she began to cry.

"I thought I'd feel revulsion for my body and have to undergo some ritualistic cleansing, wash it with Mrs. Kaona's bitter herbs, before I let you touch me. I thought I'd lost my body again, but it's come back to me these last few days. Mr. de Beaupré somehow made me understand. It's still my body. He didn't take it away from me. No one has ever taken it from me, although I thought they had for such a long time."

He wiped her face.

"Do you remember," she asked, "when we talked about vaginas, the Cooze Seminars, do you remember? Well, I think I've worked it out these last few days. It is what started everything, you know, all my trouble, a vagina. That's how it began. Under the banyan tree. It's why McCully died. He was looking for me and I was looking for Hiroshi."

He didn't understand her. He thought that she might be delirious.

"And it's what got me into trouble on my birthday. The bad thing is, I don't know what I can do about it." Physiognomy as fate, she thought. Vagina as fate. Vagina as fight. Vagina as fête.

He calmed her, and smoothed and kissed her hair and swollen face.

"I think I will go home," she said. She lay back on the pillow. "Home to the island." She smiled sadly and covered her eyes with her arm.

He did not tell her then that he had gone to Palm Beach to ask Baby to divorce him. Baby, drinking gin fizzes, had tormented him for three days before she'd grown bored and told him, laughing uproariously, that she would never, ever, not in a *millónes años,* divorce him. He said that, in that unfortunate instance, he would have to divorce her. He was also going to fight for the child. She refused to let him see his daughter and when he angrily looked through the house, he realized that the baby, Delores, had been taken away to prevent him from seeing her. "Good luck, Meester Macho," Baby screamed after him when he walked across the wet lawn to his taxi.

"Perhaps I'll bring Delores," he said to Mamie. "If you ask us."

Mamie smiled. "But not Baby."

"No, I won't bring Baby." He hesitated. "I'm going to divorce her."

He rested his head against her head. He was not sure if she believed him.

"I don't know how much my mother likes me, but perhaps it's time I found out," Mamie said.

"Who did you say died without telling you?" he asked.

"Oh, I will tell you all about it when you come to the island."

"Tell me now."

"No," she said. "I want to stop thinking about them."

He fell asleep quickly, and Mamie, not thinking about them, trying not to think about them for the first time in years, fell asleep, too.

SIXTEEN

There it was, green and gorgeous.

Mary was waiting for her at the Lihue airport with a white ginger lei she had made herself, and a bouquet of gardenias from the camp. It was raining softly, but the rain was invisible unless you caught a quick flash of it in the light, running like a school of small silver fish just below the surface. The mountains were veiled by a smokey scrim of chiffon.

The plantation house was unchanged, the old tin roof still flashing secret messages in the sun, the long beach still muddy with the stain of rich river silt. The ancient palms in the grove still shed with a sudden groan their long, dry branches onto the sandy path below, and the banyan tree, its trunk like elephants' legs, was as dank and as dusty as ever.

In the first weeks, Mamie was grateful for Mary's ability, mystifying as it had always been, to see everything on the surface. Perhaps it is a gift, after all, Mamie thought, and not a weakness. It was very comforting not to be asked questions, or to be gazed at in too sympathetic, too curious, a way. Mary did ask about Claire and when Mamie said that she had gone to Portugal with Alice, Mary simply wondered aloud what it was that travelers sought so far from home. She was not patronizing, but sincerely bewildered. She was very content at home, she said, and uneasy whenever she was obliged to leave it.

Mamie worked with her every day in the garden. She liked to watch the young boys running long snakes of canvas hose across the big lawn, and the pretty, chattering Filipino housemaids gaily throwing bed sheets over the stiff hedges to bleach them white in the sun, and the tremendously strong Hawaiian who could lift an entire tree out of the red earth by encircling the trunk with his big brown arms, like an awkward lover, and pulling the startled tree straight up out of the tumbled ground.

Mary had trained a young Japanese man, Frank, to watch over the gardens, and it was his responsibility to keep healthy the endangered plants entrusted to Mary's care. Mamie saw that Mary was respected and admired by her workers, and by the botanists and scientists who came to consult her. She asked Mary, one hot morning as they kneeled side by side in the mud, how she had learned so much about the garden.

"I don't really know," Mary said modestly. She sounded a little perplexed. "I knew nothing when I came here. Everyone was so busy, you see. It's different in the country. There is always something to be done. And I had nothing to do. The garden had not been neglected by McCully's family, but no imagination had ever really been shown in planting it. You know what I mean, I'm sure. There was the monkey pod tree by the front drive. Shower trees. Croton bushes. Some people love the croton, but there are plants I prefer to them. There were very few fragrant flowers. I had never smelled anything in my life, until then, and I certainly have never smelled anything since, like my first white ginger."

Mamie worked busily with her fingers, feeling through the

mud for the tiny lily bulbs, so that Mary would not see the tears that suddenly came to her eyes. She kept silent, as she did not want Mary to stop talking. It was the most intimate thing that her mother had ever said to her.

"I suppose it changed my life," Mary said, "that first smell of 'awapuhi. I had just married McCully."

Mamie smiled to hear her mother use the Hawaiian name of the flower. She is under the spell, Mamie thought. At last.

"I used to dream about it," Mary said. "You know how hard it is to describe a smell? Well, it is just as hard to describe it to yourself, to summon it again. After a few sleepless nights, I went up to Koke'e and I brought down ginger and everything else I could find that had a fragrance, not necessarily a sweet scent, but any kind of scent at all, anything that would survive down here in the lowland. Hiroshi sometimes drove me up and down that terrible road three times a day in the truck and I would get so carsick, I'd have to sit in the middle, right next to him, and I heard later that people, seeing us driving like that, thought we were, you know, a little too friendly. I always imagined this would be paradise on earth, if you could go to San Francisco on the weekends."

She put down her bucket and watched as Mamie deftly divided bulbs with her little knife. "Do you think you'd be good at this?"

Mamie looked at her. "I dreamed about the smell of ginger for years. I still do."

Mary shrugged and stood up stiffly. Her knees were painful with bursitis from the years of kneeling in the dirt. "I don't so much anymore," she said. "But I'm happier." She crossed the garden to a little shed where she kept her tools.

Mamie finished her work slowly. Sometimes she felt as if she were enchanted and had been set an impossible task by her mother, separating the millions of fragile, webbed ferns one from the other, or counting the transparent scales on the pink fishes the boys excitedly brought up from the dock at dusk. It was soothing for Mamie. It required her concentration and her dexterity, and she was tranquil. She worked in the dirt with the formality and calm of a young novitiate preparing the sacraments.

Before she left New York, she'd gone to see Courtney to ask if she would like to come with her to Waimea. Edwin was at Iowa giving a seminar. He had had some nasty letters after his talk on D. H. Lawrence for suggesting that women, lacking the life force called a penis, would never be able to write as vitally as men, and he had gone to Iowa in the hope of clarifying his position. He does believe it's true, Courtney had said to Mamie, about the life force. She had sounded embarrassed.

Mamie tried to convince her to go with her, if only for a few days.

"I promise, I swear, I'll let you come back," Mamie said.

Courtney smiled, a little sadly. "I mustn't. I can't." She had promised Edwin that she would type his monograph while he was away. This is sexual aggression, too, Mamie thought.

Mamie had also received an extremely angry letter from Vivi Crawford, who had returned early to New York. She included a precisely itemized bill for twelve thousand dollars for damages to the apartment. Mamie would hear from her lawyer.

Alder wrote to her, and sometimes telephoned, and she described to him the run of young yellow-striped goatfish at Hanalei and the *koli'i* plant which took ten years to mature only to produce one showy burst of flowers before it died. He wrote that he was ready to come whenever she wanted him. He'd ordered a very beautiful red snorkel and mask and fins from the catalogue of the Museum of Modern Art and she laughed when he described them to her.

"Mr. de Beaupré is sorry that you are away and asks to be remembered to you. He is not sure just who you are, exactly, but he is very fond of you," Alder said. "As am I. Not sure who you are, but very fond of you."

She slept in the screened room where she and Claire had slept as children, screened so that someone—McCully? Gertrude? —would hear them if they coughed or had a nightmare. She listened to the intoxicated fruit flies singing in the mango trees. The room was full of the smell of the white flowers that Mary had planted years ago beneath the windows, the plants fuller now and heavy, dragging with wet blossoms.

One evening, Mamie struggled across the lawn in the rain with a heavy wheelbarrow piled high with the brown seaweed she had gathered on the beach. Frank ran out from the bamboo grove to help her. He took the long wooden handles from her wet hands and pushed the wheelbarrow over the sodden grass.

She walked beside him. He was tall and slender. He did not speak Pidgin as did Mamie and the others, and he kept himself a little apart, even from her mother. His aloofness did not come from a defensive feeling of superiority or the ambiguity of his position, but from a rather matter-of-fact sense of his own equality. Mamie had watched him quietly during the long, light days. It is dangerous to mind all change, she had thought.

"Look," he said. "There's something in the *limu*." The seaweed, *limu kohu*, was called "the long-haired fish of the sea." It had a sharp smell of iodine and salt. He put down the barrow and gently parted the pink *limu* with his smooth hands and Mamie leaned over the cold, reeking seaplant and saw a white bone, perhaps a thigh bone, hidden in its soft, dense branches.

They were both wet through with the rain and Mamie's hair was black and shiny, close to her head. Frank smiled and lifted the wheelbarrow and pushed it to the greenhouse. Mamie stood in the rain and watched him until he was lost again in the chafing, cricketing bamboo.

When she came into the house through the back, Mary was waiting for her and Mamie realized that her mother had been watching her and Frank from the kitchen window.

"He's Yumiko's boy. Do you remember her? She used to work at the mill."

Yumiko's boy, Mamie thought. Yumiko was Hiroshi's sister.

"He's Hiroshi's nephew," Mary said, looking out the window. The sun was sliding into the dark and troubled sea and the palm grove behind them rattled with the heavy fall of rain.

"I'm so sorry for what happened, Mamie."

Mamie looked down at the soaked chamois gardening gloves in her hands. When she was a girl, she had thought her mother very strange for wearing gloves to touch flowers, and now she used them herself. They were very helpful, and allowed her to get a good grip where her bare hands could not hold.

Mary went to her and bent her head to Mamie's shoulder. It was as if she could not look at her. "In the banyan that day. Can you forgive me?"

Mamie looked down at her. She saw that Mary accepted her own part in the trouble and the death that began that day, and Mamie saw that her mother regretted it.

"You're shivering," Mary said, standing back and looking at Mamie.

"Yes," Mamie said. "The rain in the garden."

She smiled and leaned toward her mother, a little stiffly, but not without love, and not without pity, and she closed her eyes and bowed her head and allowed her mother to reach toward her, after all those years, to kiss her gently on the forehead.

There were many things that Mamie was eager to do. It seemed as though she had been away from home for years and years, but it was not so. It had only been eleven months. She had just missed Lily, who was on her way to Cambodia with Tōsi to look for Lily's father. She wanted to see Gertrude again, and Mrs. Kaona. She wanted to take Alder snorkeling at Na Pali. She would not be embarrassed by his red fins as she had once been embarrassed by the boy in the terry-cloth beach jacket. She wanted to teach him the old secret of luring fish with frozen green peas. She wanted a root beer float from the Dairy Queen. She had asked Orval Nalag to go body-surfing with her at Kekaha someday soon. The waves were good, she'd heard; something about a storm in Japan. She wanted to sleep alone up on the fragrant mountain. The nights had been cold. She would pick yellow ginger and she would make a fire with the peeling, gray eucalyptus. It was odd, but she could already smell the wet ginger and the curling, aromatic eucalyptus, steaming and hissing as the pale bark caught fire. *Pomaika'i au,* she thought: blessed am I.

ABOUT THE AUTHOR

Susanna Moore won the PEN Ernest Hemingway Citation and the Sue Kaufman Prize for First Fiction from the American Academy and Institute of Arts and Letters for her novel *My Old Sweetheart*. She is from Hawai'i and now lives in New York City.